Inevit

To: y'all.
We've done this twenty times.
Y'all know I luh y'all.
Thank you.

one.

Kora

Is he going to open the door?

My heels tapped out a stilted, choppy rhythm as I strode down the hall, in an unnecessary hurry to get to my destination. And then, not so much.

So I stopped.

I stood there, staring between the polished parquet floors and apartment 5C, trying to decide if I should turn around.

I needed him though.

I was frustrated, angry, and a little bit desperate, so I pushed a harsh puff of air through my teeth, squared my shoulders, and continued down the hall.

In front of the door, I took a deep breath, swallowing hard before I lifted my hand to knock. I was resigned to doing it, but still, I hesitated for a full minute, standing in the hall like a dummy with my fist raised like I was saluting the door.

Just knock on the door, Kora. It's not a big deal. But it *was* a big deal. Showing up unannounced and knocking on a man's door after eleven at night was *supposed* to be a big deal.

Shit.

I adjusted my stance in my heels, wiggling my toes against the lavish black leather of my caged booties. These weren't "*walk around*" shoes, these were "*make my calves look lickable*" shoes. Completely impractical for showing up at the door of somebody who may or may not even let you in. But then again, he *had* always liked me in a sexy pair of shoes...

I put my tongue out to lick my lips. They were long free of the deep purple lipstick I'd layered on earlier. I'd left it behind on three different glasses of white wine, and now I was wobbly on my feet, and wobbly in the head, and my emotions were... hell, those were wobbly too. I swallowed hard, and forced my fist to move.

The door swung open before my skin touched the cool metal.

Six feet and a half feet of muscled, velvety chocolate skin stood in front of me, swathed in nothing except a pair of black boxer briefs. Casually, he draped his tall body against the doorframe as he looked me up and down.

"Are you going to come in, or are you going to stand here?"

I flinched at the unusually harsh edge marring a smooth voice that at the right time, under the right circumstances, could make my toes curl just from the sound. "How did you know I was out here?"

"Fletch."

I rolled my eyes, running my tongue over my teeth before I brought my gaze back to his face. "I asked him not to tell you."

"So you could lose your nerve and run off? That's exactly *why* he told me. And besides… you don't pay him. I do. Are you coming in?"

My gaze flitted to his hand, poised at the door handle like he was itching for a reason to close it. "It depends on if you're…"

"If I'm *what* Kora?" he practically growled, after a few moments had passed without me saying anything. "It's late. I don't have time for bullshit."

"If you're going to be an asshole about it," I snapped, crossing my arms. He just looked at me, his handsomely chiseled face pulled into a bland expression. "Never mind."

I turned away, intending to storm down the hall, but he had his arm looped around my waist, lifting my feet off the ground to drag me back before I even took the first step. "Man, get your ass in here and stop playing."

"Get your fucking hands off me!" I said, shoving him away, but not until we were well inside, with the door closed. Tariq was still tall and solid from his years in the NFL, and impervious to any amount of physical force I could exert against him, but he moved anyway. He stood in front of me with his arms crossed, glaring at me, and I glared right back.

"You know you have a lot of nerve, right?" he asked, rubbing a hand over his face before he shook his head. "You come here in the middle of the night, with that mouth of yours in full effect. What is it? What's up?"

7

"I could ask you the same thing!" I tossed my purse onto the couch, then stripped off my coat, tossing it beside my bag. "You're the one with the attitude."

He laughed harder than necessary at that, head tossed back and everything. "So you're going to pretend to be surprised by that? Is that what we're doing?" Yes.

It's exactly what we were doing.

"Look," I said, glancing at him over my shoulder as I strode across the room to the bar.

"Are you going to tell me why you're mad, or not?" Silence built between us as I dropped ice into two glasses, then pulled the stopper from a decanter of cognac. My fingers shook as I poured, willing myself to appear cool and collected, refusing to look at him again before I was finished. I was placing the bottle down when I felt the heat from his body behind me.

I sucked in a breath as he snaked an arm around my waist, then used his other hand to sweep my hair to the side. "Kora, you're in *my* condo at damn near midnight, smelling like another motherfucker's cheap mass-market cologne. After I told you to stay away from him, you let him take you out, get you tipsy, let him fuc—"

"Absolutely *not*," I snapped, turning in his arms to face him.

He grunted, then put his hands against the bar on both sides of me, keeping me in place.

"But you intended to."

I shook my head, tipping my chin up to meet his eyes. "Absolutely not."

8

"The shoes say something else."

A smile tipped the corners of my mouth. "You like my shoes?"

"They're fulfilling their purpose."

I yelped as he easily lifted me off my feet, sitting me down on the bar and spreading my

legs to step between them. He lowered his mouth toward mine, but didn't touch me, grinning and pulling back when I tried to lift my lips to his. Placing his hands underneath my thighs, he gripped me, dragging me forward and making my dress hike up around my waist. The pads of his fingers dug into my flesh as he pulled me against him, leaving only the thin layers of my panties and his boxers between me and his dick.

"He hugged me," I explained, after long seconds had passed with him doing nothing. I squirmed against him, trying to create some friction, but he grabbed me by the waist, holding me still. "It was like he'd bathed in that funky shit. That's the only time he touched me."

Tariq gave me a subtle nod, then lowered his head to tease me again. He chuckled as he easily pulled his head from my attempt to grab him. "You shouldn't have been out with him in the first place, should you?"

"Tariq…"

He moved his hand between us, between my legs, brushing his fingers over the soft lace that covered my clit. He pressed down, not nearly hard enough, then lowered his head to my ear.

"*Should you?*"

9

"No," I whimpered, when he pressed a little harder.

"So then *why?"*

"He was nice! And he's sweet. And he's –"

"Not in your league. Not even in the same fucking sport."

I sucked my teeth. "According to who?"

"According to me."

"I met him at your office building."

Tariq frowned. "Even more reason to leave him alone. He's a goddamned *accountant,*

Kora. What is an *accountant* going to do with you, and vice versa? We're not even talking Wall Street money. He's barely making *Main* Street money."

"So? Broke men give good dick."

I bit my lip to keep from smiling at the way Tariq's nostrils flared in anger. A second later, one of his hands was buried in my hair, tugging my head back to make my mouth available to him. I whimpered as he nipped my bottom lip, soft at first, but then a little harder as he inched my panties aside to push his fingers into me. He outlined my lips with the tip his tongue, slowly, carefully, purposely driving me crazy.

But I didn't complain.

Instead, I pressed myself closer, hoping he'd burrow his fingers a little deeper, or finally give me his tongue, but he didn't. One hand stayed in my hair, and he pulled his fingers from between my legs, raising that hand to my face. He looked me right in the eyes as he grazed my bottom lip with his thumb. I inhaled deep, breathing in the scent of my arousal as he brought his other fingers to my lips. Still holding his gaze, I dipped my head, covering his fingers with my mouth.

Tariq's eyes narrowed as I sucked, and his grip on my hair tightened. He groaned as I slid my tongue between his fingers, tasting myself on his skin. I moved my hands behind him, gliding my hands under his boxers to press my nails into the smooth, muscled flesh of his ass, urging him closer.

Tariq was completely unhurried in the withdrawal of his fingers from my mouth, letting my tongue linger and dance over them until the last possible moment. Then he put them between my legs again with a firm thrust, burying them as deeply as they would go.

"Is somebody giving you better dick than me?" he asked, lowering his mouth so his lips were right against mine as he spoke. For a moment, he consumed the air around me, making me feel a little dizzy before he suddenly dropped his mouth to my neck, sucking hard. He hooked his fingers in me, pressing against a certain soft, fleshy spot that he knew well, and made me clench around him. "No," I answered, an absolute, undeniable truth.

Tariq's mouth crashed onto mine, pushing his tongue between my lips. Our tongues melded together, twisting and dancing as he pulled his hand from my hair to drag me closer. His dick was hard, and hot, insistent between my legs as he kissed me harder. He grabbed my face to keep me still as he licked my mouth, swallowing my desperate moans and whimpers.

11

I hooked my legs around his waist, bucking against him. "Tariq, *please,*" I purred against his mouth, raking my hands over the broad, muscled expanse of his chest. He pulled my bottom lip between his teeth, nipping it before he sucked it into his mouth.

"No. " Tariq shook his head, picked up one of the glasses of cognac bedside me, and took a swig. He savored the liquor in his mouth as his eyes raked over me, lighting me on fire with the heat of his gaze. Unconsciously – or very consciously – I pulled my shoulders back, jutting my breasts toward him.

Tariq's tongue dashed out to trace his lips, and then he grabbed the front of my dress, easily tugging the cowl-style collar down. I sucked in a breath when he tipped the icy glass toward me, letting the cold liquor dribble just above the lacy edge of my bra. He dipped his head, gifting the warmth of his tongue in contrast to the cognac as it trailed into the valley between my breasts.

He tugged my dress down to my waist, then unhooked my bra. His fingers hesitated for a moment, then gradually slid the straps down my arms and pulled away the cups, as if he was savoring the moment before he exposed me to the perpetual chill of his condo. Tariq's hands were hot and soothing as he cupped my breasts, and instantly, my nipples hardened more than they already were.

"You've been a naughty girl, Kora... tell me why I should give you anything."

"Because it's been so long. You know you miss me."

12

He chuckled. "You were married for two seconds, Kora. It hasn't been that long. And if it has, it's because you wanted it that way."

"I was married to somebody I loved, who I thought loved me. Don't you triviali–*ah!*" I bit my lip against the sweet, sharp pain as he twisted my nipples between his fingers.

"I'm not trivializing your commitment to your husband, Kora. But the fact remains that *you* chose to continue the termination of this part of our relationship after your divorce. Not me.

You chose to "normalize" our friendship, and date accountants."

"Fuck you."

He smirked, then pinched my nipples a little harder, making me whimper. "Oh I plan to.

You *need* it, bad. Especially this sassy ass mouth of yours." He touched my lips again – above and below – just barely circling one thumb over my clit, driving me insane, then trailed the other over my bottom lip. I sucked his finger into my mouth again as I pushed myself forward against his hand.

Tariq chuckled, but didn't move his hand away. He pressed harder, and I closed my eyes as tightness pooled in my belly. His thumb slipped from my lips, and he replaced it with his tongue, plunging demandingly into my mouth at the same time he thrust his fingers into me.

Another wave of moisture pooled between my legs as his free hand went to my neck.

"I think you enjoy the fact that you get under my skin," he murmured, dragging his thumb over my throat in slow, firm swipes.

I bit my lip, lifted my chin to give him better access before I smirked. "I think you're right."

He shook his head, grinning. "What am I going to do with you, Kora?"

"You could start by treating me a little better."

He lifted an eyebrow. "That's impossible. Anything you could conceivably want – everything I have… it's already yours. What more can I give you?"

My hands went under his boxers again, skirting over a thick, neatly groomed patch of coily hair to reach the smooth, velvety hardness of his dick. "This. Give me this." I pulled him free, cupping, and gently squeezing his balls in one hand, giving him a firm stroke with the other.

He gripped my neck, tugging me toward him as he leaned in, until our faces were almost touching. He reached up, brushing the silk-pressed layers of my bob out of my eyes so I could meet his gaze.

Tariq was gorgeous. Greek nose, thick lips, chiseled jaw. Intelligent, expressive eyes, so dark they were black, and locs down to his shoulders that were always impeccably groomed.

"Stop dealing with men that are beneath you, Kora. Your bitch ass ex-husband, that accountant… you can do better. Can't you?"

"Yes."

"Prove it."

"Fuck me."

"Gladly."

In one swift move, panties were aside and Tariq was inside me, stretching and filling me up. My hands went to his hips, digging my nails into his skin as he stroked. He grabbed my thighs, urging my legs around his waist before he easily picked me up, leaving himself buried in me as he walked.

"What are you doing?" I asked, hanging on to his shoulders as he crossed the room with a purposeful stride.

"Shower. We have to wash the accountant's scent off you first."

two.

Kora

Tariq and his obsession with these damned white sheets…

That was where I chose to place the blame for how brightly the sun was shining through my closed eyelids. I sucked in a subtle breath, reacting to fingers on my ass, then high on my thighs, spreading them apart to dip between. I was already wet – stayed that way when I was around him – and his fingers easily slipped and slid between my slick folds. Lips pressed to my shoulder blades, trailing kisses from one side to the other as he made his way up to my neck. His tongue swiped the top of my shoulder, making me shiver and squirm against his hand.

"Wake your ass up. Stop acting like you're asleep."

I grinned as Tariq muttered those words in my ear, then lifted my leg and entered me from behind in one confident push.

"*Mmmm.*" We groaned in unison, relishing that first stroke like we hadn't been at it all night. We *always* savored that moment like we were new to each other, even though we'd known each other forever. I was pleasantly sore, and well beyond satisfied already, so this was just a bonus. Tariq wrapped his arm around my waist, pulling me against him as he began to move.

With his arm hooked under my knee, he angled himself to drive into me at just the right angle to make me involuntarily clench around him. He thrust hard and deep, burying his free hand in my hair to turn my head. I twisted my torso in his direction, and his mouth crashed onto mine. His tongue invaded my mouth, tasting and sweeping, swallowing my sounds of pleasure as he plunged into me.

"Kora, I swear to God if you stay away from me this long again…"

I grinned into the pillow as Tariq turned me onto my stomach and then plunged into me again, using his arm around my waist to pull me onto my knees and elbows. My fingers dug into his luxurious white sheets, and I tried in vain not to cry out my pleasure as he hammered into me.

His hands moved to my breasts, twisting and tugging my sensitive nipples between his fingers until they were hard beads, aching for his continued touch. My eyes watered with pleasure and pain as he played with them, then moved his hands to my shoulders for anchor as he mercilessly drove into me.

"*Please*," I panted, gasping for breath as he stopped moving, still buried inside. One of his hands moved from my shoulder to my neck, gripping my throat with light pressure as he pushed the other hand between my legs. "Tariq, *please*," I moaned, squirming against him, but still he didn't move. Instead, he pressed his fingers to my clit, circling them as his teeth grazed the back of my neck, then sank just far enough into my shoulder to make me whimper.

"Please what?"

"You *know* what."

"No I don't."

"You make me sick."

"No I don't."

I cried out as he finally eased out of me, then slammed in again, with his hand still at my throat. He eased me backwards until I was almost upright, then kissed the back of my neck, sucking and biting as he stroked me. A fluttery, tingling tightness filled my belly as he kept moving, pinching and pulling my clit and... *Ooooh shit.* I closed my eyes tight as my body tensed, then released in a rush. Wet, sticky ecstasy dripped down the insides of my thighs as I came, with a loud cry that rasped against my throat.

Tariq grabbed me tight around the waist, keeping me flush against his body as he growled through his own release. Eyes still closed, I smiled, covering his hands with mine as his lips pressed against the back of my neck again.

"Good morning," he murmured, following the greeting with a kiss on the shoulder.

Slowly, I peeled my eyelids apart, grinning when I caught a glimpse of our sweaty, naked reflection in the full-length mirror across the room.

"Good morning to you too."

He slid out of me, then smacked me on the ass as he climbed out of the bed. "You know it's time for you to go home, right?" Tariq chuckled as I launched one of the pillows at his head, then tossed it back toward me. "Seriously though, what do you have going on today?"

"Why?" I asked, moving to my stomach with my head propped on my hands, ankles crossed in the air, watching him as he stepped into his large walk-in closet.

"Because I want you to have lunch with me today," he called out. "I have some business I need to handle this morning, but I'd like to see you again. I've missed you."

I tipped my head to the side. "We see or talk to each other almost every day. How can you possibly miss me?"

I looked up as he peeked out of the closet, meeting my eyes with an intensity that never failed to make my heart race. "Oh it's definitely possible."

He disappeared into the closet again just in time to not see me blush, and I turned over onto my back, staring up at the ceiling. I knew exactly what he meant, because honestly... I'd missed him too.

It had been hard – almost shamefully so – to stay out of Tariq's bed. As mentioned, we saw or spoke to each other nearly every day. I had good girlfriends – *great* girlfriends – but if I had to name one person as my best friend in the world, it would be Tariq.

We'd known each other since we were babies – I taught the man how to write his name. The bond we shared had been forged in more than thirty-five years of growing up together, and the relationship we had now was, well... complicated.

"So you didn't answer my question," he said, stepping out of the closet with his hands full. He laid out his clothes on the dressing table, then stopped in front of the bed, completely uninhibited by his nakedness, to look at me.

I turned over again, sitting up on my knees. "You didn't ask me a question, Tariq. You made a statement."

He cut his eyes toward the ceiling. "Okay smartass." – I smirked – "Are you free for lunch today?"

I shook my head. "Sorry handsome, not today. I already have a lunch date."

He lifted an eyebrow. "A lunch *date*? With who?"

I shrugged. "You know, just this tall, *gorgeous*, bronze-skinned—"

"So Nubia then?" he asked, the corners of his mouth twitching with a suppressed smile.

"Yes. With Nubia."

My *other* best friend in the world.

Tariq nodded. "Okay, so how about this: I'll give you my card. You and Nubia hit the salon, spa, and lunch on me. And then later tonight, you have dinner with me."

I frowned. "The salon? What are you trying to say? Are you saying something is wrong with my hair?"

His lips parted as his eyes went up to what I was *positive* was a mess on top of my head.

Between last night and this morning, wrapping it up had been the last thing on my mind, which had, undoubtedly, resulted in a bird's nest. Instead of saying anything, he clamped his lips closed and turned to head to the bathroom.

"Tariq!"

"Huh?"

"Are you saying that my hair looks bad?"

He glanced over his shoulder, a few steps from the bathroom. "I'm not, *not* saying that it looks ba—*mmhph!*" His words were interrupted by the impact of another one his pillows against his back, launched from my position on the bed. Chuckling, he bent down, and tossed the pillow

back at me. "You shouldn't have asked then, beautiful. Come get your nasty ass in this shower!" he shouted from the bathroom, and as if he were pulling me by a string, I climbed down from the bed and followed.

Tariq's master bath, just like the rest of his home, was masculine and luxurious, done in grey and white limestone. We brushed our teeth at the wide basined sink, side by side, playfully fighting for elbow room even though there would be plenty if either of us simply stepped a couple of inches to the side. After that, he pulled me into the etched glass shower enclosure and turned the water to a rainfall spray, obviously not caring that my hair would get soaked.

"A warning would've been nice!" I smacked him right on his firm ass cheek after I'd brushed the sodden strands of hair from my face, and giggled when he grabbed me by the arms, easing me against the wall. "I notice you covered your locs so they wouldn't get wet."

"You were going to wet it before you washed it anyway. I've watched you do it a thousand times," he murmured against my lips before he slipped his tongue into my mouth. I pushed my breasts against his chest, arching into him as his hands came up to cup my face. He tasted good, minty and clean and something unidentifiable, something uniquely coded to him, and I savored every drop as he licked and moved, exploring my mouth with his tongue.

Eventually, we got to the actual shower.

He washed me and I washed him, and then he climbed out to start the other parts of his morning routine. I smiled when I realized my shampoo was already there in the shower, and took a few minutes to wash my hair and coat it with conditioner before I stepped out to wrap it in a towel.

I stood behind Tariq as I gave myself enough of a rubdown to not drip all over the floor, then grabbed my body oil from his cabinet and sat down. "You offered me use of your account... is it time for my monthly reminder that I don't need your money?"

He shrugged. "Sure. And then I can remind you that I know you don't need it. Your level of *need* has never had anything to do with what I do or don't freely offer."

I rolled my eyes. "Whatever. So what are you doing today? It's Saturday, and you said you had a meeting. Who has meetings on Saturdays?"

"I do, when I finally have a chance to close a deal that my client has been bugging about for months."

I met his eyes in the mirror as I rubbed the oil in my hands to warm it. "Trouble in the boardroom?"

"You could put it that way," he said, pulling his trimmer away from his face to shake his head. "Remind me to let somebody else handle it next time, childhood friends be damned. Play tag at recess with a motherfucker thirty-something years ago, and they think you owe them personal service."

I giggled as I massaged the oil into my skin, leaving behind a pleasant tingle and the faint scent of vanilla, citrus, and almonds. "Is that a jab at me?"

Tariq scoffed. "Never, beautiful. I'll insult you outright when I feel inclined, and I know you'll give me the same respect. It was a jab at—"

"Braxton and Lincoln Drake," I smiled. "I know. You still crushing on their sister?"

"Crushing? Nashira is gorgeous, but no. I have another prospect in mind." He winked at me, and I shook my head.

"Mmmhmm."

I finished moisturizing my skin and left him there in the bathroom. I grinned when I saw his clothes laid out on the dressing table. Quickly, I snagged his black label Ralph Lauren buttondown and slipped it on, fastening the buttons as I walked over to the mirror.

"Ah, come on, Kora," Tariq groaned a few seconds later, when he stepped out and saw me still in front of the mirror. I watched his reflection as he pulled on a pair of black boxer briefs, charcoal and cranberry dress socks, and then tailored pants in a slightly lighter gray. He tugged a black ribbed tank over his head, then stalked across the room to stand behind me. "Are you trying to make me late?"

"Why would I do such a thing?"

Tariq chuckled, dipping his head to nuzzle my neck. "Didn't we already establish that you enjoy making my life more difficult than it has to be?"

My giggle turned into a moan as Tariq's tongue touched my skin, dipping inside the shirt collar to trace a path from the base of my neck to my ear. I closed my eyes, melting against him as he pulled my earlobe between his teeth, tugging a little before he sucked it into his mouth. His hand went under the hem of the shirt, brushing the top of my thighs before he slipped between, urging them apart.

It was amazing, honestly, how sensitive I was to Tariq's touch. I'd been with – and enjoyed – other men, but eventually, you got used to the same person's touch. Not tired of it, or unaffected by it, not even that it lost any of its pleasure, just… used to it.

But every time Tariq touched me it was like a brand new experience. Electric, vivid and *so* damned good.

He eased his fingers into me, pressed his thumb to my clit, and moved both in concert
with his tongue against my neck. He'd touched me like this a thousand times before, yet here I was, already about to come unglued.

"You never answered about dinner," he muttered against my ear, then bent to nip my neck.

With my eyes still closed, I shook my head. "I don't think I can do tonight. I need to make notes on—"

"Think harder." His hands stilled, and I let out a groan of protest as he nipped my neck again. "Think harder, Kora."

"Don't do this," I whined, trying to rock against his hand, but he held me immobile.

His lips brushed my ear. "You want to come?"

"Yes."

"You want *me* to make you come?"

"*Yes.*"

My body involuntarily trembled as he pressed against my clit with his thumb, then touched his lips to my neck, then shoulder. "Then think harder about dinner."

My feet came off the floor as Tariq's arm moved around my waist, hauling me against his body as he drove his fingers into me again. He pumped hard, hooking his fingers into me until he found that little spot again, and worked me until my legs were trembling as I came.

He lowered me to the floor and then licked me off his fingers, smirking at my wobbly state as he reclaimed his shirt. He pulled it on, buttoning it as he headed back for the bathroom.

At the door, he turned to look back in my direction.

"Kora?"

"Yes?"

"About dinner…"

I swallowed, taking several long blinks before I turned to face him. "Text me the details."

three.

Kora

Nubia's voice carried over the hum of the blow dryer.

I smiled when I heard her calling my name, being her usual dramatic self.

"Koraaaa! Helloooo? Can you hear me Koraaaa?"

I shook my head as I shut the dryer off, rubbing product together in my hands before running them through my blown-out hair. The muted thump of her footsteps sounded as she crossed the plush carpet in Tariq's bedroom, and I heard her moving around in his closet. Rolling my eyes, I started the process of flat-ironing my hair back into my sleek bob.

I didn't hear a peep from her as I finished the first quarter of my head, so I yelled out her name. A few seconds later, her massive hair appeared in the doorway. A second after that, I saw Nubia.

She bore a striking resemblance to the black Wonder Woman after whom she was named. Deep golden-brown skin, a head full of thick, blonde streaked coils that she usually wore like a

lion's mane, and a face that was, simply put, gorgeous. Big brown eyes the same dark gold as her skin, pouty lips, perfect nose. She stuck her head into the bathroom, one flawlessly sculpted eyebrow raised. "Why am I not at all surprised to find you here?"

I cut my eyes toward her, then back to my reflection in the mirror as I carefully parted my hair, then raised the flat iron to smooth the section. "What's wrong with me being here?"

"Nothing I guess," she shrugged, then stepped fully into the bathroom, with her thumbs hooked in the belt loops of her jeans. I parted and straightened another section while I waited for her to say whatever was coming next. "Except..." Nubia flashed me a bright smile, leaning against the counter with her arms crossed. "The fact that you *swore* you were going to stop doing this."

"Stop doing what?" I avoided her gaze as I finished straightening the front of my hair, then carefully pinned it out of the way.

"Tariq."

"Hmm?"

"We're doing it like that?"

"Doing what like what?"

Nubia sucked her teeth, then stepped closer to me, pulling the comb and flat iron from my hands to take over the back of my hair. "Acting like you *didn't* tell me you weren't going to sleep with Tariq again."

"I *didn't* sleep with Tariq..."

She scowled. "Liar."

"I'm not lying that much. We spent hardly *any* time sleeping."

28

"Ha ha. You're funny. Look at how hard I'm laughing here," she said, gesturing with the comb to her deadpan expression as she passed the flatiron through my hair. "In all seriousness though Kora, I don't understand you and Tariq. Lord knows I've tried, but…"

I frowned at her in the mirror as she parted another section. "You say that as if we're anomalies. Tariq and I have a perfectly normal friendship."

Nubia's face crumpled in disbelief. "Who exactly are you telling *that* lie to?"

My mouth opened for a snippy comeback, but closed just as quickly, because… "Both of us."

"Thank you," Nubia trilled, grinning as she pulled the comb through my freshly straightened strands. "Cause there is *nothing* normal about whatever the hell you and Tariq are doing now, or ever did. Or ever *will* do, for that matter."

"You don't think you're going overboard?"

She raised an eyebrow at me, and unclipped the last section. "Kora, I just picked out an outfit for you from *your* section of *his* closet. I don't have any male "friends", even ones that have tasted the kitty, who keep a section for me in their closet."

"I can't believe you went in his closet," I lied, trying to deflect from the truth of what she said. "You know he barely likes you." – another lie.

"Then why did Fletch not even hesitate to let me up here, and into Tariq's apartment?"

I laughed. "Because Fletch wants some ass."

Nubia sucked her teeth, shaking her head as she pulled the flat iron through my hair again. "Whatever girl. Tariq *loves* me, don't play."

"Does not."

"Does too." She put the flat iron on the counter and then pulled her cell phone from the pocket of her distressed designer jeans. She tapped a few buttons, then put the phone on speaker, placing it back down on the counter. "*Shhh.* Listen."

The phone rang several times as she went back to helping me with my hair, and then finally, a recognizable baritone voice came over the line.

"How can I help you Nubia?"

"*Hiii* Tariq," Nubia sang, winking at me in the mirror. "How are you?"

"I'm good. Getting ready to head into a meeting. How are you?"

"I'm wonderful!" She placed the flat iron down again, then propped a hand on her hip. "I know you're a busy man, so I won't keep you, I just have one little thing I need."

"I'm listening."

"Tell me you love me."

I raised an eyebrow at her in the mirror, but she clamped a hand over my mouth just as I opened it to ask what was going on. She raised a finger to her lips and scowled at me as deafening silence came from the other end of the phone. After a long moment, Tariq finally spoke again.

"Nubia, are you serious right now?"

"As a heart attack." She grinned, keeping my mouth covered. "Come on. Out with it." Tariq let out an audible sigh. "Nubia Perry, Goddess of Everything... I love you."

Nubia threw her head back, sticking her tongue out as she laughed. "That wasn't so bad, was it T?!"

"I swear, I cannot stand your ass."

"Don't be like that!"

"Goodbye, Nubia."

"*Byeee!*"

The phone chimed to let us know the call had ended, and Nubia pulled her hand away from my mouth.

"What the hell was that?!" I asked, turning to face her.

She immediately grabbed me by the shoulders, turning me back around to finish with my hair. "*That* was the first of my winnings in a little wager I placed with one Tariq Evans."

I frowned. "Wager?"

"Mmhmm." She nodded, then smiled at me in the mirror. "You see, I knew this was going to happen, so when he asked me about you after your divorce—"

"Wait, why did he ask *you* about me, when he could have just asked *me* about me?"

Nubia wrinkled her nose. "The same reason any man asks a woman's friends about her.

To get the real deal. This was when you first decided you were just going to be "regular" friends with him. He asked me to lunch, told me he was concerned you were mad at him, and just not saying anything. He – correctly, might I add – gauged that something, since your divorce was different. And obviously that something is the fact that you were no longer spending your lonely nights in his bed."

"Nubia…"

"Where is the lie?" she asked, then put the flat iron down and unpinned all of my hair. "Right, there isn't one. I told him you were still processing your divorce, and not to worry, because your "friendship" would be back to normal in no time at all."

"Why would you say that?"

She lifted an eyebrow. "Because I try to make the truth a habit. Anyway, noble as always,

Tariq wasn't so sure. He said that once you set your mind to something, you were typically unable to be swayed from it. So, if you'd charted a new path for your friendship, it was probably the course you two would be taking."

"And all of this is coded language for whether or not he and I would be sleeping together?"

Nubia smiled as she combed my hair into a style, then tossed the comb onto the counter.

"I mean neither of us explicitly said it, but it was understood."

"I need new friends."

"Oh please, you'll never find a more perfect friend than *moi*. In any case, Tariq was so sure that I bet his ass you two would be close as ever. He bet that you would stand your ground, and because you didn't, his Hersheyness has to tell me he loves me any time I ask for the next month."

"But he was upset with me for—never mind." I rolled my eyes. "What did he win if I held out? And how was it going to be decided? Was there a time frame?"

"A month," Nubia declared as she headed out of the bathroom. I followed her, stopping at the dressing table to look at what she'd picked out. "And if he won, I had to go on a date with one of his friends."

"Seriously?! You only gave me a month after a divorce to hold out?" I looked up from the deliciously soft sweater Nubia had chosen for me, wondering if Tariq had purchased this because of how the mustard color would pop against my deep brown skin. "And which friend?"

"It wasn't a month after the divorce. You'd already been divorced a few months at the time of the conversation. And the friend Stephen Foster."

I dropped my robe, then stepped into Tariq's closet, opening my drawer to pick out underwear and put it on. "So, not just *a* friend, his *best* friend. Now why on earth would you have to lose a bet to go out with Steph?"

"Because my interest in Tariq's friends is zilch. I don't do athletes – current *or* former.

Remember?"

I stepped back out, clad in midnight blue lace, then reached for the pair of jeans to pull them on. "How could I forget? Your ass was *gone*."

"Oh whatever." Nubia rolled her eyes, propping her chin on her hand as she watched me button myself into the slim-fitting jeans, then pull on the sweater. "You can't talk about *anybody* being "gone" when you and Tariq have been

33

"friends" for thirty damned years and you still can't leave those *benefits*, alone."

I shook my head, then moved to look at myself in the mirror, pleased with how I looked.

"We're *not* friends with benefits, Nubia. Just friends—"

"Who *happen* to fuck each other. Right. That's normal stuff. I mean, my "friends" keep this season's new Giuseppes waiting at their house, in my size, all the time," she said sarcastically, gesturing toward the brand new black cutout booties – a gift from Tariq – resting on the dressing table.

I snatched the shoes off the table and put them on, then headed back to the bathroom for makeup without responding to Nubia's words. There was no need, not really. *She* knew, I knew, and *he* knew, that not much about our friendship was "normal".

Nubia and I had known each other a *long* time. Not as long as I'd known Tariq, but long enough that she was more than just my friend – she was my sister. She'd been there through good, bad, ugly, and everything in between. As confused as she pretended to be, she knew exactly what the dynamic was between me and Tariq.

"So listen," Nubia said, her hair appearing in the doorway before she did, again. "All jokes aside, Kora, you're thirty-six. He's thirty-seven. Your crazy asses are damned near forty years old—"

"And you aren't?"

"That's beside the point."

I smirked, then went back to carefully lining my eyes in dark brown pencil. "Then what *is* the point?"

"That none of us are getting any younger. I know you love that man, and I know he loves you. *Why* are you two still playing around with this "just friends" shit? Why don't you make it official?"

I shook my head as I replaced the pencil in the makeup kit, then picked out a lipstick in a deep plum. "Really, Nubia? You're going to act like you forgot Tariq is…"

"Fine? Independently wealthy? Single? *All the way*, for real heterosexual…"

"And *crazy*," I laughed. "You forgot his ass is full-blown crazy."

"Yeah, about you."

I finished applying my lipstick, then turned to face my friend. She was giving me a

"look", part amused, part bewildered.

"Nubia," I said, placing my hands at her shoulders. "As unconventional as our friendship is, this dynamic is what works for Tariq and me. As long as it's not romantic, we vibe."

"Kora." Nubia put her hands on my shoulders, mirroring my stance. "I need your ass to understand that this is crazy."

I shrugged. "Crazy, or perfect? I get great sex from an amazing man, while maintaining my personal space and freedom. What more could I want?"

She lifted an eyebrow. "I don't know, love? Companionship? Someone to hold you at night?"

"Who says I don't get that?"

Nubia laughed as she dropped her hands from my shoulders. "Oh, I'm *sure* you get all of that. From Tariq. Because that's your damned man!"

"He's *not*," I giggled, stepping out of the bathroom. I picked her Kate Spade up from the bed, handing it to her as I headed into the main living space. "We tried it before, remember?" I let out a heavy sigh as I picked my own bag up from where I'd left it on the couch the night before. When I turned, Nubia was right behind me, with her arms crossed.

"That was a long time ago," she said. "You were both young, in the public spotlight, super busy with your careers. You don't think it would be different now?"

"Not a risk I'm willing to take."

"So you're saying you *do* want him, you're just afraid of losing your friendship if it goes bad again?"

I nodded. "Yes, exactly that." I started to swing my purse up on my shoulder, then stopped. "Wait a minute, *no—*"

"Uh-uh-uh," Nubia said, a grin spreading across her mouth as she wagged a finger in front of her. "You said what you meant, so there's really no point in denying it. Besides. you're just confirming what I already knew."

My face pulled into a scowl. "Your ass always thinks you *know* something," I snipped, then turned on my heels to head for the front door.

"Because I always *do*," she called over my shoulder as she followed me out of Tariq's condo. "Go ahead and pull your key to his place out Kora, so you can lock the door."

I sucked my teeth as I, indeed, pulled out my keys. "Having a key to his place is *not* out of the ordinary! I only ever use it if he's not here anyway."

Nubia smirked. "Right. Like, when you stay over after a night of filthy sex."

"Nubia…"

"*What*? Come on, Kora. We've had this conversation what, once a quarter, for the last… how many years? That man loves you, and you love him. Be together."

"It's not that simple."

"Why not?"

"*Because*," I said, dropping my keys back into my purse. "It's just complicated."

Nubia cut her eyes toward the ceiling, then back at me. "But does it *really* have to be?"

I opened my mouth to respond, but she'd already turned on her heels and started down the hall, yelling "*Bring your ass on, you've given me a headache only new shoes can fix.*"

I shook my head, then followed her, but my mind was still wrapping around what she'd said.

She and I *had* been having a repeat of this same conversation for a long time. We started having it about a year after Tariq and I mutually decided that a formal romantic entanglement just wasn't working for us.

"more" with Tariq was a bad idea. They were awful enough in just the form of memories to know that I never wanted to be immersed in them again.

So yes, I loved him, and there wasn't a singular doubt in my mind that he felt the same. But I loved him entirely too much to risk losing him – or myself – again.

Right?

The little voice in my head that would usually yell back *"hell yes!"* was conspicuously absent, and as I followed Nubia onto the elevator, I chewed at the inside of my bottom lip. *Where the hell was that voice*, reminding me of dodging photographers, of the jealous tirades, of screaming at each other, and arguing, and all the things that *didn't* happen when I simply didn't consider him mine.

Yes, it was psychological bullshit, the idea that any real difference was made in our relationship by the simple use – or none use – of a certain title, but that didn't make it less true.

For whatever reason, when he wasn't "my man", it really didn't bother me when Tariq was out partying, being connected to hot celebrity women, actually sleeping with some of those women, whatever. But as *soon* as we decided to be official, it was like somebody flipped a switch and opened a door, and angry, jealous girlfriend Kora came charging out. When we shifted back into just being friends again – with a few new "benefits" – that switch flipped back the other way.

It never bothered me to see Tariq with someone else, because when *I* needed him, he made me a priority, and the opposite was true as well. If he needed me, for anything, I made myself available. Even if he and I weren't going to be together, that didn't mean we didn't want something permanent – just not with each other.

So we played the field.

We dated.

However unconventional our friendship was, it worked. And as much of a mess as our

attempt at being a couple was, I wouldn't take it back, because since then, we'd only grown closer.

Every once in a while, one of us got serious about someone. We had a rule between us, that if there were someone we were serious about we would keep things between us platonic.

Neither of us wanted to cheat on, or play with another person's emotions, so we kept by that promise –whether or not the person we were with actually believed it.

"Have you even heard a word I've said to you?" Nubia asked, rolling her eyes as the elevator doors slid open.

I shook my head a little, bringing myself back into the present and answering her question. "No, I didn't. I was thinking about something."

"Something like…?"

"Nothing really. Just trying to figure out where you keep the motor on your mouth."

Nubia sucked her teeth, then stepped onto the glossy wood floors of the lobby. Fletch,

one of Tariq's assistants/bodyguards came from the front desk to greet her. I watched their exchange with a smile

40

as I exited the elevator, even though my thoughts were still a bundle of confusion.

I could run through all the reasons in my head that Tariq and I would never work, but for some reason, today, those reasons felt a little hollow. For some reason, last night with Tariq – the things he'd said, the way he reacted to my presence, the way he'd touched me… something about it was different, but I couldn't quite pinpoint why.

Maybe because it had been a few months since we'd been intimate? I'd seen Tariq nearly every day since the divorce, but was trying my hand at *not* ending up between his sheets. We'd talked, and eaten together, hung out, but at the end of the night, I went back home, and slept in my own bed. I hadn't said anything to him about it, but we were so in tune with each other that he picked it up anyway.

There had been no flirting, no innuendo, just our normal platonic friendship, from the length of my marriage, and before. Why I didn't just tell him, "hey, I think we should stop sleeping together." was something I had no answer for. I just knew I was trying to prove a point to myself, that our friendship *could* exist without sex, but Tariq had never given me a reason to doubt that. Paul, on the other hand… I sighed, hard.

After a quick greeting with Fletch, Nubia and I headed out, into the perfect early fall weather. I breathed deeply from the crisp air, trying to cleanse the stubborn thoughts from my mind, but they wouldn't budge. No matter how hard I searched my head for my normal indignation at the thought of being with Tariq, I couldn't find it. My conviction that what I had with him was enough was nowhere to be found.

Maybe because of the divorce.

I mean, that wound was still fresh. It hadn't even been four months yet, and I was still hurt, still angry, still embarrassed. It made sense to seek comfort with my friend, who was there for me through anything, even a marriage he didn't want to happen. That was it.

That was *definitely* it, it had to be.

There was no crazy shift in feelings, no sudden change of heart. I was just emotionally raw, reading too much into some things, and not enough into others. He was just as touchy-feely with me as he'd always been, it had just been a long time. I wasn't *really* considering a second chance relationship with Tariq, I was just newly divorced, and trying to figure things out.

Nubia and I turned the corner toward the boutiques downtown, and my shoulders sagged

in relief. Instead of immersing myself in my thoughts, I tuned back into whatever she'd been talking about this whole time, and pushed my focus to shopping.

Perfect distraction from trying to believe my own lies.

four.

Tariq

"So I heard about your little bet."

When I glanced at Kora, she had her face pointed up towards mine, her eyes hidden behind designer frames with dark lenses. It was late – dark out – but she wore shades anyway, supposedly to protect her eyes from the harsh wind that had kicked up, turning a mild day into a cold night.

She had an eyebrow raised behind her glasses, and a smile tipped the corners of her mouth as she looked away from me, down to the hot, sticky cinnamon roll in a cardboard container in her hands. *"We'll share it,"* she'd insisted, stopping at the street vendor and looking expectantly in my direction for the cash she rarely carried on her. I handed it to her, with not enough hesitation, because I was notoriously bad at saying no to Kora.

It was half-gone, and I *still* hadn't gotten a bite.

"So Nubia really can't keep anything to herself then, huh?" I asked, shaking my head.

Kora laughed. "Oh, she keeps plenty to herself. Just not from me." She forked another piece of the cinnamon roll into her mouth, moaning a little as her lips closed around it. I looked away, pointing my gaze ahead of us, to the corner where we'd be turning next.

We'd had a great time at dinner – like we always did – talking, laughing, keeping things light, and upbeat. But now that dinner was over, this was just like Kora, to hold out and wait for the conversation she really wanted to have.

"Sooo," she said, when she'd finished chewing. "Don't try to deflect. Tell me about the bet." She laughed at my exaggerated groan. "Don't act like that. You're the one betting against me. Don't get all shy when I want to talk about it."

I shrugged. "I'm not getting shy. And I didn't bet against you. I bet *on* you – and lost, by the way. If anybody should be getting scolded…"

Kora gasped, then playfully smacked me on the shoulder as we rounded the corner to her building. "That's so…"

"Accurate?"

"I was going to go with ridiculous. How exactly do you lose a bet based on whether or not someone will sleep with you? You could have easily won by keeping your dick to yourself."

I chuckled, shaking my head as I followed her into her building, then watched her key in the code that would give access to the interior doors. "Kora, I lost the bet the moment you decided to come to my door."

She froze, with her fingers still hovering over the keypad. She turned a little, her eyes still hidden behind those dark lenses, bottom lip pulled halfway into her mouth, worrying it between her teeth.

I *really* wished I could see her eyes.

On Kora, those were the windows to everything. She was an actress through and through, easily able to bottle and alter the emotions that showed on her pretty face. But those eyes of hers – big, heavily lashed pools of honey-specked mahogany, set against velvety skin just a shade or so darker than cinnamon – they told it all.

Which was the *real* reason for the shades, whether or not she admitted that.

So what was she, a woman who so rarely kept anything from me, holding back? Was she

embarrassed that she'd failed at her goal of a completely platonic friendship for us? Wanting to go right back into that, but unsure of how to let me down gently? Still reeling from her quickie divorce, but trying to put on a brave face? Or something else?

"What does that even mean?" Finally, she stopped looking at me, and turned to finish keying in her code to the door. It let out a low chime, and then the electronic sounds of the locks sliding open echoed down the hall.

"What does what mean?" I asked, following her down the hall to the elevator, leaving the warm scent of sugar and butter and icing in our wake.

"That you lost the moment I decided to come to your door."

"What do you think it means?"

She stopped in the elevator and turned to face me as the doors closed, whipping off those glasses to finally show me her whole again. Those big browns, that dark cinnamon skin, regal cheekbones and full lips… everything about Kora gave off a "queenly" vibe – from that gorgeous face to her perfect posture to her beautifully toned legs, standing in a way that she always looked like she might break into dance.

"If I knew, Tariq," she snapped out in a clipped tone, even though her eyes spoke amusement, "I wouldn't have asked, would I?"

"You're notorious for asking questions you already have answers for, just to see what I'm going to say." I walked past her when the elevator opened again, continuing to her apartment, where I waited beside the door. I lifted an eyebrow at her, then inclined my head toward the locks. "Come open the damned door, girl."

"Excuse you?"

"Is your hearing going bad? I mean, you *are* getting closer to forty now, so…"

"Fuck you, okay?" She grinned, reaching into the purse hooked over her elbow, keeping a careful hold on her dessert as she rummaged for her keys. She closed the short distance to the door, unlocked it, and stepped inside.

I was right behind her, grabbing her arms to turn her around, pinning her against the door as soon as it had swung closed. She hadn't even flipped on a light yet, but the blinds that covered her big front windows were open, and moonlight streamed through the sheer drapes.

Her expression was blank, only breaking into a smile when I released her long enough to take the things she held in her hands, depositing them on the table by the door.

"What are you doing?" she asked, her words coming out in a whisper as I lowered my mouth to hers.

"I'm about to answer your question."

"What question?"

She grinned, and then I did too, reaching up to cup her face in my hands. "You asked me what it meant when I said I lost the bet as soon as you decided to come to my door. And you implied that I bet against you, which isn't true. I know you very well, Kora. When you put your mind to something, when you make a decision, you're very good at following through. If you told Nubia we were going to be strictly platonic, I had no reason to believe otherwise, so yes, I wagered on it. But I can't tell you no, Kora. If you were coming to me, with intimacy in mind, it was happening. Bet or not."

I caught the tiny hitch in her breath as I pressed my mouth to hers. Felt the subtle tremor of a moan in her throat as I nibbled her bottom lip, then brushed it with the tip of my tongue. She was sweet, hints of sugar and cinnamon glazing her lips as I pushed my tongue between them to taste her mouth. My hands kept her face tilted up toward mine as I kissed her, cherishing the pliant, pillowy softness of her lips, the sweetness of her tongue, and the warmth of her hands at my waist, then under my blazer, then tugging at the buttons of my shirt.

When I pulled back from the kiss, she averted her eyes, and I narrowed mine.

What the hell is up with her?

Before I could ask, my cell went off in my pocket. I glanced at the screen before I answered, giving Kora a *hold on a second* gesture as I eased away, letting her free from her place against the door.

She slipped away, grabbing her cinnamon roll, but leaving her purse and keys. She was dressed in something I'd purchased for her, from her section in my closet. Heels that highlighted her legs, jeans that emphasized her ass, and a plush, oversized sweater that kept slipping down her shoulder, offering a peek at the bare skin I wanted to touch so bad.

But we were supposed to be keeping it friendly.

That's what she was saying, without saying it, I realized in a rush of awareness as I ended my call. The avoidance for the last few months, the hiding of her eyes... last night was just a moment of weakness for her. This morning was finishing it off.

She kicked off her shoes, leaving them near the door. "That was Julissa?" Oh yeah.

She was *definitely* putting me back in the "friend" lane.

I nodded, then took off my jacket before following her to the kitchen where she perched herself at the counter. "Yeah. Wanting to know if I was available for a late dinner."

She smirked. "Guess you should have checked with *her* for dinner plans first, huh?"

"Don't do that."

"You need to go use the bathroom or something to make some space?"

"Kora…"

"*What*?" she asked, breaking into a peal of giggles. "Don't be all serious Tariq, I'm kidding. What did you tell her?"

"That I had dinner already, with you."

Kora cringed. "Oh."

"Oh? That's all you're going to say?"

"Mmhmm." She stabbed another piece of her dessert with her fork, and then – "that is *all*

I have to say about you telling your girlfriend you can't have dinner with her because you were out with another woman." – and stuffed the piece in her mouth.

I shook my head, fighting the urge to smile. "I wasn't at dinner with "another woman", I was at dinner with my lifelong friend. And besides that, Julissa is *not* my girlfriend."

"Does *she* know that?"

"She does."

Kora sucked her teeth, looking at me with her face pulled into a disbelieving scowl.

"Tariq please. You've been giving her time, attention, gifts, and good dick. She thinks you're her man."

"I've been clear."

"You think that matters?" Kora laughed again, then climbed down from her seat at the counter to open the refrigerator. "I thought you knew women a little better than that, my friend."

I blew out a breath, swallowing my growing irritation with how she was acting. Turning in her direction, I watched as she pulled a glass water bottle from her fridge, which I immediately pulled from her hands. I sat the bottle on the counter, then slipped an arm around her waist, drawing her against my chest.

"What is going on with you?" I asked, using my free hand to tip her chin up to face me.

"Seriously. Don't give me any bullshit."

She focused her gaze on something over my shoulder. "Nothing."

I turned her chin a little to the right, so her eyes actually met mine. "Kora, come on."

One moment she was holding on to that stoic façade. Two blinks later, her eyes were glossy, and she was fighting against my hold on her face. I let go of her chin, but kept her pulled close against me until she looked up again, and finally whispered, "Paul."

My jaw tightened the moment her ex-husband's name came off her lips. "What about him? Is he bothering you? Is—"

"No." She shook her head, then closed her eyes for a moment before she met my gaze again. "He just… in his divorce petition, he essentially claimed I defrauded him."

I drew my eyebrows together in a scowl. "*What*? How?!"

She sighed. "He said that I'd made him believe that I loved him, when I didn't. That I was incapable of loving him, because of my relationship with you. That we could never fully commit to each other, when I was having my emotional needs met by you."

My eyes narrowed a little more. "That's…"

"Completely accurate." Kora shrugged her way out of my arms. "It's true, Tariq, and that's why the judge bought it. I mean, how would you feel if the woman you loved… if it didn't matter if you messed up, or didn't listen, or understand her sometimes, because she had a male bestie she used to fuck, who will be there to fulfill those roles for her when you won't?"

I scoffed. "Wouldn't happen."

"Pretend it did."

"Then I would step up my goddamned game with my wife. What kind of whiney, worthless man blames a woman's friendship on the demise of his marriage? If he can't compete, or make himself invaluable, it sounds like a personal problem to me."

Kora rolled her eyes. "It's not that cut and dry."

"Oh, but it is. Remember what I said, Kora, about men that are beneath you? It's not just about economic status. When you first told me you were serious about Paul, I didn't approve, but I didn't stand in your way either. I didn't disparage your relationship with him, even though he wasn't somebody that I felt deserved my respect – or yours, for that matter. I never gave him a reason to feel threatened, and a

51

real man would have recognized that. He wasn't good enough for you."

"Against your impossible standards for me, who could possibly be "good enough"?"

I let a grin curl on my lips as I smoothed my eyebrows with my thumbs, then straightened my collar. "Well, I mean…"

"Oh, of course," Kora laughed, smacking me on the shoulder. "*You* meet your standards.

And we *both* know how that turned out."

I wanted to remind her that we were basically kids at the time of our ill-fated romance. Early twenties, young black celebrities trying to keep our relationship out of the public eye while the media paired us with any other celebrity who happened to be in the vicinity. I remembered secret bathroom quickies, holding hands under tables, acting like we barely knew the other existed, and then laughing about it later, when we were finally. But looking in her eyes, I knew *she* remembered screaming matches rooted in jealousy, begging me not to kill the stage manager who'd looked at her a little too long, and having to apologize to – and pay off – the groupie whose ass she kicked when she caught her trying to sneak into my hotel room one night.

The not-so-good parts.

"You act like it was all bad, Korrine."

Her expression softened, and she smiled a little as she shook her head. "No. It wasn't *all* bad, not at all. I'm not saying I would take it back, but it was bad enough that we both know better now, right?"

52

I shrugged. "You weren't *that* crazy."

"But *you* were," she laughed. "Seriously, Tariq. I don't want to risk our friendship like that again. You mean too much to me."

"And yet, you blame your divorce on me."

"I'm not blaming it on you. I'm blaming it on *me*," she said, shaking her head. Part of my responsibility as a wife is making my husband feel essential to my life, just as I would want to

feel essential to his. I can't do that if I'm so physically and emotionally invested in you. I think it would be wise for us to get used to being completely platonic friends, so that we actually have a chance to connect with someone else. Somebody like Julissa."

I scoffed. "And who is your "somebody" going to be? Another accountant? Paul?"

"No and no, asshole," she said, lifting an eyebrow at me. "Somebody new, I guess. But in any case, we'll be able to move forward without the ambiguity."

"Without ambiguity huh? So what was last night then?"

She blinked, and then shook her head. "Last night was me needing you. Was that okay?"

I took her hands, pulling them up to my mouth to plant a kiss against her fingers. "It will *never* be a problem for you to need me Kora. *Never.* Have I ever made it seem any different?"

Kora shook her head, then smiled as I leaned in to kiss her forehead. "No. Never."

"Are you okay now?"

It took her a second, but she nodded, then pushed herself up on her toes to kiss my cheek.

"Yes, I am. Go see your girlfriend."

"She's *not* my— you know what, I'm not even about to let you mess with my head.

Goodnight, Kora."

She grinned. "Goodnight, Tariq."

She walked me to the door, where we exchanged a last hug before I put on my jacket and she let me out. I waited to hear the lock click into place before I started down the hall, taking a moment to pull out my phone.

I scrolled down to Julissa's name and hit the "call" button.

She sounded out of breath when she answered, like she'd run to catch the phone.

"Did I catch you at a bad time?" I asked as I stepped onto the elevator, pressed the button for the lobby, then leaned back against the mirrored wall.

"No. *No*, not at all." Her answer was eager, quick. "I'm glad you called me back. I thought maybe you…" She was quiet for a few seconds, and then came back. "Never mind.

What's up?"

"Nothing. Just keeping my word. I said I would call you back. What are you doing?"

"Just at home, alone. Bored."

I shook my head as I walked off the elevator, and headed out of Kora's building. I recognized the invitation in her words, but after being with Kora, it wasn't one I was about to accept.

"Get dressed. Just because I'm not hungry doesn't mean I can't take you to dinner."

five.

Kora

"Come on. Come *on. Come on!* Do you have to look like something stinks? You're supposed to be turning me on, and looking like that, I'm about to tune you out!"

I sucked my teeth, shaking my head as I watched my actors perform the dance routine that would lead into the reprisal of the title song of the show – *The Chase*. It was a very sexy, high-energy routine, and most of the women were giving it everything, which was something I required at every rehearsal.

Get used to giving it your all, so when it's time to perform you can give it a little more.

Those words – *my* words, were framed in the breakrooms, bathrooms, dressing room, rehearsal rooms, and offices. Everywhere someone who mattered to a production put on by Warm Hues Theatre might be, that sentence beckoned, daring them to be better, work harder, to *impress.*

At the moment, I wasn't impressed at all.

My star performer, the one whose face had already been printed on a billion flyers, slathered across social media, plastered all over entertainment news – was on a *billboard*, for Christ's sake – was giving me nothing.

"Arch your back, flip your hair, make me want to fuck you, Dawn, that's the point here, is it not?!"

She said nothing, just rolled her eyes as the choreographer reset the music, urging the girls to start from the top of the routine. I crossed my arms, tuning the other women out to focus on Dawn. They had it down – she didn't.

Dawn was playing the role of Robyn in the show. A beautiful, seductive young jewel thief being pursued by a rookie FBI agent with something to prove. In her "regular" life, Robyn was the main attraction at a burlesque show, joined by four other women who formed a band of thieves.

In the scene we were on, one of the biggest dance numbers in the show, Robyn was found out, and she knew it, but she and the girls were dancing for their freedom – keeping the agent – Kyle Jamison – and his cohorts distracted long enough for their allies to help them escape.

Dawn's ass was up there dancing like she *wanted* to go to jail.

She was a beautiful girl. Strikingly so, with deep golden-brown skin, high cheekbones, the kind of body that was perfectly balanced between curvy and athletic – the kind of body most dancers would kill for – and a mane of thick natural curls that rivaled Nubia's. Young, eager, talented... *perfect* for the role of Robyn.

If only the girl would find some discipline, *somewhere.*

Fatigue from last night's partying was all over her face. And really? Not just her face. Her arms, her legs, her hands, her feet. She was sluggish, and stiff, and—

"*Goddammit, Dawn,* your timing is off, and now—"

I stopped, swallowed hard, and took a deep breath.

"Cut the music," I snapped, then took the few steps that would put me right in Dawn's face. "Why are you here?"

She raised a neatly arched, blonde tinted eyebrow at me. "What?"

"You heard me. Why are you here? I know it's not to be a part of my show, not with this lackluster mess you're giving me right now. You are supposed to be the *star.* You were *chosen* for this, over thirty other girls, including the four behind you, who wanted this spot. And you have the nerve to pop up here with bags under your eyes, wearing yesterday's tank top, dancing like you're the only stripper in an empty strip club. Do you think I won't replace you?"

At *those* words, the threat of getting replaced, the stank attitude dropped from Dawn's expression, and her tired eyes widened with fear.

"No ma'am."

"You're damned right. We only have three weeks before this show opens, and I am *not* above getting a new Robyn if it makes the difference in those opening reviews. I will not allow you to drag this production down. Do you understand?"

She averted her gaze. "Yes."

"Good."

With one last cutting look, I turned around and started to walk off, but I stopped, and whirled back around.

"What did you just say?" I asked, my words amplified by everyone else's sudden silence.

Dawn shook her head. "Nothing. Whatever. Can we get back to work?"

My lips spread into a grin. "Oh, my dear. No, we can't. Because I could have sworn that once I turned my back, you mumbled something under your breath about me *"getting my ass up here to see how hard it is"*. Did I imagine that?"

"I–I didn't mean—" *"Did I imagine it?"*

"No."

"I didn't think so." I pulled my sweater over my head and tossed it into a chair, leaving on my camisole and the soft, slim-fitting leather pants I wore with my Jimmy Choo platform pumps. *"Move,"* I demanded of Dawn, and she scurried aside to watch as I cued for the music and then took the place of Robyn, in the middle of the line.

A little surge of adrenaline rushed through me when the beat dropped on the music, and my body immediately moved with the other girls. Rolling hips, swinging hair, into the eightcounts that matched the tempo of the song. Strong, confident, concise movements with no ambiguity. A clear purpose of ass in your face, sexy distraction. The sensual, seductive number came later.

I moved through the routine – one I'd overseen and helped create – with ease, and hadn't even worked up a sweat by the time it was done. When the music ended, I looked pointedly at Dawn, then motioned for her to get back in place as I moved to get my sweater. I pulled it back over my head,

60

careful not to get any lipstick on it, then took a position near the edge of the rehearsal stage.

Right in front of Dawn.

"Okay. Now, if we're done with *that*, let's start from the top."

~

I pinched the bridge of my nose, hoping the pressure would help ease the headache steadily building between my eyes. With my free hand, I held my tablet up in front of me so I could lean back as I watched a run through of *The Chase* play on the screen. If everything fell into place, it would be really be an incredible production.

Warm Hues Theatre's last show had been a deep, emotionally stirring piece that had garnered a lot of critical acclaim. Sold out house every night the show ran, rave reviews from the press, a true breakout project that engraved our name in the category of theatre elite. I'd served as assistant director for that production, saving it from a director who was more concerned with screwing the ingénue than putting on a great performance.

She got fired, I got hired, and *The Chase* was my show.

My *first* show as head director.

I had no delusions that *The Chase* would get the kind of national attention that *Light Up the Dark* had received, but that was kind of the point. I was confident in my ability to put on a show, but too-lofty ambitions for a debut project had

61

been the demise of more than one young director. I refused to let that be my fate.

So: *The Chase.*

It was campy, sexy, and fun, the kind of show where I could get my feet wet as a director, while still putting on a fabulous production.

If everything falls into place, I reminded myself.

I mostly ignored the actors on the screen, focusing instead on the lighting design. For the run through, it had still been rudimentary, but even then I could see how much that element was going to shine. Deep, vivid blues and purples ruled the color palette, with laser lights creating special effects, spotlights emphasizing certain parts of the stage or the actors. A little bubble of excitement built in my chest as I watched it play through, and—

"You know you didn't have embarrass me like that, right?"

I lowered my tablet to look toward my office door – now open – to find Dawn standing there with her arms crossed. I smirked as I lowered the tablet to the desk, pausing the video before I motioned for her to come in.

"I understand how you might be confused, but *I* didn't embarrass you. You embarrassed yourself by not performing at the level you're capable of."

"Everybody has "off" days, right? I'm tired. We've been rehearsing seven hours a day, six days a week for the last three weeks." She plopped herself down into the chair across from my desk, rolling her eyes when I gestured for her to straighten herself up.

"Get used to it, because after next week, we're going to *ten* hour rehearsal days. Five hours on, a two-hour break, and then five more hours. You need to drink more water, get in the gym, get some caffeine in you, something. Whatever it takes so that the girl that earned the starring role in this show is the same one who shows up for rehearsal. *That's* who I expect to see every day."

"I'm just *tired*. You act like I'm messing up left and right."

"Today you were. And tired is not an acceptable excuse around here. You should have taken your ass home from whatever you were doing last night and gotten some rest. No one told you to go out on a Sunday night, when you knew we had rehearsals today. There is no reason not to be fresh for practice. I mean, you walk around listening to this girl, what's her name? That popstar you *love*…"

"Pixie?"

"Right," I nodded. "Pixie. That girl gets on stage and dances her ass off to a routine, in heels, and does it flawlessly, every time. While she's singing – also flawlessly. Her background dancers? Flawless too. She and her team are serious about their craft, and it *shows*. I'm not going to sit here and accept *I was tired,* or *I woke up late* or, *I was hungry,* or any other lame ass

excuses, Dawn." I stopped to glance at the time. "Go on your lunch break, eat some leafy greens and protein, no bread, no sugar, and come back ready to work. Or I *will* give another woman your spot."

Dawn let out a deep sigh, pouting as she pulled herself up from the chair to stand in front of my desk. "I thought there would be way more perks to my mother directing the show."

I cleared my throat, trying to soothe a subtle, itchy sort of tickle that had been nagging me all day, then smiled. "You thought wrong, sweetheart. No privileges. No special favors. You earned your role solely on merit, so you're going to have to do the same work I would require of anyone else if you want to keep it."

At only twenty years old, Dawn was still learning the ways of the world – especially

when it came to the professional theatre. She'd been immersed in it since before she was born, danced and sang as a little girl, performed in small school productions whenever she could, but that was very, *very* different than the "real world" of entertainment.

I was already anticipating charges of bad parenting for allowing Dawn to be cast in such

a highly sexual role. And honestly? I kind of really didn't want her to do it. But this was her life, and her career, and I knew how badly she wanted it. I was *not* about to tell my (just barely) grown daughter she couldn't audition for a role.

Out here, she was the child of a two-time Tony award winning, "triple-threat" Broadway starlet. The grandchild of a woman who danced, sang, and acted her way into *three* Tony awards, and was, in the late sixties, referred to as a "modern Lena Horne". If she didn't perform at her very best,

64

and if her very best wasn't damned good, Dawn's success would be branded as the product of nepotism, and that was a stamp of disapproval she'd never get past.

And honestly? I was fighting that same battle. I wanted my directorial debut to be considered good because it was *actually* good, not because my mother was the legendary Kathryn Oliver. Not because I was given special treatment because my friends in the industry felt bad for me. There were many who would grade me with a more critical eye because of those two things, and I wanted those accusations stopped in their tracks.

So rather than hear whispers that Dawn only got – or retained – the part because I was her mother, I pushed her. Rather than spark the rumor that I was bad at casting, I made my daughter prove herself. Rather than throw her at the mercy of some (possibly) perverted creep of a director, like the one I replaced, for her first role, yes, she could work with her mother.

As long as she *worked.*

"I'm gonna tell Tariq on you."

I let out a laugh that turned into a fit of coughs, which I calmed with a swig from my water. "Girl, tell him! Both of you can still get your little behinds swatted."

"Momma, ew! I don't want to think about you *spanking* him!"

I shrugged. "Then don't."

"But now you've put the visual in my head, and I was about to go have lunch with him!"

I smiled. "Well, think of the spankings *your* ass got instead, and tell him I said hello."

For two weeks, I'd successfully avoided being alone with Tariq. We'd shared a few meals since that awkward after-dinner conversation, and several phone calls, but I was trying my best to curtail a situation where I might end up saying more than I should.

Especially now that he was seeing Julissa.

He wasn't serious about her – yet, at least – and I knew that because he moved slow, first of all, and because he would have made it clear. But, she was great for him, from what I could tell. Smart, successful, sexy. The kind of woman who would, eventually make a great life partner for him. Maybe his wife, mother of his kids… *ugh. Whoa.*

Wait a minute… why the hell does the thought of that make my stomach hurt?

In any case, it wasn't fair for my uncertainty to overshadow the possibility of what he could have with her. As much as I teased him about her, Julissa Santos had the potential to make Tariq a happy man. And more than anything, that was what I wanted for him.

Dawn shook her head at my teasing, but a smile played at her lips. "Bye momma."

"Bye sweetheart, I love you."

"I love you too."

She turned for the door, and as she approached, her mouth spread into an even bigger smile before she quickly tempered it, trying to look unaffected. I frowned a little at her change in demeanor, then followed her gaze to the doorway,

66

where I laid eyes on the reason for her attempts to play "cool".

Special Agent Kyle Jamison.

Or, as he was known *off* stage, Donovan Perkins.

Ideally, I never would have cast a twenty-five year old in that role, but his chemistry with Dawn during auditions had been undeniable. Together on stage, they were smoking, hot enough to burn the theatre down.

And that was where I preferred they *leave* the fire.

Donovan was, to put it simply, *gorgeous*. Deep, dark brown skin, thick curly hair cut into a short Mohawk style, chiseled features – face *and* body – and the boy could move like nobody's business. His singing was passable, but his acting was strong, and this wasn't his first show. He was already building a reputation as a hard worker in this industry, which was incredible for him, but he was building a reputation as something else too.

A womanizer.

I did *not* want his little ass with my daughter.

Never mind the fact that he had *just* very publicly broken up with Pixie, who was Dawn's current pop idol. He already had Dawn – and every other heterosexual woman on my cast and crew – wrapped around his finger.

I cleared my throat again, trying to break the long, lusty gaze they were giving each other. "Can I help you, Donovan?" I asked, maybe a little more curtly than I should have.

He took his sweet time looking away from Dawn, then turned his eyes on me. "Yes, boss lady, you sure can."

I quelled the urge to roll my eyes. "What is it?"

"Well, I ran it by Micah first, but he said I would have to come and talk to you." *Must be some bullshit then.*

If my assistant director, Micah, had told him he had to talk to me about it, the answer was almost certainly about to be a big *no*.

"That doesn't tell me anything, Donovan. Make your point."

He flashed me a big smile, showing off a mouthful of perfect teeth. "Ms. Oliver... you know I used to have the biggest crush on you, right? I remember being fifteen years old, watching you in that commercial where you were "the girl of my dreams", and you were wearing this –"

"*Donovan, what do you want?*"

"Oh, my bad, I did get a little off track didn't I?" he asked, still smiling as he tucked his hands in his pockets. "Well, it's like this: I have to miss a week of rehearsals so I can go dance in this show—"

"The hell you do. *What*? Listen, if you miss a whole week of rehearsals, you may as well kiss your role goodbye, because I *will* put someone else in it. *Permanently.*"

"Come *on*." He let out a heavy sigh, then licked his lips. "I have to do this, I'm under contract."

I shrugged. "Which you didn't disclose when I hired you, and asked about any prior responsibilities you may have that might cause a conflict."

"I wasn't thinking about it!"

"Oh, I know *that*." I shook my head, taking another sip of water as that tickle built in my throat again. Suddenly, I felt exhausted. Was I really about to have to replace his ass, three weeks before we opened?

"Kora, *please*. I'm begging you. They're gonna sue my ass if I don't show up, and I know they're not gonna give me a break, cause it's Auriel's show."

"Auriel?"

"Pixie."

I lifted an eyebrow. "Oh." *Shit.* They *would* sue his ass.

I filled my cheeks with air, then slowly pushed it back out through my teeth. "Okay... when is the show? How many nights? Where?"

"It's next weekend. Two nights, in LA."

I sucked my teeth. "Two nights?! Then why the hell do you need to miss a whole week of rehearsals?"

"I mean... it's LA. I can't go out there and *not* turn up a little b—"

"Get away from my office.'

"Wait, wait," he said, finally stepping inside. He flashed a smile at Dawn before he looked back at me, pleading with his eyes. "Kora, *please*?"

Rolling my eyes, I sat back in my chair. "Mr. Perkins, I will give you *two* days off from rehearsals, plus your normal Saturday off. It *is not*," I said, raising my voice when he opened his mouth to speak, "A negotiation. *At all*. Goodbye. Both of you."

I waved Dawn and Donovan out of my office, directing them to close the door behind them so I could lay my head on my desk. That exhausted feeling that I *thought* was the result of their ridiculous requests was beginning to feel like something else.

I picked up my phone to send a message to Micah, but as soon as I turned on the screen, Tariq's name was there, notifying me of a new message.

"Saw this and thought of you – T.E."

That message was right above a link to a video, which I tapped to follow, and then tapped again to play. It was a gorgeous woman on a stage, full band behind her, a mic in front of her, but when she opened her mouth to sing… *Oh, I'm going to kill him.*

"Oh really? A video of a woman's voice replaced with bleating goats reminds you of me?"

"No offense though. – T.E."

"I will drag your ass by your locs, negro."

"Ooooh, is that a new kink for you? Are you turning into a sadist on me? How are you? Haven't heard from you all day – T.E."

"Been busy all day. Trying to get this show in order, and I feel like shit."

"Like shit? What's wrong? – T.E."

"Throat being weird, headache, suddenly feel like I got hit by a truck. Normal stuff."

"Go home. –T.E."

"Can't. Did you not catch what I said about getting this show in order? It's a mess right now."

70

"What would happen if I bet my left nut that you were exaggerating this 'mess'? – T.E."

"You'd still be in possession of a full set of testicles."

"Right. So go home. I'll come check on you later. – T.E." Meaning, be alone with me, in my apartment? *Hell* no.

"I've gotta run. Meeting Dawn for lunch. – T.E." I smiled.

"Yeah, she told me. Thank you for always being so present with her."

"Just doing my sworn duty. I'll see you later. Go home. Rest. – T.E."

Shaking my head, I read over that last message again, knowing it was mostly pointless to respond. Tariq was going to do what he wanted, and what he wanted was to see me.

We both knew I wasn't saying no to that.

Besides, I *did* feel like crap, and this was how sickness always hit me. Fine one moment, half dead the next.

I backed out of the message thread with Tariq, and tapped in Micah's name to bring up the ongoing conversation I had with him. I told him what was going on with me, about my concession to Donovan, and urged him to, in the second half of rehearsals, stay on Dawn's ass.

And then, I did as Tariq had requested.

I took my ass home.

six.

"So you'll talk to her?"

"I'll talk to her."

"Don't just say it though, I need you to like, actually do it."

"I said I'll talk to her."

"For real?"

"You're pushing it."

I shook my head, trying not to smile as a huge grin spread across Dawn's face. "Thank you Tariq!" she said, wrapping her arms around me for a hug.

"You're welcome baby girl, but I'm not playing with you. I expect the best from you just like your mom does, and I'm *not* going to bat for you just so you can slack off."

Dawn stepped back, eyes wide. "It won't happen again, I promise."

"We'll see. Go ahead and get back to rehearsal, I'll see you later."

"Okay! Bye!"

"Bye."

She gave me a kiss on the cheek, and then a parting wave, and I sighed as she walked off.

I had no idea why I'd agreed to ask her mother to be a little easier on her, other than the fact that like her mother, I had trouble telling her no. Something about those Oliver girls made me hell bent on making them happy.

As Dawn exited the building that housed the office space of Foster Evans, my finance firm, I turned to head back for the elevator.

"Well she was pretty," I heard from behind me, and I pivoted in the direction of the voice. "But I never would have guessed you like them so young."

I chuckled a little, then pushed my hands into the pockets of my slacks. "Ah, you're not jealous are you, Julissa?"

She smiled, then closed the short distance between us, using her hand to steady the large designer bag swinging from the bend in her elbow. Julissa Santos was attractive, to say the least. A corporate finance lawyer – one of the youngest partners at her firm, which was housed in the floor above where my offices lived. Thirty-four years old, no crazy ex-husband or kids – that I knew of. Flawless golden skin, seductive brown eyes, and the body of a social media "model". It didn't go over my head that she was – physically, personally, professionally – the height of some men's fantasies.

"Not jealous.
Just observing the
competition." *Whoa.*

"Competition? That twenty-year-old *little girl* is Dawn, my goddaughter. Kora's daughter," I explained,

74

but something in Julissa's expression made me stop. "But you already knew that didn't you?"

Her eyes went a little wider, and then she gave me an embarrassed smile like it was nothing, but it told me plenty. She *was* "observing the competition".

Competition being *Kora*.

Shaking my head, I turned and started for the elevator again, knowing she would follow.

We made our way up to my office in relative silence, and I couldn't help wondering what was going on in her head.

"Are you mad at me?" she asked, as soon I closed my office door behind us, shutting us away from the reception area.

I lifted an eyebrow. "Mad about…?"

"About me looking into your *friend*."

A deep breath was necessary to tamper my annoyance over the inflection she put on that

word. It wasn't as if it were outrageous, or even surprising, that she would be curious about my relationship with Kora. Close friendships between men and women were still seen as an anomaly, and if I wanted to be very, *very* honest – which I kind of had a rule about anyway –

Kora and I weren't the pair to use to argue in favor of them. The romantic partner – male or female – always thought their partner used to have, wanted to have, was currently having, or would have in the future, sex with that "best friend". And when it came to me and Kora… that was true.

I shrugged. "Age of the internet. Everybody googles everybody. It's not a reason to be mad."

"Good," she nodded, not bothering to shutter her relief as she sat down in the chair in front of my desk. "I don't mean to be 'that' girl, but you know how people talk. I mean, there are all kinds of stories about you and her, rumors that you two are secretly married, that you're the reason for her divorce, cause the marriage wasn't legal in the first place. That Kora's daughter is actually yours…"

I dropped into the seat behind my desk, and reclined back. "You need to stop believing everything you read on those message boards and blogs."

"I don't. I just trying to figure out where I stand with you. And I feel like if I know where you stand with *her*…"

"Kora is my friend."

"*Just* your friend?"

"Yes."

"So you're *not* sleeping with her?"

"No."

"Have you slept with her before?"

"That is absolutely not your business."

Julissa reared back like she'd been hit, then let out a hiss of air through her teeth. "Wow.

So, yes then?"

"It's not a yes or a no, I'm saying that it doesn't concern you."

"If you and I are going to be together, it absolutely does concern me for you to be "best friends" with a woman you're screwing."

I chuckled. "Okay, let's get a few things clear. First, you and I are not "together"."

Her face dropped into a scowl. "Then what are we doing?"

"Getting to know each other. Julissa, the first meal we shared as anything other than colleagues was less than a month ago, and we've only been out a few times since then. I *like* you, yes, but this possessive thing you're doing... we aren't there yet." *Shit.*

Julissa blinked hard a few times, then ran her tongue over her teeth as she crossed her arms and sat back. "So, us sleeping together. That means nothing to you?"

I pushed out a heavy sigh. "We had sex a few times, yes. That's how this started, as just that, and *then* decided we enjoyed each other's company, and actually talked. Sex doesn't tell me shit about who you are, so no, in terms of us working toward an actual relationship, us sleeping together *doesn't* mean anything. You having or not having sex doesn't increase or decrease your currency with me."

She rolled her eyes, then turned away from me. "Whatever, Tariq."

"Oh, it's whatever now?"

She scoffed, standing up. "Uh, yes. It is. What else am I supposed to say when you're basically telling me you're not interested in me?"

"That's *not* what I'm saying to you, Julissa. If I weren't interested, I wouldn't be entertaining this conversation. At all. What I *am* saying is that I'm not a man who rushes things, and I'm not a man who will be rushed. I

77

do not consider us to be *together* yet, and us having sex is not relevant to that decision. You don't have to accept that – I'm letting you know where *I* stand, so you can make an informed decision."

She lifted an eyebrow. "Decision?"

"On if we're moving forward or not. Maybe remaining in a "getting to know you" phase isn't acceptable to you, and you want to termina—"

"No!" Julissa shook her head, and her expression softened as she slowly paced in front of my desk. "No, it's not like that. Getting to know each other is fine, it's just... how am I supposed to handle your "friendship" with Kora if we *do* go past this phase?"

"Well first you stop putting that little pissy inflection on your words when you talk about her. She's my oldest friend, and anything even hinting at disrespect towards her isn't going to fly with me. Secondly, you trust me. That's pretty vital, to a relationship. If I tell you that I'm not sleeping with someone, you trust that I'm not, and if you can't..."

She stopped, right in front of me. "But what if it's not *you* I don't trust? What if it's *her*?

I know how women can be—"

"But you don't know Kora. You know the old stories you read on the little gossip blogs about her. She and I have known each other more than thirty years, and she's never been anything but respectful and supportive of *every* relationship I've been in, throughout our friendship."

78

Julissa ran her tongue over her red-painted lips, subtly shaking her head again. "So you're saying I should put intuition and common sense to the side, and just believe that this woman could possibly just be somehow immune to you?"

I grinned. "Immune to me? I'm *that* desirable, huh?"

"Tariq..."

"What?"

She sucked her teeth. "Can you be serious, please?"

"I *am* being serious," I said, leaning back in my chair. "Listen, you can believe whatever you choose to believe about Kora, but if you try to force me to make a decision between continuing my friendship with her, and pursuing a relationship with you..."

Julissa lifted an eyebrow. "Then what?"

I sat forward, resting my elbows on the desk. "Kora's place in my life is very, *very* secure."

She sucked her teeth. "And mine isn't. Got it." Again, *shit.*

"I'm not trying to be an asshole here, Julissa. I'm just not a fan of ambiguity. I like you. I'd like to continue seeing you, until we've reached a point where we're both comfortable with taking a further step. My friendship with Kora isn't negotiable, but if it's a deal breaker for you, I understand that."

Julissa dropped her gaze to her manicured nails, then fingered the gold bracelet on her wrist before she looked up again. "Okay."

I cocked my head to the side. "Okay? Okay... *what?*"

"Okay, as in, I understand your position. I get it."

"So are we good?"

She took a deep breath, cutting her eyes toward the ceiling, but a few moments later, her mouth began to spread into a smile. "Yes," she said, nodding. "We're good."

"You're sure? You're a beautiful, desirable woman Julissa. You don't have to settle for something that makes you uncomfortable."

She rolled her eyes. "I know that. You haven't said anything that doesn't make sense, you know? And, I like you, and I see potential there, so yes. I'm sure."

I nodded. "Good. You want to make some plans for this weekend or something?"

"Actually, what are you doing tonight? One of the partners is really into theatre, and he got us all tickets to this play..."

I cringed. "Tonight isn't a good night."

"Ah. Are you working on portfolios?"

Sitting back again, I scratched my head. "Yes and no. Kora is sick, so I was going to go sit with her, and work from her place."

Julissa just looked at me for a long moment, and then said, "Oh." She stood, draping her purse over her arm again, then came around the desk. I sat back as she leaned in, pressing her mouth to mine for a kiss. When she drew back, she smiled. "This weekend, then."

I nodded. "This weekend."

She sashayed out of my office, and before the door closed behind her, Stephen walked in, pausing in the doorway to watch her leave. "She is... *whew*."

"If *whew* means stressful, yes. Yes she is," I said, chuckling as I opened my laptop.

"Uh oh. Trouble in paradise? Let me get the fuck out of here before it rubs off on me."

I sucked my teeth. "Negro, *please*," I laughed. "You know damned well you're not keeping anybody around long enough for *trouble in paradise*."

"I would if you'd hurry up and make me and Nubia happen." He crossed his arms over his chest and stared up in the air, like he was daydreaming. "Man," he shook his head. "Now that woman is—"

"Not at all interested in your ass," I said, logging on to my computer.

He twisted his mouth to one side, incredulous. "How do you know?"

"Because she *told* me." I glanced at Steph over my laptop, and shook my head. "She doesn't want you. Says she doesn't "do" athletes."

"Well that's because she hasn't been *done* by the right one yet," he said, rubbing his hands together. "Give me her number."

I laughed. "I am *not* giving you her number."

"I thought we were boys, Tariq!"

"We are, and I'm still not giving you that woman's number."

Steph groaned. "Man, I *knew* I should have partnered with Paul instead."

I looked up again as a vein started throbbing at the side of my head, and Steph cringed at the look on my face. "Too far?"

"Yeah," I nodded. "Too far."

Me, Steph, and Paul – Kora's ex-husband – went way back. We'd all gotten championship rings in our respective sports in the same year – football for me, rugby for Steph, and soccer for Paul. We were asked to do a little documentary together, a motivational thing for young black kids. All three of us agreed, and we ended up becoming friends.

Somewhat.

Steph and I were close like brothers, and Paul was more like the extra, because I never

quite trusted him. Something I couldn't quite put my finger on didn't curl all the way over with him. But on the surface, he was cool.

Mostly.

There was an underlying sense of rivalry with him, but I didn't mind, because I could compete – I usually just didn't care enough to bother. He wanted the finest woman, biggest house, flashiest car, whatever. As long as what *I* had was bad – in a good way – that was enough for me. And that bothered the shit out of Paul.

For whatever reason, he had some underlying issue with me, and I ignored it, and him. When I left the league because of an injury, that shit was probably the best time of his life. He pretended to be sorry for me, but if he could have gotten away with it, I really believe he would have thrown a party. That's just the kind of person he was, but it was like nobody could see it except me. Which was fine.

When he stopped playing, he moved to my city. All of a sudden, he was interested in a finance degree. Out of nowhere, he's a financial advisor too. Everything that I was doing, he was doing it too, trying – and failing – to be better at it than me.

I decided not to let it bother me, because really, what effect did it have on me? I wasn't concerned with him while he tried and tried to do… whatever he was trying to do. Unfortunately for me, it wasn't that easy. It took him long enough, but he finally identified the one thing that would actually get under my skin. My weak spot.

Kora.

And just the thought of that still made me sick to my stomach.

"I still can't believe she married Paul, man. I thought for sure you and her would—"

"Steph, come on man."

He raised his hands. "My bad. I know that's a sore spot for you. Business?"

I nodded. "Please."

His demeanor immediately changed, and he took the seat in front of my desk. "Okay.

About this deal with the Drakes…"

seven.

Tariq

She wasn't answering the door.

My first thought was "*Damn, I guess she really is taking this 'avoid Tariq' bullshit seriously.*" Eventually, I would call her on it, but in the meantime I'd just been giving her the space she obviously wanted. But not answering the door – or her phone – for me? No, this was something different.

I shifted the bags in my hands to one side, to pull out my keys. I maneuvered the one she'd given me into my hand and unlocked the door, closing and locking it behind me, then paused for a second. The relative silence was clue number two that something was really up.

On the rare occasion I used my key to get into Kora's place while she was actually home, no matter the reason, she came from somewhere fussing at me about coming in unannounced.

We both knew it wasn't *actually* a problem, but I let her fuss, then we argued, and then we made up – which was most likely the purpose of the manufactured disagreement.

Today? No curse out.

I put my bags down in Kora's kitchen and left my shoes and jacket by her front door, then followed the low sound of music filtering through her apartment. It was the same soulful

R&B playlist I'd heard countless times over the years, which she gradually updated with new artists and new music over time. If I thought about it hard enough, I could probably remember exactly when she added something to her mix. I helped her create the original damn near twenty years ago. We'd come a long way from making sure a blank tape was in the boom box so you were ready to record when your song came on the radio, but she *still* had a tendency to call and ask me "hey, have you heard this yet?" about every new song before she added it.

Kora always put that same playlist on when she was cleaning, or working, or—

"Damn, you really are sick, aren't you?" I muttered under my breath as I looked through her bedroom doorway. The bed was still made, but she was sprawled on top of it with her head buried in the pillows, and the Blakewood State University blanket I'd sent her as a gift almost fifteen years ago spread on top of her.

A smile came to my face before I could help it, and I quietly made my way to the bed.

The day I got drafted to the Connecticut Kings– first round pick – Kora hadn't been able to make it, because she had a show. The next day, there were pictures everywhere of her coming out for curtain call with this very blanket around her shoulders. We were honestly still "just" friends back then, and I know for a fact it wasn't her intention, but that was, to me, where the rumors about us got started.

Sitting down beside her, I slipped a hand under the blanket to rub her back. I wasn't surprised that she was bare underneath, because she hardly ever wore actual clothes if she was at home. She responded immediately to the stimulation of my hand against her skin, pressing herself against it like she recognized my touch in her sleep. She groaned a little, then shifted her position from face down in the pillows to sleepily staring at me with her head turned to the side.

"*Hey*," she whispered, her voice sounding scratchy, like her throat was dry.

I smiled. "Hey yourself. What's going on with you?"

She shrugged as best she could, then buried her face in the pillows again.

I shook my head, then went into her bathroom, rummaging until I found what I was looking for. When I went back to her, she let out a few moans and groans that were definitely curse words, but she let me put the thermometer in her mouth. A few seconds later, it chimed to let me know she had a mild fever.

"Hey gorgeous," I said, pushing the wild, tangled strands of her hair out of her face, and nudging her to open her eyes. "I need you to tell me your other symptoms."

Her face wrinkled into a scowl. "It's just a sinus infection, I'm fine."

"How do you know?"

"Doctor. I stopped before I came home."

I raised an eyebrow about that. Kora hated going to the doctor, avoided it as much as she possibly could. "How do I know you really went, and aren't just trying to get me to leave you alone?"

She opened her eyes. "Prescription on the counter for me to take if it doesn't clear up on its own. I can't afford to be sick right now, not with the show in three weeks."

I nodded. *That* sounded more like her. "Okay. You hungry?"

As tired as her eyes were, they lit up for a second. "*Yes.* Are you feeding me?"

I chuckled, then bent to kiss her hot forehead. "You know it."

First though, I stopped in her bathroom and pulled the stopper for her jetted tub. I started the water – warm, but not hot – then looked through her bottles of essential oils until I found lavender and peppermint. I added drops to the water, then rummaged around again for a scoop of chamomile bath salt, grinning when I saw that she actually had it.

"Come on," I said, as I stepped back into the bedroom. She had her head buried in the pillows again, so I peeled the blanket back, then eased my arms under her to pick her up.

"What're you doing?" she mumbled into my neck as she snuggled against me for the trip back to the bathroom.

"Doesn't smell familiar to you?"

"I'm all stuffy," she said, but lifted her head up as we entered the bathroom, and pulled in a congested breath through her nose. It took a little bit, but after a few moments, she grinned at me as I lowered her into the rising water of the bath. "Oh man, am I really about to get the Mama Tamille treatment?

I chuckled, then nodded as I crouched beside the tub to meet her eyes. "Complete with chicken soup if I can pull it off."

"I feel special." She gingerly moved herself to the front edge of the tub where I was, using her arms as a pillow to lay her head down. "Thank you."

"You're welcome." I kissed her forehead again, then stood. "You know that woman would kick my ass if I didn't take care of "her Kora"."

"That's the only reason, huh?"

I shrugged, then winked at her. "Why else?"

I chuckled at the way she tried to hide her smile, then left her in the bathroom. I turned her music up a little bit on my way to the kitchen, then dug into my bags to see if I could turn the

Cajun chicken pasta I'd planned to make for us into my grandmother's chicken soup.

I ended up getting Mama Tamille on the phone for a few minutes to help, and by the time I found myself turning down the pot to let it simmer, almost an hour had gone by. After a quick

cleanup, I went to check on Kora, grinning when I saw that she'd fallen asleep. I carefully eased her out of the tub and into a bath sheet, then carried her back to bed, where she snuggled in under the covers and promptly drifted off to sleep again.

While she slept, I fired up my laptop to work. Tonight was all about research – making sure the crazy business ventures some of my clients wanted to pump money into actually made financial sense. I was knee deep in trying to figure out if Braxton Drake's most recent endeavor – the purchase of a block of commercial businesses – was worth it when my phone chimed.

I smiled at the screen, then shook my head.

"So... about that soup, Nurse Evans? ;) – K.O."

I closed the laptop and went into the kitchen to ladle spoonfuls of soup into bowls for us, with big pieces of the cornbread Mama Tamille had insisted I make. I found a serving tray in her pantry, and loaded our food, some orange juice, water, and a quick hot toddy onto it, then carried it back to her room.

Kora was still where I'd left her, laid out on her side, but she sat up when I came in. "I already feel a little better," she said, moving to one side of the bed so I could have the other. "That bath blend *never* fails."

"Never. And I see that you had everything on hand, too."

"Of course. Your grandmother's wisdom did *not* fall on deaf ears."

I left the tray with her long enough to retrieve another, and then I settled onto the bed beside her to eat. I listened while she told me in an increasingly raspy voice about the issues with the show – mostly Dawn.

"I swear that child runs my nerves in the ground," she said, sipping from her hot toddy.

"And it's not even because she's not good. If she wasn't good, I could accept that. No problem, you weren't meant to be on stage. But Tariq, Dawn is a *natural*. Sings like a hummingbird, acts like a chameleon, has the grace of a damned gazelle, but she's…"

"Young?" I suggested, shaking my head. "The girl is twenty years old, Kora—"

"About to be twenty-one."

"Okay, about to be twenty-one. Still young. Still learning. Still figuring shit out. You have to take it a little easier with her."

Kora frowned. "Take it *easier*? Tariq, I have spoiled that girl rotten. Her rent, her living expenses, her time at Juilliard – which she decided was "too hard" – all of that has been funded by me. And don't think I don't know you give her a monthly allowance, because I saw the boots she had on today, and I know she can't afford those with what I give her."

I opened my mouth to speak, but she shook her head. "I'm not upset about that. I mean you're her father, basically, you know? Definitely the closest thing she's ever had to that, so I'm not going to begrudge you wanting to do things for her, nor am I going to interfere, I don't want her to miss out on the work she should be doing *now* to solidify her career. When I was her age—"

"You had a lot more to prove. Twenty years old with a four-year-old daughter, and you'd made it to Broadway. Famous mother to live up to. Critics to prove wrong. Dawn doesn't have that same spotlight, because you've shielded her from that. You protected her."

I left off saying that she'd done a much better job at that with Dawn than her own mother had done with her.

"Kora, Dawn is going to be just fine. Once she performs that opening night, gets those first critiques from outsiders, she'll straighten up. She's used to naturally being the best, not *having* to work for it. You remember what the director at Juilliard told us, right? Dawn was easily one of the best students she'd ever seen, but as soon as they tried to push her beyond that, is when she shut down. Just let her move at her own pace."

Kora sighed, then sat back against the pillows, closing her eyes. "I guess you're right."

"I *know* I'm right."

I gathered up our dishes and trays, and took them into the kitchen for a second round of clean up. When I came back, I found Kora in the bathroom, rinsing her mouth from brushing her teeth. Her movements were still sluggish, but she seemed like she felt a little better.

She'd wrapped her hair up in a scarf, and instead of her bath towel, she was in a robe. The air was permeated with the scent of her brown sugar body butter, and her skin was glowing like she'd just rubbed it in.

"I forgot how bad that bath soak dries my skin out," she said when she saw me. "I opened that towel and I looked like I was ready to get dropped in hot grease."

I laughed, then wrapped my arms around her from behind, meeting her eyes in the mirror.

92

"You feel better though?"

She nodded. "Quite a bit. I'm still ready to go to sleep again though. The sinus pressure is killing me."

I pressed my lips to her temple, then nodded. "Yeah, you still feel a little warm. You want me to do the foot massage with the eucalyptus?"

Her eyes went wide, and she turned to face me. "You would?"

"Absolutely."

"Then *hell yes*."

We shared a laugh as we went back to her room, where we settled on her bed after grabbing the oil blend. She sat up against the headboard as I warmed the oil between my hands, then rubbed it into her feet. In less than five minutes, she was asleep.

I tucked her under the covers, and started to slip out, when she turned over. Barely opening her eyes, she mumbled, "Will you stay with me?" She and I both knew the answer to that question.

I'd showered before I came by, so I had no qualms about pulling off my jeans, sweater, or the tee shirt I wore underneath. I slipped under the covers with her, and she immediately scooted against me, pressing her overly warm body against me.

Her ass was pressed right against my groin, and I couldn't help my reaction to that. Friends, lovers, whatever, once we crossed that line, Kora always had that effect on me. But I had to squelch it. Had to ignore that overwhelming itch to touch her, because that's what she wanted, apparently.

But then, she turned toward me, pressing her hands against my chest as she buried her face in my neck. Slowly, but surely, her hands drifted down, until she had my dick wrapped in her fingers, gripping me through my boxers. "Tariq," she rasped, her sore throat taking the smooth edge out of her normally sensual voice.

"You're sick," I rumbled back, shaking my head as she opened her eyes, looking me right in mine.

"More reason that we should. We'll both feel better." She moved her hand inside my boxers, cupping and gently squeezing me.

I groaned. A little voice in the back of my head told me to move her hand, get out of the bed, but a different voice, speaking much, much louder, reminded me that it wouldn't be the first time we'd slept our way through a little cold or sinus infection before.

Kora turned onto her back, dragging the blanket down, and taking the belt of her robe with it. The room was still illuminated by the soft, dim light of her bedside lamp, so I could easily see her glowing brown skin bared to me.

Beautiful handfuls of full breasts, tipped with dark brown nipples that made my mouth water. Soft, flat belly adorned with a tiny silver ring, leading to the smooth, bare treasure between her legs.

One hand was still in my boxers, and she squeezed me again as she moved her free hand between her own legs.

94

She opened them wide, spreading herself apart with her fingers, and that was where I lost my resolve.

Kora grinned as I climbed on top of her, brushing her hand aside once I was free of my boxers. A moment later, I pushed inside her, groaning as her body clenched around me.

"You're hot as hell," I whispered into her neck. The fever had her burning up. So damned hot, so damned wet, so damned *sexy* when she whimpered my name, pushing her nails into my biceps as I buried myself in her as deep as I could go. She bit down on her lip, digging into it with her teeth as I began to move. Slow, deep strokes that pulled little moans from her at the end of every one. Friction that was sweet and savory at the same time, driving me a little bit crazy with every plunge.

This was home.

Kora was home.

I recognized that in her, and I knew she recognized the same in me, but the craziness of when we tried to be together before... I knew why it felt impossible, and I didn't fault her for that. I got it. I got *her*. But damned if the feeling she gave me didn't make it seem impossible to be with anybody else.

So where did that leave us?

When having an *us* was infeasible, but nobody else quite measured up, what the hell did we do? We went after the Pauls and Julissas of the world, and hoped for the best.

But right now, I wanted to just enjoy what we *could* have.

Sex with Kora was predictable in the best kind of way. I knew she'd be responsive to every touch, could count on her to be intuitive, to move and adjust, arch at just the right angle, exactly when I needed her to. I knew her body through and through, just the right spots to touch to make her melt.

I plunged into her and stayed there, sliding my hand down her thigh until I reached the back of her knee. Just a light stroke of my thumb while I was anchored deep inside her, and she opened her mouth, gasping, then giggling as she dug her nails into my waist.

"That's cheating," she murmured, closing her eyes as I moved again. I ran my tongue along the crease between her neck and jaw, making her shudder, then brought my face up to hers.

"How?"

"Because you know what that does to *mmmmm.*" She arched her back away from the bed as I did it again, pressing her breasts against my chest. When she relaxed again, I brought my lips back to hers, trying to kiss her, but she angled away. "What are you doing?"

I stopped moving to raise an eyebrow at her. "What does it *seem* like I'm doing?"

"Trying to kiss me while I'm sick."

"It's a sinus infection, you're not contagious like that."

"But I'm still gross. No kissing."

I scowled, then hooked her under the legs and plunged as deep as I could get, making her let out a hoarse little yelp of pleasure. Keeping her thighs pinned around my waist, I leaned forward again, getting right in her face. "How are you going to tell me I can't kiss you?" I asked as I ground into her, making sure there was friction against her clit.

"I'm *sick*," she insisted.

"And I don't give a shit," I insisted right back, releasing her thighs so I could cup her face in my hands. I kissed her forehead, the tip of her nose, her cheeks, her jaws, her chin, her temples, then came back to center, letting my gaze flicker down to her lips. "I'm just trying to get close to you, Korrine. Can I do that?"

She closed her eyes, then let out a sigh before she opened them again, locking with mine.

"No tongue."

"No tongue," I agreed, then lowered my mouth to hers.

I pressed gently at first, just little pecks and brushes, since she had her lips closed tight. I shifted to little nibbles and licks as I stroked her, and she slowly relaxed until I was able to pull her bottom lip into my mouth, sucking and biting before I released it. I moved my hand, wrapping my arm around her waist to draw her as close as I could as we made love.

Eventually, I dropped the other hand too, slipping it between us to rub circles against her clit. Kora slid her hands away from my back, moving them over my chest and shoulder, to my neck, and then up into my locs to urge me closer. I lowered myself onto her, being careful not to crush her under my weight as I drove into her again and again.

I could feel the tension building in her body, knew she was getting close. Her hands went to my shoulders again, digging her nails deep as her legs began to tremble. Every little whimper or moan that left her body seemed to make me harder. She still felt hot as hell, and so slippery wet that I was drowning in her, and it was *so* goddamned good.

When she climaxed, it came with a rush of extra wetness that made me slip a little deeper, and a chorus of sexy cries and purrs that were music to my ears. Her body clenched around me, gripping me tight, and I exploded in her with a growl, burying myself as far as I could get.

After a few moments passed, I collapsed on the bed beside her, staring up at the ceiling. I turned to her, intending to say something, but her eyes were closed. Subtle, congested snores started to fill the room, and I chuckled softly, shaking my head as I slid away from her and out of the bed to get to the bathroom.

I relieved myself, then washed up, and took a warm towel into the bedroom to clean Kora up too. She barely stirred, only mumbling an annoyed complaint as I got her out of her open robe, replacing it with an oversized tee shirt from her drawer – a royal blue and gold NFL relic of mine. After retrieving and getting back into my boxers, I turned off the lamp and joined her in the bed, where again, she snuggled close. I wrapped my arms around her, gently stroking her back as she fell into a deep sleep.

I closed my eyes too, running through my tasks for the next day in my head. Finish my research for the Drakes, meet with Steph about our company portfolio, call my grandmother back and schedule lunch for next week... and what else? ... What else? *Talk to Julissa about weekend plans.*

Oh.

Yeah.

That.

Kora shifted in my arms, and guilt swept over me.

Less than twelve hours ago, I'd been talking to Julissa about trusting me, basically insisted that Kora and I weren't sleeping together, and yet... we'd slept together. Again. I blew out a sigh.

Maybe Kora was right.

I couldn't possibly make a meaningful connection with somebody else when I was so invested in her. Not saying that I wanted to drop our friendship – that wasn't an option. Would *never* be an option – but I couldn't keep relying on intimacy from her.

What I'd said to Julissa earlier, about sex not increasing her currency... was that only true because I knew I could turn to Kora if I wanted an experience that actually *meant* something?

To my credit, I'd been clear with Julissa that she and I weren't together, but still. After the intense level of intimacy I'd just shared with Kora, it barely seemed fair to expect her to compare. The only way to make it work with

Julissa, or anybody else, was to remove myself from a position where I was tempted to draw parallels.

It was a good plan in theory, but how the hell was I supposed to put it into action?

eight.

Kora

I woke up feeling great.

Still sick physically, but mentally and emotionally, I was good.

And it would be downright silly to give credit for that to anything or anyone except Tariq.

He was gone from my bed now, but when I'd woken up throughout the night, he'd been right there, letting me use him as my own personal body pillow. In the very early hours, when

the sun had first started filtering into the room, I'd laid there watching him. Eventually, I realized that my breath had fallen into sync with his, and not for the first time, my thoughts drifted to things they shouldn't.

Things like: what would *really* happen if we tried again?

That was the problem with being as close as we were. How could a man sacrifice a night that he needed for work to run you essential oil baths, cook you chicken soup, and make *good* love to you, without leaving you thinking about forever?

Impossible.

I rolled into the spot he'd left and inhaled deep, breathing in the subtle hint of *him* that still lingered in my sheets. His body heat was long gone, but I could hear the occasional movement from elsewhere in my apartment, letting me know he was still close by.

Reluctantly, I climbed out of the bed, trudging into the bathroom to pee. I washed my hands, brushed my teeth, washed my face, then stopped short of pulling off my scarf to comb down my wrapped hair. There was never a need for me to be "put together" with Tariq. He'd seen my best, sure, but he'd almost seen my very ugliest worst, and didn't seem swayed by either.

I left the scarf on.

I exited the bathroom and wandered out into the main area of my apartment, and was only a little surprised to find him in my kitchen, at the stove. "I was just about to come get you," he said, not looking up from what he was doing. "Sit down."

At the counter, there were plates, cups, and forks set up, and as I approached to sit down, Tariq served scrambled eggs onto the plate in front of me.

"Wow, I get breakfast too?" I asked.

He nodded, then slid a plate of thick cut bacon across the counter. "Yeah. You didn't smell it from your room?"

Snagging a piece of meat, I shook my head. "Nope. Still stuffy."

Tariq frowned, then grabbed my prescription bottle from the other end of the counter, putting it in front of me.

"You should probably go ahead and start taking those antibiotics, so you can get ahead of it before it gets bad."

When I agreed, he went to the refrigerator, and poured a glass of orange juice for me. I downed one of the pills, and he topped off my glass, then finished serving both of us breakfast like it was nothing.

Because for him it *was* nothing.

Taking care of me was just a natural thing, as it had always been, for both of us. It

brought tears to my eyes, thinking of all the times he'd put himself out there for me, never with an expectation of receiving something in return. Just because he loved me, like nobody – *nobody* – else ever had. Probably ever would.

But love wasn't *enough*. Not when you lived your life under the lights, with half the world watching your every move. Scrutinizing and digging into painful past memories, analyzing and predicting the motives of every step you take in the present, and betting against your future.

Me and Tariq though, we thought we were smart. Nubia and Steph were the only people who knew for a *fact* that we were anything more than friends, and at the time, they didn't even know each other, so it was perfect. On both sides, our publicists swore that the young, hot, sexy, and *single* angle worked in our favor. Not just for fans, but for roles, and endorsement, for our perception in our industries.

A young, talented Broadway star should just *know better* than to think she could tame the hottest young wide receiver in the NFL. And a gorgeous footballer, the most exciting rookie, fresh out of college, the charming, playboy face of his team… what did it say for him if he chose a bougie woman from *musical theatre*?

So whatever.

We left them out of it. Snuck around to be together whenever we were in the same city, before the age of a smartphone in every hand. But part of being a celebrity in a secret relationship with another, was watching the media not only pair them with whoever was convenient, but make a damned convincing case for it as well. It was the kind of thing that played on any little doubts or insecurities you had, especially when you were young and experienced with relationships. *Especially* when the person they swore just got caught in a hotel room with someone else was the only man or woman you'd ever loved.

And that wasn't even getting started on the people that actually were potential threats. Flirtatious stage managers and hot young actors who were known for charming the panties off their co-stars. Slender-bodied cheerleaders with those saccharine smiles, and groupies who knew the team schedule better than the players and had the freedom to travel on demand. The people who had the benefit of close proximity to the person you loved, and could fly under the radar while seeing them every day.

Tariq and I weren't wise, or mature, or *confident* back then, and every single one of those weaknesses showed. It got ugly. *Very ugly.*

Constantly fighting ugly.

Ignoring phone calls ugly.

Potential assault charges ugly.

But Tariq was right when he argued that things were different now. In the thirteen or fourteen years since we'd made that attempt, we'd evolved, we'd learned, we'd grown up so much since then. We weren't the same people at damn near forty as we'd been in our early twenties, so maybe…

"Tariq," I said, then took a deep breath when he looked up. He took a bite from the bacon in his hands and then rounded the counter, looking expectantly at me as he sat down.

"Kora, what is it?" he asked, when I still hadn't said anything.

"Umm, your locs." I coughed into my elbow, trying to clear the sudden tightness in my throat. "You're starting to look a little fuzzy. Messing up your whole GQ vibe you like to give off."

He sucked his teeth. "Oh, you've got jokes this morning, huh? Maybe if *somebody* hadn't been avoiding me for the last two weeks, I wouldn't be 'looking a little fuzzy'. So what's up? Do

I need to look for somebody, or…?"

"I've got you." The offer rolled off my lips before I could catch it. I'd gone with him to get his locs retightened enough times that the technique was ingrained in my mind, and for the

last few years, I'd done it for him. It was a "thing" for us. Old black movies on Netflix, with plenty of snacks, while he sat between my legs for me to twist his hair. We were

105

supposed to do it last week, and I'd canceled, in my quest to get out of being alone with him.

"We can do it this week," I said, doubling down. It wasn't fair to him for me to isolate myself out of our friendship because of my own doubts. But were those doubts fair to either of us? What the hell were we doing? This was crazy, for us to be here, settling for other people, when we really wanted each other.

It was nuts.

It was time to stop it.

"Thank you."

My eyes went wide. "What?"

"*Thank you*," Tariq repeated, lifting an eyebrow at me. "My locs?"

"Oh! Oh, you're welcome." I smiled at him, then filled my mouth with food, hoping to ease my nerves a little before what I wanted to say next, so I wouldn't change the subject again. We ate in silence for a few minutes, and then finally, I took a long swig from my orange juice before I spoke. "So, um, about last night."

Tariq sighed, then nodded. "Yeah, about that. What you said before… I think you're probably right."

My eyes went wide. "What I said?"

"Yeah." He shrugged, then leaned forward, propping his elbows on the counter with his arms crossed. "The whole platonic friendship thing. I guess you're right, you know?" *What?*

"There's no way we can keep interacting with each other on such an intimate level, and hope to build anything meaningful with someone else." *I said that?*

"And not just once we're "serious" about them, because it's almost like it's tainted from jump, if we know we can still turn to each other for certain things." *What?*

"And really, I *do* get why you're reluctant to give us another chance. We ended up not being very good to each other, and almost lost our friendship in the process, which is... shit, it's scary to think about." *Yeah, it is.*

"And I don't want that for us. Losing your friendship isn't an option for me." *Me either.*

"So last night was a bit of a revelation for me. I agree that we should let go of anything extra, and focus on being "just" friends. All the time." *Wait a minute though—*

"I want to be fair to Julissa." I was going to throw up.

There it was. The argument I'd made to him, over and over, rephrased in his words and given back to me. I'd finally done it. Finally convinced him that we shouldn't risk our friendship again, that we needed to... that we... *Holy shit.*

"Yeah," I said, in a voice that was about a billion times more cheerful than I felt. "That's good. Probably for the best."

Our eyes met, and I saw none of the uncertainty I was hoping for as he gave me a little nod. "Yeah."

I looked away. Coughed, then coughed again, and again, then excused myself to handle my manufactured coughing fit in the privacy of my bathroom. I locked the door, turned on the water, flipped the toilet cover, and then sat down to cry my damned eyes out.

What the hell just happened?

One minute, I'm getting ready to tell him that yes, I want to give *us* shot. I'm willing to take that chance again, for him, and he… wants to be fair to Julissa. *Fuck* Julissa.

I dropped my head into my hands. I didn't really mean that, but shit. How *should* I feel when the man I wanted was…

Shit!

I nearly jumped out of my skin when a knock sounded at the door, and Tariq's voice carried from the other side. "Are you okay?"

"Yes," I yelled back, punctuating it with a cough. "I just need a second," –*cough* – "Post nasal drip, you know?" – *cough* – "This is why I didn't want you kissing me last night," –*cough*

– "I'm all gross."

I quickly washed my face, using cool water to try to calm some of the redness from my eyes. When I opened the door, he was standing there on the other side, worry etched into his expression.

"I think I'm going to lay back down. I don't feel well, at all."

At least that was true, and Tariq nodded. "Alright. I actually need to try to get into the office today. You think you're going to be okay?"

"Yes. I'll let Micah know I won't be at the theatre today, and I'll get some rest in. Dawn should be happy for the break," I said, laughing, which turned into my first real cough of the day.

Tariq gave me a half grin. "Yeah. Probably so. I'll come check on you again at lunch time, bring you something to eat."

"You don't have to do that."

"I don't do anything for you because I have to Kora. Always because I want to." *Jesus, take me now.*

I smiled. "Well, in that case."

"Yeah, whatever," Tariq chuckled, then grabbed my hand and squeezed. "Hey, you sure you're okay?"

"It's just a sinus infection."

"I'm not talking about that. I'm talking about me and you. Are we good?"

I scoffed, pulling my face into what I hoped was a convincing frown. "*Of course.* Yes. I mean... Julissa... she's cute or whatever I guess." "Kora..."

"I'm kidding," I shot back, forcing myself to laugh. "Julissa is a beautiful woman, Tariq. Smart, successful. I like her for you. As long as *you* like her, and she's good to you. As long as she makes you happy. You know that's all that's ever mattered to me. I owe you that."

Tariq shook his head. "You don't *owe* me anything."

"I do. I *do*," I insisted, squeezing his hand. "I love you."

"I love you too." I closed my eyes as he pressed his lips to my forehead, squeezing them tight to try to hold back my tears.

I coughed again, pulling away from him as I shook my head. "Hate to cut our little sentimental moment short, but that bed is calling me."

"Go lay your ass down, patient zero," he said, gently pushing me in that direction. I did as he said, burying myself in the blanket and pillows, wishing I could fall into them and disappear. Twenty minutes later, he came into the room, and I kept my eyes closed and my face buried. He hovered for a second, then kissed my barely exposed jaw before he left again.

It wasn't until I heard the front door close behind him that I sat up, and bawled my eyes out over him. Then I climbed my ass out of bed and got into the shower, so I could go to work. Never before had I so desperately needed a distraction.

I clutched a mug of hot tea in my hands as I watched Dawn and Donovan interact on stage. Special Agent Jamison had just saved Raven from certain capture, and instead of the grateful deference he expected, she met him with angry defiance – an attempt to cover her intense attraction to him.

They were *killing* these roles.

I kept my face impassive, but seeing my daughter move effortlessly around the stage, delivering her line crisply, clearly, with an emotional depth that *she* brought to the role – not just what the writer had put on the page – made my heart full enough to burst. Donovan was doing a wonderful job as well, but my *baby… God, I really needed this.*

A few days had gone by since that morning with Tariq at my apartment, and we were fast approaching the weekend. Somehow, I'd been able to maintain my composure with him when we were together, instead of just avoiding him. We'd talked, we'd had lunch, I'd touched up his locs. All while pretending that I was really okay with being just his friend. But Tariq wasn't stupid. That man knew me like he knew the alphabet, and at least once a day, had asked me what was wrong.

I'd been playing it off that I was just still feeling iffy after the sinus infection, but eventually that excuse would be gone, and I would have to figure something else out. Not a lie, because I hated lying to my friend. When he asked me, *"Are you okay?"* in that warm, rumbling tone, I needed to be able to say, without reservation, *"yes"*.

Thirteen years.

That's how long I'd loved Tariq as more than just my "friend" without the pleasure of being able to call him mine. In the course of those years, I'd screwed, dated, loved other

111

men, but I knew that ultimately, inevitably, my heart would always come back to him. But loving someone and *belonging* with that person weren't always the same thing, and Tariq and I were the poster children for that. Never quite on the same page, never quite the right timing, and despite our love, life moved on.

So back to those thirteen years.

In that time, I'd come to understand that trying to "get over" Tariq wasn't a thing that would happen. It was a pointless endeavor. What *would* happen was that I'd meet someone. I'd like him, and he'd like me. I'd make sure he was good in bed, aspiring to greatness, and *then* I'd open my heart – the portion that was available – to him. He'd fill it up, and I'd fill his, and we'd love each other, and be content. There might be some false starts, and dead ends, but that's how it would go, until we tired of each and moved on, or like with Paul – got married.

And maybe *still* moved on, as he had.

The point though, was that I wasn't on some fatalistic, *I'll never be happy with anyone else,* type of trip. Because I knew I could, knew that eventually, I would. But that didn't negate the fact that *he* was the one I wanted. Acknowledging that I was fully capable of a life as just his friend did nothing to minimize that in my heart, he would always be *it.*

It just wasn't meant to be.

So instead of pining, I needed myself a damned boyfriend – but it wasn't like I had the time or energy to find one right now anyway.

112

Dawn and Donovan's scene ended, and I approached the stage, offering them a wellearned smile. "Good work Donovan," I said, addressing him first as he came to the edge of the rehearsal stage. "My only note for today is that when Kyle kisses Raven in that scene, you don't *have* to stick your tongue down her throat. You're both talented actors, and you bring a lot of chemistry to the scene. The audience gets the point either way. So, you know, feel free to keep your tongue to yourself."

Donovan smiled. "My bad, boss lady. I may have gotten a little caught up in the scene."

I looked over at Dawn, standing a few inches behind Donovan, trying her best to look occupied by her feet, then back to him. "Understandable. But when you're on stage, let's keep it professional, please. Go. Go get something to eat."

I dismissed him, and then turned my attention to Dawn. "I must say, that what I'm seeing from you today? *This* level of performance confirms why you received this role over anyone else. When you display it this way, no one will watch you on a stage and even think about *me*, let alone claim that your success is only because you're my daughter. *You* – just *you* – on your very own, have been flawless today. Keep it up."

Dawn's lips had parted in surprise over my first line of praise, and remained open while I finished. They moved a few times, like she was trying to figure out what to say, and when a few seconds passed with no response from her, I shook my head. "Close your mouth. Go take your break."

I turned to head to my office, and was a few steps away before Dawn said something that stopped me in my tracks.

"*Mama!*"

She said it loud enough that several people –set designers, stage hands, other actors – looked up, and looked at us. I pivoted back in the direction of the stage, slowly, with my

eyebrow somewhere near my hairline. When she wasn't using it to her benefit, Dawn was very, *very* insistent on not reminding people that she was my daughter, so that *Mama* was a surprise.

Dawn glanced around, then looked back to me. "I mean… Kora."

I bit the inside of my lip to keep myself from laughing. "Yes?"

"I…" she swallowed hard. "Thank you."

I nodded. "You're welcome. Break. Lunch. Eat. *Now.*"

She nodded back, then turned to exit the stage, and I turned too, keeping my expression blank until I was out of the rehearsal theatre and in the hall that led to my office. Then, I looked down at my teacup and let myself break into a big, goofy, completely unrefined grin over the fact

I knew I'd just made my little girl's day.

"I really wish I was the one who'd put a smile like that on your face."

My head popped up, in the direction of the voice that carried down the hall. The air left my lungs when my eyes met with his, and a grin spread across his handsome face as he moved closer. When he reached me, he put his hands in his pockets and let his shoulders drop into the posture of a man who was completely relaxed, while I struggled to keep my heart rate contained. "Hello Kora."

I ran my tongue over my lips. "Hello Paul."

He was, just as he'd been a few months ago when I last saw him, gorgeous. Golden skin, beautiful honey-toned eyes, strong, chiseled features. His grin grew a little wider. "As always, you look amazing. It's good to see you."

"Thank you. Is there something I can do for you?"

Paul's smile faltered a little, but he kept it on his face as he shook his head. "Damn, that's all I get?"

"You divorced me, Paul. So, yes."

He nodded, and that grin finally dropped as he looked down at his feet, then back up at me. "I guess that makes sense."

Our eyes meet again, for a long moment, and I'd be lying if I claimed not to feel anything. We'd dated for almost a year before he proposed. Were engaged for six months, married for six months after that, and then, in what had to be the fastest proceedings ever, he'd divorced me, claiming that I was in love with my "best friend". Which was true.

So maybe I didn't have too much room to be mad.

Truthfully, Paul had never been anything but good to me. He was kind, and charming.

Handsome, and successful. Gave great advice, knew when to listen and not try to "fix" things. I cared for him very much, and over time had grown to love him.

We had our marital woes, like everybody else. He would retreat to his corner, and I'd go to mine, we'd talk to our friends for guidance, to figure out how to proceed.

Problem was, one of my friends was Tariq.

They weren't exactly friends, but they weren't enemies either, for reasons neither of them ever divulged to me. I appreciated that neither of them were petty enough to pull me into their beef, and I was certain that if Tariq thought I was in danger of any kind with Paul, he would tell me. But that didn't happen. The one thing I knew for sure was that once Paul and I started dating, any positive feelings Tariq may have held for him were gone. He never spoke ill of Paul, or disrespected our relationship in any way, but I felt his quiet disapproval, and eventually stopped looking to him for advice. We remained friends, totally separate from my marriage, but for Paul, that didn't fly.

He pushed, and pushed, and pushed a little more, wanting a major downgrade in our friendship, not understanding that I loved him, but not *nearly* enough that removing Tariq from my life would ever be an option.

So he divorced me.

"Again, what can I do for you Paul?"

"I wanted to make sure you'd updated your retirement paperwork, life insurance, healthcare, all of that since the divorce. Making sure you're still covered."

116

I lifted an eyebrow. "We never combined any of that, Paul. I'm still covered on all fronts, and you aren't one of my insurance beneficiaries. But you didn't *really* come here to ask something you could have called or emailed me about, did you?"

An embarrassed grin crossed his face, and he lifted a hand, running his fingers over his short, impeccably waved fade. "No. No, I didn't."

"Okay," I laughed, leaning against the wall behind me, my mug still tucked in one hand.

"So am I going to have to ask a third time?"

He shook his head. "No, you don't. I came because I wanted to ask you in person if you would consider having lunch with me."

My eyes went wide. "*Oh.* Um, why?" I asked, letting my face pull into a scowl.

"To catch up." He ran his tongue over his lips, then took another step forward, into my personal space, leaving barely a foot between us. I watched his hand move until it touched mine, and held my breath as he entwined our fingers. "I miss you." – I swallowed hard – "And the divorce… I've been wondering if that was a mistake. If I acted too abruptly. If we should have… I don't know. Tried counseling, or something like that. I feel like we didn't even *try*. So… I wanted to talk to you about that."

"No." I slipped my hand from his, shaking my head as I eased away. "What's different now? What changed? Why *now*?"

117

He raised his shoulders. "Nothing changed. I've just been thinking. Like I should have back then, before I called a lawyer. Look, I'm not asking you to make a big, sudden decision. I just want to talk to you."

"Paul..."

"Lunch?" He smiled at me, that perfect, beautiful smile of his, and I had to bite the inside of my jaw to keep from smiling right back. "No pressure," he said, reaching for my hand again, and running his thumb over my palm. "Just a meal in the middle of the day, plenty of people around, too early for margaritas..."

I laughed, then shook my head as I met his eyes. "Let me think about it."

His eyes widened, in pleasure and surprise, and he nodded. "Absolutely. My number is still the same."

"Okay."

"Okay."

He hesitated for a second, then quickly brought my hand up to his lips. He kissed the back of it before he released it, and then with a parting wave he was gone.

I looked down at my cup of tea – now cold – and pushed out a heavy sigh. I didn't know what to think about the timing of Paul's little pop up. Maybe a little birdie had told him I would potentially be ripe for a new – or recycled— companion?

Finding out that he knew about Tariq and Julissa wouldn't surprise me, because the circle of black finance professionals in our area was pretty small. And if he *did* know, then what? Was that really a bad thing? Was it really

118

so strange to feel a little more secure knowing that the person you felt threatened by in your relationship was dating someone else?

I continued down the hall to my office, knowing exactly how I'd spend my lunch hour today – on the phone with Nubia dissecting this. Whether this would be a welcome trip down memory lane, or an awful lesson in revisiting the past, I really didn't know. But it was something to mull over, and it was *definitely* right on time.

nine.

Kora

"Say something."

"Uh-uh."

"Seriously?"

"Mmmhmm."

"So you're not going to say anything. At all?"

Uh-uh." "Nubia!"

"*What,* Kora?! Shit! You're messing up my spa vibes, damn."

Nubia's forehead was wrinkled in annoyance as she shifted in her individual volcanic mud bath, and if they weren't currently covered by a cool mask, I knew she'd be rolling her eyes at me.

"The sooner you answer me, the sooner I can stop *messing up your spa vibes,* mean ass."

Nubia gasped, then sat up, turning in my direction like she could actually see me through her mask. "*Mean ass?* Me?! You're ruining my much-needed relaxation to talk about goddamned *Paul* of all the people in the world, but I'm the mean ass? Oh. Okay."

"Yes, I'm talking about Paul," I said. "Don't look at me like that."

121

"How do you know how I'm looking at you?"

"Because I took off my mask, that thing itched."

"I hope you break out."

I sucked my teeth. "And *that's* why I called you a mean ass. Now, can we get back to my dilemma?"

"What dilemma? The one where your silly ass finally convinced the man you want that he *shouldn't* want you, and now your insecure ex-husband is sniffing around trying to get you back?"

I rolled my eyes as I sat back, sinking deeper into my mud. "Yes. That one."

When she put it like that, it really did sound pitiful, and I guess it was. I'd roped myself into both situations, and the only thing I could do at this point was keep moving and hope for the best.

My nerves were still on edge from the run-in with Paul the day before, and though I'd talked this to death with Nubia already, I still wasn't sure what I wanted to do. At this point, there was nothing *to* do about the situation with Tariq.

Paul though… that was something to consider.

"So are you going to have lunch with him, or not?"

I sighed. "I mean, it's just lunch. Going to lunch isn't saying *I want you back*, right?"

"Or is it?" Nubia shrugged, and then sank lower in the mud too, keeping her head balanced against the rolled towels that made a makeshift pillow. "Otherwise, what is your purpose? He's your *ex*, Kora. And everybody knows what happens after the *let's just clear the air and get some closure* lunch."

122

I lifted an eyebrow. "No, everybody doesn't. Is that a thing?"

"Yes," Nubia scoffed. "One of you calls the other up with some sentimental bullshit. You get together at some nostalgic place, end up reminiscing about the good times. Next thing you know, he has a finger in your ass, his tongue in your yoni, and you're wondering if you should give it another shot."

I tossed my head back and laughed, and a second later, Nubia joined in, giggling as she used her fingertips to pull up her mask, then reach for her glass of champagne beside the tub.

"Sounds like firsthand experience to me," I teased, sipping from my own flute.

"That's because it *is*," she shot back, shaking her head. "So, the question is, do you want him back?"

"*Should* I want him back?"

"I can't answer that for you."

"The hell you can't," I laughed. "You *know* me."

With her mask propped against her forehead, Nubia narrowed her eyes at me, then took a deep breath. "Okay. Fine. Let's go over it *again*."

"I'm listening."

"Anybody with eyes can see that you and Tariq are in love, and have been for a long ass time. Paul and Tariq knew each other, which is how the two of you met in the first place. He knew Tariq wanted you, and he pursued you anyway, just to prove he could get you."

123

My face twisted into a scowl. "How could you possibly know that?"

"Because I know *men*. So, we can make that strike one for Petty Paul."

"Petty Paul?"

"I said what I said." Nubia gave me a scathing look, then pulled her mask back down over her eyes. "Next – Paul made you happy. He's charming, he's handsome, he had a damned job, he was good to you, and as far as we know, faithful. He gets points for all of that."

"No. We were *married*, so being faithful is a given. He shouldn't get points for doing what he was supposed to do."

"Kora, you underestimate the occurrence of men who do what they're "supposed" to. Trust me. He gets points for it. But we can take away points for him being so insecure about your friendship with Tariq that he divorced you. Everybody knows you can't oust the opposite-sex bestie unless they're *actually* fucking. And you and Tariq weren't…?"

"*No!* Nubia, you know I wouldn't have done that, and even if I'd tried, Tariq wouldn't have gone for it. We *don't* screw people over like that."

"Right. You just pretend to be emotionally available until they get sick of your bullshit and move on. Of course."

My mouth dropped open. "Okay, whose side are you on here?"

"Common damned sense. But since you and Tariq are so clearly boycotting that, and ignoring the inevitable conclusion, sure Kora. Go to lunch with Paul. Be clear with him that you don't fucking *know* what you want right now, because you're newly divorced – from him."

I chewed at my bottom lip. "Just like that, huh?"

Nubia nodded. "Just like that. You're talking to him, and probably going to screw him too. But neither of those is saying you want to get married, or even *date* him again."

"I'm *not* screwing Paul after one lunch," I laughed. "And no, not getting married, not dating, not... hell, you know what I think I need? Like, a year of not being committed to *anybody*. A palate cleanser."

Nubia let out a loud yelp. "Girl, *please*. You know as soon as... never mind."

"As soon as *what*?"

"Never mind."

"Nubia..."

"Girl, I said never mind! I think you have a lot happening right now, with Dawn, and the show opening soon, so I think some time focused on just enjoying your life would be good for you."

"Really?"

"Yes, *really*. Now can I get back into my relaxation please?"

"*Yes*, thank you."

"You're welcome," she mumbled, and I closed my eyes, running back over our conversation in my head.

Just lunch.

Just lunch.

Just lunch.

Couldn't really cause any harm... right?

~

Tariq

"Could you *not* do that, please?"

I ducked my head, dodging another attempt from my grandmother to – presumably – check my forehead for a fever. We were in the middle of a restaurant, and her antics were causing a little bit of a scene.

"Well, if you'd just be still, I could get it over with," she said, aiming her hand at me again, and frowning when I dipped away.

I chuckled at her expression, putting my hands on her shoulders. "I'm not sick."

"But my Kora was."

"*Two weeks ago.*"

My grandmother pursed her lips in annoyance, propping her hands on her hips. "And things incubate, don't they? Bring your head here, boy. We're old folks, we can't afford to be getting sick."

"Speak for yourself, old woman."

I grinned as my grandfather stepped around Mama Tamille to shake my hand. I returned his gesture, pulling him

126

into a hug that I knew would make her jealous, and sure enough, she gave up on her quest to check my temperature so she could draw me into an embrace.

They'd purposely chosen a flight with a layover, so that we could have this visit. I loved the hell out of these two, and was glad that they'd made time between their jet-setting flights around the world to have lunch. They were always on the go, always doing something new, since they swore that was the key to a happy life. To anybody passing by, they probably looked more like my parents than grands – and really, that was pretty accurate.

My grandmother and grandfather had raised me from the time I was born. They took care of me, and had pushed me in school and sports, so that by the time I made it to college I had several paths I could take for my future. I finished a bachelor's in business before I went to the NFL, and after I got sidelined with a knee injury I never quite recovered from – last play of a championship game at that – my grandfather introduced me to his business: finance.

"We went to see your mother about a week ago," my grandmother said as I pulled out her chair so we could sit down. "I hope you're planning a trip soon. She kept asking about you. She wants to see you."

"Yeah." I opened my menu as soon as I sat down, trying to look preoccupied. "My normal visit."

Mama Tamille nodded. "Good. She's been having a hard time, you know?"

"I heard."

"And she's still your mother, you know, even if—"

127

"Tam," my grandfather spoke up, with censure in his voice. "Leave the boy alone. He said he was going to see her."

She narrowed her eyes at him. "I'm just making sure."

"I'm going," I said, putting my hand over hers. "I already have my flight booked, already have the time blocked out of my schedule, all of that. It's handled."

Mama Tamille nodded, adjusting the rope of pearls around her neck. "Good. I just don't want you to forget about—"

"I *won't*. Trust me."

No, *really*. No matter how much I may have wished for a different reality, my mother was who she was – and it was impossible to forget.

I squeezed my grandmother's hand and turned back to the menu, wondering if it were too early in the day for a good single barrel whiskey. If the conversation was going to continue like this

"So where *is* my Kora?" Damn.

Definitely going to need that whiskey.

I looked up to meet my grandmother's eyes, and immediately decided that was a bad idea. Tamille Evans was a woman who could see right through you if she snared you with those deep brown eyes. I *still* had memories of whippings with switches from her garden.

"You know Kora's show is opening next week, right?" I asked, deciding that the menu was a safer place to rest my gaze.

128

"Yes, we're supposed to be flying back for that, to see Dawn perform."

"Well, when she gets close to show time, she likes to stay close to the theater during the day so she can be available. She was like that even when she was working on the stage crew.

This is her first show as director, so I knew I wasn't going to be able to get her away for lunch."

My grandmother let out a sigh. "I'm going to have to call that girl. It's been way too long since I've laid eyes on her in person, and I don't like that." *Yeah, join the club.*

Once again, Kora was avoiding me. It was becoming way too common between us, but Kora was her own woman – what was I supposed to do about it? I could push, yeah, but I tried not to overdo that. She deserved to be able to decide if she wanted to see me or not, and for me to

respect it, but still. If it went on too much longer, I wasn't above a surprise pop up to see what was going on with us.

In any case, I was pretty sure I knew why she was being distant. She claimed to be okay with me and Julissa as an item, but she always seemed to disengage whenever she came up as a topic of conversation – *exactly* like I'd been with her about Paul.

I didn't like his ass, and I especially didn't like her *with* him. But who she liked wasn't up to me, and she wasn't being mistreated, so I made it my business to mind my business. I wasn't going to talk bad about him to her, but I also didn't want to talk about him, period. I had a strong suspicion that Kora's feelings about Julissa were similar. So between being busy with the show, and living life, she probably found it simpler to avoid being around me. Sooner or later, she and I would address it.

In the meantime, my grandparents and I ordered lunch and spent some time catching up
while we ate. It wasn't until we were preparing to order dessert that my grandmother looked up, and nudged me.

"Tariq, I thought you told me Kora wouldn't be available for lunch since she likes to stay around the theater?"

"Yeah," I said, taking a drink from my water. "That's how she's always been."

My grandmother lifted an eyebrow. "But that's her, right over there, isn't it?" She pointed over my shoulder, but before I could turn around, she's already stood up, and whisperyelled, "*Kora!*" across the restaurant. A big smile came over her face, and by the time I could wipe my mouth and look behind me, sure enough, Kora was walking our way, looking... *Goddamn.*

Hair perfectly styled, makeup flawlessly applied, body looking like the definition of sin in skin-tight jeans and high-heeled boots that came up to her thighs. The white blazer she wore made the outfit a *little* more conservative, but that was canceled out by very few closed buttons on the shirt she wore underneath, putting her cleavage on full display.

Okay.

130

Maybe I was exaggerating.

Honestly, it wasn't over the top. She looked amazing, and she hadn't crossed the line into being *overly* sexy for a restaurant – especially one like *Butter*, which was frequented by celebrities – in the middle of the day. Still, a vein began to throb at my temple and my fists clenched, because I saw who she was with, and I knew she'd dressed for him.

Motherfucking Paul.

Kora's gaze was locked on my grandmother, and she wore a huge smile as the two women embraced.

Paul's eyes were on me.

I was suddenly glad I *hadn't* had that whiskey, because with a little liquor in my system, I was very likely to have punched him in the face. Instead, I met his smug ass expression with a bored one of my own, only smiling when Kora was finished hugging my grandfather, and then turned to address me.

"Tariq, you didn't tell me your grandparents were going to be in town today." *And you didn't tell me you were being all cozy with Paul.*

I smiled. "Because I expected you to be busy preparing for the show. I didn't want to infringe on that, but I see you aren't as busy as I thought you were."

I caught the slight narrowing of her eyes before she turned to Mama Tamille again. "I am so sorry to have almost missed you. I wasn't expecting to see you guys until the opening next week, but I definitely would have made time for lunch with you."

"Obviously," my grandmother said, with a glint in her eyes that I recognized well. "I see you made time for a lunch date." She looked over Kora's shoulder to Paul, who pulled a smile to his face, and gave a little wave.

Kora's eyes went wide. "Oh! Um, you guys remember Paul, right?"

Mama Tamille's nose wrinkled. "Hm. Of course. I remember your ex husband. It's wonde… it's nice to…" she sighed, then nodded. "We see you, dear."

Kora bit down hard on her bottom lip as my grandmother gave Paul a sugar-free syrupy smile, then retook her seat, busying herself with the dessert menu. My grandmother loved Kora like she was her own, so I knew Paul's presence had everything to do with the dismissive air she was giving off now.

"Well," Kora said, her eyes still wide. "I *do* need to get back to theatre, so we're going to head out, but you guys are still joining us at the cast party next week after the show, right? I'm sure Dawn will want to see you."

"As long as you'll have us, sweetheart." My grandfather kissed Kora's cheek before returning to his seat.

After a few more exchanged goodbyes, Kora and Paul moved on, but my blood was boiling as I sat down again. What the *fuck* was she doing with him? I knew Kora had probably taken a car, and would be able to respond, so I slipped my phone from my pocket to send her a text.

"Thought you said you were NOT getting back with ole boy?"

"So she's back with *him*, huh?" Mama Tamille's voice broke into my thoughts as I waited for Kora to respond. I ran my tongue over my teeth, then shrugged, and she shook her head. "I really thought you two would have stopped this silliness by now, and gotten together.

What exactly is the hold up?"

"I—" My phone buzzed, and I glanced down to read Kora's response.

"Who said anything about being back together? We had a meal, we talked. – K.O."

"What could his ass possibly have to say to you? He filed the papers, right?"

"Tariq, are you going to answer my question?"

I looked up at my grandmother's stern expression, and swallowed hard. "I... Kora and I just seem to work better as friends."

She rolled her eyes. "So it has nothing to do with that little Mexican girl you were in those pictures with?"

"I'm fully aware that Paul initiated our divorce. We talked about the same stuff you talk about with Julissa I guess. Do you need a copy of the minutes from the conversation? –
K.O."

I sighed, then returned my attention to the table. "Julissa isn't Mexican."

My grandmother lifted an eyebrow. "She *looks* Mexican. And the headline said—" *Former football star gets cozy with Latina hottie.*

133

Yeah, I knew exactly the headline she was talking about, featuring pictures snapped of

Julissa and I as we left dinner a few nights before. I'd cursed when I first saw them, after

Stephen emailed me the link to the story. The writer was referring to us as an "it" couple, and saying that we must be close to engagement because of her analysis of our body language.

Hell no.

That little analysis couldn't have been further off.

We hadn't even discussed being official or exclusive, and I wasn't anywhere near ready for us to have that conversation, but that's not what the media said.

"I saw it," I said, thinking about that whiskey again. "But Julissa is Dominican."

"Whatever the little heifer is, is *she* why my Kora is sharing oxygen with that silly assed ex-husband of hers?" my grandmother asked, accepting a fresh martini from the waiter.

"I don't know why Kora is with Paul." I shrugged, then looked down at my phone to reply to her last message.

"No need to get pissy about it, I just asked a question. Hope you're not giving him room to weasel his way back into your life…"

"Well you need to find out, and make sure that fool doesn't get a chance to hurt her again. She was heartbroken when she found out he was divorcing her. And I haven't even seen her break down like that before. Well, not since…"

134

She sighed a little, then shifted uncomfortably in her seat as she downed the rest of her martini. "You know…"

Yeah.

I did.

And even though what Paul had done wasn't nearly on the same level, seeing her hurting, *period,* unleashed a sort of rage I barely knew how to handle. The only reason I hadn't kicked

Paul's ass was because I'd promised her I wouldn't. But if he hurt her again, I couldn't make any guarantees.

"And then that mother of hers… that poor girl. It's a wonder she turned out as well as she did. Can you imagine if they hadn't moved in next door?"

I shook my head. "No, actually."

But not for the reasons my grandmother was talking about, however valid they were. If they hadn't moved in next to us when I was three years old, Kora and I would have very likely never met at the park in the self-contained, upscale subdivision. We wouldn't have been classmates in the same private kindergarten and become friends, wouldn't have remained that way through all those years. I wouldn't have been there when she needed me, and vice versa.

Way too many "wouldn't haves" that I really didn't want to think about.

I finished up lunch with my grandparents, and then saw them off to the airport. Next

week would be a longer visit with them, for a few days, and then the week after that, I'd be getting on a plane

135

myself to see my mother, which was a trip I simultaneously dreaded and looked forward to.

For now though... I needed to figure out what was up with Kora. She didn't respond to that last text – my clear sign that I'd pissed her off – so I knew I'd be making a phone call or a drop-in visit later. After seeing her with

Paul... it was time to push it. ～

It took me a day or so to pin her down, and when I did, her face when she saw me was priceless. I took the thirty-minute drive to Kathryn Oliver's house for dinner at Dawn's request, and I was reasonably sure she didn't mention that invite to Kora, or Kathryn – Kora's mom.

That suspicion was confirmed when I rang the doorbell and Kora answered, her mouth dropping open when she saw me on the other side, holding a bottle of wine.

"Surprise, surprise," I said, handing her the bottle as I stepped inside without waiting for her to invite me, and took off my coat. "I finally caught up with you. I hope you see now that you can't dodge me."

She sucked her teeth. "I haven't been *dodging* you, I've... been busy."

"Busy dodging me. Just say it, gorgeous."

That "gorgeous" was no exaggeration. As much as I *did* love to see her dressed up, today she was in my favorite look for her. Fresh faced, hair pulled back, simple long sleeved tee shirt, and jeans. With the wine bottle hanging from one hand, she propped the other hand on her hip.

136

"Fine. I was dodging you. Because I don't feel like hearing about how Paul is bad for me, or a terrible person, or any of that."

I sucked my teeth. "I wasn't going to say any of that."

She tipped her head to the side. "*Really?*"

"Hell no." I smiled. "I was going to say all of that, plus some more, but…" I shrugged. "I can safely assume you don't want to hear it."

"And your assumption would be correct. Mostly because I'm *not* dating Paul."

I kept my shoulders high, not allowing them to sink in the sweeping relief I actually felt. I nodded. "Okay. Are we cool?"

Kora scraped her teeth over her bottom lip, and shifted on her bare feet. "You're not mad about me not responding to your texts?"

"I was. But I'm really not interested in fighting with you Kora. Especially not about him, not when I know that nothing I can say will change anything." I extended a hand toward her. "So are we good?"

She looked at my hand, then let out a heavy sigh. "Yeah."

I lifted an eyebrow. "That sounds convincing…"

"Sorry." She shook her head, and then took a few steps forward, closing the short distance between us to accept my hand. Her eyes were big as she looked up at me, and then glanced over her shoulder. "It's just, being here, you know? With her." she kept her voice low, and her shoulders drooped as she met my gaze again. "No matter how much time passes, I can't get over that awkward feeling. But I'm fine. Just mommy issues."

"You know you aren't alone with those," I said, placing my hands on her shoulders. "Are you going to be okay?"

She smiled, but it didn't reach her eyes as she nodded. "Of course. Aren't I always?"

"You're good at pretending."

There was a noticeable hitch in her breath as she looked away, and before I could say anything, Kathryn's voice carried in from the dining room.

"Who was at the door, Kora—*oh*," she said, when she saw me. "Hello Tariq."

Even though I knew Kathryn Oliver was well into her sixties, she barely looked older than Kora. In fact, there weren't many differences between them. The same warm dark copper skin, big brown eyes, pert nose, full lips. As a young teenager, I'd held a little bit of a crush on Ms. Oliver from next door, even snuck to the video store to find her movies to watch with my friends.

The reality of who she was, not just what she looked like, had killed those fantasies.

"Hello Kathryn."

She stiffened at my use of her first name, but said nothing about it. Instead, she lifted her chin a little higher, not quite looking at me, but past me. "I guess Dawn invited you?"

"Yes. I hope it's not too much of an intrusion," I said, even though I knew full well that it probably was – I just

138

didn't care. Our disdain for each other was mutual, but only warranted on my part. Kathryn Oliver didn't like me because I didn't like her, but we loved Dawn and Kora, so we figured out how to make it work.

She clenched her jaw, then said, "Of course not. We're actually ready to sit down and eat. You two come along." Without meeting my eyes again, she turned and headed back out of the hall, and I dropped my hands from Kora's shoulders.

"Tariq, please try to get along with her today?" Kora asked, grabbing my face between her hands. "Can you be good?"

I grinned, then took her hands, kissing her fingers before I headed toward the dining room, saying over my shoulder, "Aren't I always?"

My smile grew wider when, just faintly, I heard her mutter, "You're good at pretending."

I *was* good though, and not just at pretending. I was nice, and not just because Kora asked. Dawn was already sitting down, so I took the seat beside her, and we ate. Through dinner, the conversation mostly centered on her. Her feelings about the upcoming show, what was going on in her life, etc. Kathryn was serving peach cobbler when Dawn left in a rush of excitement to go hang out with her co-stars. She was banned from sugar "So everybody could see her abs" so she wasn't interested in watching us indulge.

Her absence left just me, Kora, and Kathryn.

But I'd still try to be good.

"Have they started calling you yet?" Kathryn asked Kora, sitting back in her seat with a glass of Riesling.

"Has who started calling?" Kora asked, then spooned another bite of Kathryn's peach cobbler into her mouth, and I did the same. Despite my feelings about the woman – she could cook her ass off.

"All those reporters, and the people from the news shows. Usually I just get a call from my publicist when someone wants an interview, but you kids these days, with the internet blogs, and the TMZ. I have folks calling my house, calling my cell phone, emailing me. I had to turn that social media stuff off, with all the alerts going off all times of night. But everybody wants to know something new about Dawn, with the show opening soon. What was she like as a little girl, where her father is, who she's dated. I told those people to stop calling me, and that one who wouldn't leave it alone, the one with the TV show, I just asked how much the check needed to be."

Kathryn stopped talking to sip her wine, as if everything were normal, but my heart slammed to a stop in my chest. Across from me, Kora's eyes went wide, and she started shaking her head. "Mama, please tell me you're joking about offering to pay people off."

Kathryn frowned, looking confused. "No, why would I joke about that? I want them to leave it alone, so I asked what it would take."

"*No. No, no, no.*" Kora's face crumpled, and she dropped her head into her hands with a low moan, as

Kathryn looked on in continued bewilderment, and then turned to me, looking for an answer.

I shook my head, swallowing hard to table my frustration. "By offering money to these people, you essentially held up a big flashing sign that there's something to hide. They aren't going to leave this shit alone now. You didn't learn that from your publicist?"

"I... I don't usually handle these things! I have people for that."

"And you didn't think you should call your people for *this*?"

"I was trying to be helpful!"

I grunted. "Yeah. Sure. Thank you so much for that. Great fucking job."

"Okay, listen to me, young man," Kathryn snapped, putting down her empty wine glass. "You will watch your tone with me in my house, first of all. Second, I was just trying to protect my grandchild."

I scoffed. "Of course you were, and what about your daughter?"

Kathryn sputtered, "Yes! Kora too! Protecting them has always been my priority!"

"Always?" I threw my head back and laughed. "Always, wow. You're funny. The only person you've ever been interested in protecting is yourself, even now."

"How dare you?!"

I scowled. "Ms. Oliver, I should ask the same question of you. You're acting scandalized, as if you've ever been in

141

the running for mother of the year. Have you forgotten how *I* was the one who—"

"Tariq, *stop it!*" The distress in Kora's voice made me hold my tongue. She looked up from between her fingers, shaking her head as she slowly pulled her hands away from her face to turn to Kathryn. "Mama, he's right. You shouldn't have paid anybody. That's as good as telling them outright that there's something we'd rather nobody know."

Kathryn sighed deeply, her voice cracking as she spoke. "I was just trying to help."

I snorted, crossing my arms, and Kora shot me a look across the table. "I know mama."

Kathryn reached over the table, covering Kora's hand with hers and squeezing it as her eyes filled with tears. "I know I've made mistakes with you in the past, Korrine, but I've been trying to make amends, no matter who won't let it go."

Kora looked at me, and swallowed before looking back at her mother. "I know, mama."

"I love you," Kathryn continued. "You and Dawn mean the world to me, and I know I haven't done the best I could, but I'm doing my best now to make sure nothing hurts you."

Kora dropped her gaze, and slid her hand away. "I know, mama. Just please don't say anything else to any reporters, okay? They call me too. I don't know how they get the number, but somehow they always do, and they email, and they tweet, but please... just don't say anything else."

"I won't. I *won't*, I promise."

Shaking her head, Kora pushed away the rest of her bowl and left the table. Silence lingered between me and Kathryn for a long time before she shifted in her seat, and I knew she was getting ready to make some appeal to my sympathy, so I pushed myself away from the table too.

"Tariq."

I groaned, then stopped my movements to look at her. Her eyes were glassy, a blend of emotion and intoxication from that third glass of wine she was on.

"Yes?"

"I *love* my daughter. Not a day goes by that I don't wish I'd done things differently."

"I don't need to hear this from you Kathryn."

"You do." She nodded, then reached for her empty glass again, fingering the stem. "I've said it to Kora a million times, but you're the one who still seems stuck on it, so—"

"No." I shook my head, propping my hands against the back of the chair I'd just exited.

"I'm the one who *seems* stuck on it, but Kathryn I hope you don't think your daughter isn't still affected by what you did, because she is. She *has been.* She *will be,* for the foreseeable future, because that shit is ingrained in her. It's part of who she is, whether or not you see it. *I* see it.

And as long as that's the case, yeah, I'm still going to be stuck on it too."

I didn't give Kathryn the chance to say anything else, because I didn't trust myself not to curse her out if she continued with her misguided attempt to get me on her side. I stalked out of the living room, and after thinking about it for a few seconds, I ventured to the back porch, where I – correctly – expected to find Kora.

"You know," she said as soon as the door closed behind me, and I stepped outside with her. "Even though this isn't the same house, even though *that* house is hundreds of miles away I still have a hard time coming *here*. How screwed up is that?"

She was standing at the deck railing, staring out over the lake, and I wrapped my arms around her waist when I got to her. "Don't do this to yourself."

"Don't do what?" She shrugged. "Owning the truth about yourself is supposed to be healing, right? Well you asked me if I was going to be okay, and I'm not. Not with being here, thinking about the media dragging out something I want to just put behind me." She turned to face me, and the streams of tears running down her face made my throat clench. "I can make myself be okay with a lot of fucked up stuff. Getting divorced, us not being together, you and Julissa. I can handle it. I can be okay. But *this*…"

"*Shhh.*" I cupped her face in my hands, kissed her wet cheeks, then her forehead before meeting her eyes. "Do you want to leave?"

She sniffled, then nodded. "Yes."

"Have you called for a car yet?"

"No."

"Then come on."

She immediately agreed. We took a second for her to say goodbye to her mother, got her shoes, got her coat, and then we were out. We climbed into my Range Rover for the drive back to the city, and Kora fell asleep on the way.

She was grouchy when I woke her to get her up to her apartment, but by the time we got up there, she was a little more awake. She wouldn't let me help her out of anything, but I stayed until she emerged from her room in a robe I knew she would be out of as soon as I left, to climb into the shower.

"Do you think it's going to be okay?" she asked, pouring herself a large glass of wine.

"The only people who know wouldn't say anything, so nothing to worry about?"

I nodded. "Nothing to worry about. You have bigger things to devote your energy to.

Show opens in three days."

Kora shook her head. "Don't remind me." She closed her eyes and took a big gulp of her wine, and when she opened them again, her gaze landed right on me. Something in her expression seemed so desolate that I took a few steps closer to her in the kitchen.

"Kora," I said, grabbing her hand. "Are we *really* good? You've been avoiding me a lot, and I don't know. I'm usually able to figure you out, but lately you're a mystery to me."

She laughed. "That's funny, Tariq, because I feel like you see right through me. Glad to know that's not the case."

She lifted her glass, draining the rest of her wine and I shook my head. "What does that even mean? I don't hide anything from you, Kora. So why would you...? See what I mean? A mystery."

For a long moment, she held my gaze, but then she blinked, and a gloss of tears coated her eyes. She turned away from me, pulling her hand from mine to pour herself another glass of Syrah as she cleared her throat.

"Kora," I said, slipping the glass from her hand to put it down on the counter. At first, I entwined my fingers with hers, but even though I was right in her face, she kept her eyes averted.

So I released her hands, cupped her chin instead, tipping it up toward me. "Talk to me about what's going on with us right now. This distance that's happening, you pulling away from me like this... we don't do this, Kora. This isn't *us*."

She sucked in a breath, blinking hard as several tears escaped her eyes. "You're right – it's not. But Tariq, you can't possibly have thought that things wouldn't be different. I mean, we're making a huge adjustment, saying that we need to keep an appropriate level of intimacy between us. So where I usually would have asked you to come and lay with me right now, hold me... I can't. We can't do that anymore, and that's hard for me, because this is a time that I could damned sure use it. I'm in limbo right now. Changes with me and you, chaos from the play, and now a concern about if my past is going to become tabloid fodder, how that's going to affect my job, and more importantly, my *daughter*. So forgive me if I seem withdrawn. I'm not upset with you, I'm just..."

146

"I get it," I said, releasing my hold on her face. Instead, I wrapped my arms around her, pulling her close. "I'm sorry for—"

"No! *No,*" she repeated, looking up to meet my gaze. "There's nothing to apologize for.

Especially not for *you.* It's just different. I still love you. You're still my best friend. I'll still burn down your entire fucking life before I let anything change *that.*"

I chuckled, then reached up, swiping tears from her cheeks with my thumbs. "Damn right." She smiled at me then, and the sudden urge to kiss her was so strong that I licked my lips. Something in her expression shifted, and I could swear she pushed herself a little closer, subtly raised her mouth closer to mine before she closed her eyes, and shook her head.

"You should probably go." She maneuvered herself out of my arms, and retrieved her wine, downing half of it in one gulp.

I cleared my throat. "Yeah, you're probably right. So I'll see you later?"

"Yeah. Of course, Tariq. We'll get through this little valley, and we'll be fine."

"I know." I nodded, then approached her again, pressing a kiss against her temple before

I backed away. "Bye."

Kora raised her glass to her mouth, finishing it off as she walked me to the door. "Bye."

I paused for a minute on the other side of the door, hoping that all those things we'd said were actually true. The last thing I wanted was to lose Kora as a friend, especially when this "just friends" shit wasn't even my idea.

My cell phone rang as I started down the hall. I pulled it from my pocket, expecting to see Julissa's name, but it wasn't her. I frowned at the screen before I answered, and that frown stayed on my face while I took the call.

When it was over, I let out a deep groan, then stashed the phone back in my pocket. Swallowing hard, I braced myself for what was sure to be a complete mess, and turned around to knock on Kora's door.

ten.

Kora

"I'm going to *kill* her ass."

I'd made that statement at least twenty times before Tariq helped me out of his sleek black Range Rover, allowing me to steady myself on my feet before we moved again.

"Just calm— *shit*," he muttered under his breath, already knowing that *calm down* was the absolute wrong thing to say to me. There wasn't any damned *calming down* to do. As a matter of fact, I wasn't nearly upset enough. The half bottle of wine I'd drunk before I found out about this mess had me too mellow.

A door opened at the building in front of us, and Officer Wiley looked out, waving us toward him. That was the direction Tariq led me in, and I tugged his arm, getting his attention.

"I'm. Going. To. Kill. Her," I repeated, when he met my eyes.

He let out a heavy sigh, then shook his head. "In front of the police?"

"That's where she chose to clown, why can't I?"

Tariq stopped, staring at me for a second before amusement tipped the corners of his mouth in the glow from the floodlight on the building. "You sound *just* like my grandmother right now."

We stepped into the building, and I watched Tariq and Officer Wiley shake hands before he turned to me, and I tried to look like I wasn't nervous as hell. "Goddamn, you're even finer in person."

My eyes went wide as he extended his hand toward mine. Tariq had explained on the way that he knew Officer Wiley personally, but he –obviously – hadn't mentioned that this man was *fine*. Honey-brown skin, sculpted jaw, strikingly green eyes… he could have been a cousin of Paul's in looks, but even my former-soccer player ex-husband didn't have a body like *this*. He wasn't in uniform, but instead in a black tee shirt with SECURITY printed in white letters on the front, stretching across his broad chest.

I accepted his hand, and my eyes went even wider when instead of shaking it, he cupped it in his, then covered it with his other hand as he stepped a little closer. "I'm Officer Garret

Wiley, ma'am. I am so sorry to have to interrupt your evening with some—"

"Garret, motherfucker I will shove that badge down your throat if you don't talk to her in a normal voice, man."

A big – gorgeous – smile raked over Officer Wiley's face at Tariq's words, and he winked at me before he shrugged, then tossed a scowl over his shoulder at Tariq.

150

"You threatening an officer of the law, while he's trying to conduct official police business?"

"Trying to get ass isn't official police business fool."

Officer Wiley scoffed. "Depends on who you ask." Some of the silky-smoothness dropped out of his voice as he turned back to me. "Anyway, I know your girl is off-limits," he said over his shoulder, then addressed me, actually shaking my hand before he released it. "I'm just messing with Tariq. Follow me, Ms. Oliver. I'll show you where your daughter is." And *that* brought me back into the reality of what was happening.

The potent aroma of coffee permeated my nose as he led us through the building, and into a private office in the back. Distantly, I could still hear and feel the loud thump of music from the open mic night happening in the front.

"Now," Officer Wiley said, blocking my view inside the office as he turned to face me. "I called Tariq because I knew I recognized this young lady from his office, and he introduced her as his god-daughter. The knucklehead over there," – he gestured to his left, where I presumed

Donovan was sitting—"I heard the women going nuts over him. I had a feeling it was going to be a big deal if I had to put them in cuffs." He reached in his pocket, then put a plastic card in my hand. "I'm going to pretend I don't know this is fake."

I looked down at it, and my eyes went wide as I realized it was a fake ID, telling the blatant lie that Dawn was *twenty-five*. I tried my best to swallow my rage as Officer Wiley stepped around me, and told Tariq in a low voice, "I do *not* want to see a bill from your ass for the next few months."

"I've got you. Thank you for having my back on this," Tariq replied, his voice low.

"What exactly happened?"

"Some hothead got upset because someone stepped on his shoes. Donovan tells him to chill, it's not that serious, they start arguing. Hothead's lady joins in, so Dawn joined in too. Little bit of shoving, but me and Cason get to it and shut it down before it gets too bad. We tell everybody involved to get out, get some air, walk the shit off. Instead of doing *that*, they come into the back hall, trying to fight. I separated everybody, and then I called you."

Shaking my head, I stepped into the room, rolling my eyes when I saw Dawn seated at a table, with her head down. Donnie was across from her, arms crossed, head back, staring up at the ceiling.

"I need one of you dummies to tell me this is a dream, please." Both of their attention snapped toward me at the sound of my voice, and they both looked terrified.

Good.

"This has to be some sort of fucked up nightmare," I continued, glancing back and forth between them, "because there is no way that in *reality,* the two headlining stars of my show, which opens in *two days* almost got their silly young asses arrested for public intoxication, disorderly conduct and goddamned underage drinking! Dawn!" I snapped, and she nearly jumped out of her seat, eyes wide. "Little girl, why would… *why?!*"

152

I rolled my eyes as Dawn burst into tears, shaking her head and blubbering some bullshit about how she didn't mean to get drunk.

Sucking my teeth, I approached her side of the table, and knelt close to her. "Maybe I would accept that excuse from you, if you weren't *too young to drink in the first place!* And *you*," I turned quickly, jabbing a finger in Donovan's direction, "I shouldn't have hired your ass, or should have let you go for the first unprofessionalism you displayed. But I was patient. I was kind. I honestly believed that the two of you would pull it together, and come through for me, but obviously, I thought *wrong!*"

Donovan opened his mouth to speak, but I shook my head, holding up a finger. "Oh no don't you dare. I don't want to hear any excuses, I don't want to hear your dumb ass reasoning, and I don't want to hear any apologies. Both of you – *fired.*"

"Why?!" Dawn and Donovan chimed at once, standing up. They both started talking, but I held up a hand for silence.

"I *don't want to hear it!* You should have considered the consequences before you decided to drink enough to get your asses in trouble. You could be in jail right now. Your saving grace is the fact that Officer Wiley had money to invest and called Tariq for help. The only reason your dumb asses aren't all over the internet right now in handcuffs is because you know somebody that knows somebody. Your careers are still extremely young. Getting drunk, getting arrested... that's the reputation you want to build? That's

153

what you want the public to see? You think you're going to get hired like that? I can tell you now, the answer is *no*."

Donovan let out a heavy sigh, then scrubbed a hand over his face. "But getting fired isn't a good look either."

"Not my problem. I'm not your mother, and I *am* hers, but she's grown. I can't ground you, I can't send you to your room, I can't revoke your privileges to the mall. But what I *can* do, is hand down a real, grown up consequence to your childish, immature ass decision."

"*Mama*—"

"Dawn, please. It's not up for debate. Take me home please," I said, turning to Tariq, who hadn't said anything yet. His eyes were wide too, like he was waiting on his scolding as well. I walked past him, and back to the door we'd come in at the back of the coffee shop – my *favorite* coffee shop – and waited there. A few minutes later, Tariq joined me, and we walked back to his vehicle in silence.

He waited until we were moving to say anything.

"I called cars to come and get them." I said nothing, only nodded.

"You don't think firing them is harsh?"

I sucked my teeth, crossing my arms as I stared out the window, watching the buildings go past. "Hell no. I think you feel bad for Dawn, and don't want to see her upset. I think she has you wrapped around her fingers."

"They're kids, Kora."

"Not in the eyes of the law, Tariq. And not in the eyes of the media. Their black asses are going to have a hard enough time being taken seriously in this industry without

154

arrest records and negative headlines. They lucked out of getting arrested tonight, fine. But they obviously aren't taking their roles in this show seriously if they can do something to jeopardize it two days before it opens. Can you image the spin on the story? Instead of it being about their performances, about their talent, it would be about drunk and disorderly conduct. Too many people have worked too hard to have it overshadowed by this."

"And you don't think firing the two stars is going to fuel rumors?"

"Tariq, leave me the fuck alone."

"Damn," he chuckled. "I'm just trying to get you to step back and think about this."

I huffed. "Yeah, I'm about to take a step back and put my foot in *your* ass too. Not even an hour ago, I was telling you that I was feeling anxious and overwhelmed, like too much shit was happening. And now here come these two, who should honestly know better, and you want to defend their silly asses."

"I'm not defending them."

"It sounds like you're defending them."

"I'm not. I get it. They messed up, and I understand why you don't want to let that go unpunished. But firing the stars of the show you've been slaving over for months? Come on, gorgeous. If you follow through with that, you're really hurting yourself, and causing more stress. You've got to come up with another punishment. Make them eat laxatives and spicy food or something."

I couldn't help myself – I laughed at that, and smacked Tariq on the arm. "Damn fool."

He didn't do anything but chuckle in response, and the relative silence in the car after that gave me time to really think about his words. Now that my own little buzz was wearing off, I was more disappointed than angry with them. Especially at Dawn. Getting into a fight because of Donovan? *Seriously?* I raised her better than that – or so I thought.

But outside of that, Tariq did make a good point. Was I letting anger overshadow common sense? It certainly wouldn't be the first time my emotions had taken over my ability to make the best decision, so it wasn't outside the realm of possibility.

Maybe they would learn a lesson if I followed through on firing them. But it would definitely make it around the theatre world that they'd been fired – together – from their first major show. Donovan had professional dance experience, a handsome face, a famous ex, and the fact that he was a man to fall back on.

Dawn did not.

Their dismissal would follow both of them though. And there was no telling what pulling in both understudies at the last minute would do to the quality of the show. And I'd be lying if I said I wasn't concerned for how my relationship with Dawn would be effected. *Maybe I should reconsider… but I don't want to punk out either… hmmm…* My phone chimed, and I expected it to be Dawn. Instead, it was Nubia.

156

"Have you seen this? – Wonder Woman"

I hadn't told her yet about this mess with Dawn, but I tapped on the link that was included at the bottom of her message. It led me to a video someone had posted on social media, but I couldn't make out what it was from the static thumbnail. I tapped the "play" button, and audibly gasped as Dawn's voice filled the car, singing one of the songs from *The Chase*.

She was on the stage at Urban Grind, singing with all her heart about being caught up in love with someone she shouldn't want, and the audience was captive.

"Hey, that's Dawn isn't it?" Tariq asked, and I nodded as I stared down at the screen. Despite my anger, I actually smiled too at the *huge* grin that crossed Dawn's face when Donovan joined her on stage, wrapping an arm around her waist as he harmonized with her for the bridge.

I scrolled down a little to read the comments, and my smile grew even bigger.

"OMG, they are so cute together! #relationshipgoals"

"This girl can saaaaanngggg! Who is this?!"

"That's @DawnOliver, and @DancingDonJuan, from Pixie's video and tour!

Cannot WAIT to see these two live! Already got my tickets! #TheChase #TheatreJunkie

#BlackTheatreRocks"

"@DawnOliver…damn girl! Hair, skin, body, voice goals like shit! #heyboo!"

"Where is my #cryface emoji?! @PixieBadAss is gonna drag this girl by her hair, who is this all hugged up with @DancingDonJuan?!"

"#TheChase?! The folks in it sound and look like this?! I'm sold!"

"Yo, this @DawnOliver chick is bae af!"

"@DawnOliver inbox about to full of creeps... myself included. Y'all see the ass on this girl?!"

"Her voiiiccceee, OMG!"

"This girl is who they put at the gates of heaven to welcome people, gotta be."

"About to order tickets for #TheChase RIGHT NOW!"

Some of the comments I saw made me roll my eyes, but overwhelmingly, they were positive. The video said it was uploaded two hours ago, and it already had nearly thirty thousand likes, and had been played almost five times that many times. I was getting ready to hit play again when another message from Nubia came through.

"Wait until the world sees her on stage for real! Baby girl is going to be a star!" I let out a heavy sigh.

Was I really prepared to take that from her?

No, Warm Hues Theatre wasn't Broadway, but we weren't anything to sneeze at either.

We were well respected, we sold out shows. More than one star had been made in this theatre, and it could absolutely be a springboard for success. Did either of them deserve to lose that over a mistake?

158

We pulled up at my building, but I made no moves to get out of the car. Tariq reached over to grab my hand, squeezing my fingers between his.

"What's on your mind?"

"These kids," I said, with a deep sigh. "I was sure about firing them when I said it, but now... not so much."

Tariq shrugged. "You're allowed to change your decision. And I'm not just saying that because it's Dawn. I'm saying it because yes, I do remember that you said earlier you had a lot on your plate. I'd hate to see you make a huge change like this without looking at all angles. I don't want you to regret it."

"You mean you don't want me whining to you *when* I regret it."

He grinned. "Yeah. That too. So what are you going to do?"

I tightened my grip on his hand, then looked down at my phone. After a few long moments, I picked it up, and started a group message with Donovan and Dawn.

"Tonight is your lucky night... but I swear to God if either of you mess up again..."

eleven.

Tariq

I sat in front of the computer for a long time, staring at the email until the letters on the screen began to swim in front of me. *It's just a confirmation email. A reminder,* I told myself, but that didn't do anything for the twinge of anxiety it had sparked in my chest.

Flight information. Hotel confirmation. Schedule blocked off for several days. Trips to see my mother were a production that had to be carefully coordinated and planned for best results. They were draining enough on their own, but if my timing was off, or any other arbitrary variable was out of sync, I could kiss the idea of a "nice" visit goodbye.

"Couldn't sleep?"

Finally, I tore my eyes away from the screen, following the source of the question. Julissa was standing at the door to my home office, draped in nothing but a shirt – *my* shirt, from earlier in the night – with only a few of the buttons closed. Which was interesting, to say the least, since when I left her in my room, she'd been fully clothed.

I knew what she was doing, and if my mind wasn't on my mother, I probably would have at least been amused, but as it stood, I had to swallow a bit of annoyance before I nodded, then clicked away from the email on the screen.

"Yeah. Came to catch up on some work instead."

It was true. Working had been my original intention when I left my bedroom, and I'd even gotten a little bit done before that email caught my eye.

Julissa sauntered into the room, making a show of yawning and stretching her arms high so that my shirt slid upward, showcasing toned caramel thighs. Bodily, she got the reaction she wanted from me – I got hard thinking about her bare skin underneath, but I gave away nothing with my expression.

"I have some things to catch up on myself," she said, stopping in front of the desk. She pressed her fingertips to the smooth mahogany surface as she stared down at me in my seated position. "I've been putting in hours like crazy. That's why I've been a little MIA the last week or so."

I nodded. "I understand. I thought that might be the case, with what happened tonight." She gave me an embarrassed smile, then shrugged as she looked away.

Julissa and I had been out to dinner earlier. While there, we'd spotted on her partners from her firm. Well, *I* spotted him, because old boy was staring at us hard as hell even though he was with someone, and I mentioned it to Julissa. When she saw who I was talking about, her mood had changed, almost like she was in trouble. Like she should have been home working instead of at dinner.

A glass of wine, a few cocktails, and I could already tell she'd overdone it, but instead of taking her home, like I wanted to do, she insisted we go to my place for *after* dinner drinks, which was the original plan. I agreed, but I had no intentions of giving her more alcohol.

Turns out, I didn't have to have that conversation with her anyway. She passed out on my couch about five minutes after we arrived, and I took off her shoes and coat and put her in my bed. So add the late hour, the alcohol, and the admission that she'd been overworking herself, and the falling asleep made sense.

What didn't make sense was her current state of dress.

"What happened to your clothes?" I asked, sitting up, propping my elbows on the desk.

Her gaze drifted back to me. "They weren't that comfortable for sleeping. I woke up with the button on my jeans digging into my skin, and once I was up, I felt like I needed a shower.

You weren't in the bed, so I figured you were working or something. I went ahead and took the shower, but after I got out, I didn't have anything to wear. So I went to your closet, thinking I could grab a tee shirt..."
Oh, shit.

"But the first thing I saw was this little section of women's clothes. *Really nice* women's clothes. Do you have a woman living with you?"

I scrubbed a hand over my face, and shook my head. "No."

She lifted an eyebrow after a moment passed and I didn't elaborate. "No? That's all you're going to say, just *no*? No explanation?"

163

"Do you want the truth?"

She jerked her head back. "What? Uh, *yes*, I want the truth. Why wouldn't I?"

"Because last time, it was pretty clear that I upset you, and I'm not out to do that."

"Wow." She sucked in a sharp breath and stepped back, crossing her arms over her chest. "So they're Kora's clothes, is what you're about to tell me. Your "friend" has clothes at your home, in plain view. You didn't even have enough respect to put them away while I was here?"

Immediately, my face dropped into a scowl. "*Inside my closet* is not plain view. You took it upon yourself to go snooping, and found something you didn't like. I *didn't* think that maybe I should hide what's in my closet to accommodate your impromptu sleepover at my house. It has *nothing* to do with respect."

She sucked her teeth. "It has *everything* to do with respect. If we're together, I expect to not have another woman rubbed in my face!"

"I'm not rubbing another woman in your face, you're *looking* for shit."

"You have her clothes in your closet, and I'm not supposed to think you're sleeping together?"

"I'm *not* sleeping with Kora, and we've had clothes in each other's closets since before I even had a place of my own. It's a habit we picked up as goddamned teenagers, something we do to take care of each other."

"I'm supposed to believe that?"

I sighed, then sat back in my chair. "Julissa, you can believe whatever you want, but I've never been anything but honest with you. Never disrespected you. You're pissed off because I'm not bending over backwards for you, and I'm not sure why you think I don't see that."

"Is there something wrong with wanting to be bent over backwards for?"

I shrugged. "Absolutely not. But that's *earned*, through time and shared feelings. We've been casually seeing each other for less than two months, and I don't do the whirlwind relationship thing. I'm not that guy, and I didn't think you were that woman. You approached me about sex, no strings attached. We happened to evolve past that, to getting to know each other further. Last time we had this conversation – because it *feels* like the same conversation – it became clear to me that you were reading more than I was into sex. Is that a fair interpretation?"

She rolled her eyes, then nodded. "Yes."

"So, I said okay, let's eliminate sex from the equation, to be respectful of your feelings. We agreed. I'm not stupid, Julissa. You showering here, walking around naked – I see you.

You're trying to entice me into breaking our agreement, and in the two weeks since we put that little "rule" into place, this isn't the first time you've tried."

"Because *I'm* not stupid," she snapped, dropping her arms from her chest to point a finger at me. "You're a man – if you're not getting it from me, you're going to get it somewhere."

165

My mouth twisted to the side. "Or not. What kind of—listen, I can't speak for every motherfucker on the planet, but I'm not so obsessed with sex that I can't go a couple of months without it. The point was to show you that I'd become interested in you, not your pussy, but even that's getting twisted into something else now."

"Months without sex?"

"Yes, that's what I said. Is that so strange, that it might take me months to know if I want to be in a committed relationship with someone?"

She rolled her eyes. "No, it's strange for a man to willingly go without sex for months."

"It's not my normal practice, no, but I just explained why I was willing to do it. Didn't you *just* say you wanted to be bent over backwards for? So how…?" I raised my shoulders in confusion, then dropped them as I put a hand to my forehead, trying to massage away my building headache. "Julissa, I like you, but this is draining. I'm not going to keep having conversations like this, when we've only been seeing each other outside of sex for a damned *month*. Either my friendship with Kora is acceptable to you, or it's not. Either we're taking this slow, or we're not taking it at all."

"And what about what *I* want? Hm? All of this is about you."

"You should be doing the same thing! Before we commit, making sure that our wants are aligned. I'm not asking you to compromise anything – I'm telling you what *I* won't be compromising on, so you can decide if that works for you or not."

166

When our eyes met again, hers were glossy, and I pushed out a heavy sigh, because

goddamnit. Here it was again, her reacting as if I'd said something purposely hurtful when the intention was the exact opposite – *not* hurting her, or any woman for that matter, by being direct. It was something that my grandparents had instilled in me, and I took it seriously. It was important, they said, to be clear about my intentions, even if it wasn't necessarily what the other person *wanted to hear*, so it couldn't be said that I'd misled or tricked anyone.

And it was still a problem, somehow.

"Julissa…" I stood up, rounding the desk to put one hand at her waist, using the other to tip her face up toward mine. "I'm sorry, if I offended you. That's not my intention, at all. I just need us to be on the same page, and there's no shame in it if you aren't feeling it."

She flicked her gaze away from me, blinking back tears before she looked at me again. "I just want to understand where I stand with you. I don't feel like that's too much to ask."

"It's not. I'm telling you where we stand right now. You have to stop trying to rush this, and just relax. We're still casual right now. If that's not what you want, don't settle for it. If you aren't enjoying our time together…"

"We have a good time together," she said, with a subtle nod. "It's just… I don't know.

I'm going to put my clothes back on and go."

I frowned. "You sure? It's late, and you're welcome to stay until morning."

167

"I'm sure. I need to sort through my thoughts."

"Okay. I understand." I released my grip on her waist and stepped back, watching as she turned and headed for the door. She paused just on the other side of the threshold, but then kept moving, and I called Fletch to make sure she made it home safely when she was ready.

Once she was gone, I took a shower and settled into bed myself, wishing I could tell Kora about this shit. I knew she'd give me the real deal, without sugarcoating it, to let me know exactly what I was doing wrong with this Julissa thing. Before, I could talk to her about any and everything, but our relationship seemed to be in a different place now.

It had only been a day since that talk in her apartment, the same night Dawn got in trouble with Donovan. She'd said then that there would have to be a change in how we interacted, but what that meant hadn't sunken in for me.

Until now.

Now, it felt like it didn't matter what happened. Together or not together wasn't really that relevant at all.

It was almost like I was losing her either way. ～

"I don't care what kind of cars your teammates drive – a Maybach is *not* a good use of your money."

Across from me, one of the NFL's latest breakout stars sat rolling his eyes. Jordan Johnson was young, reckless, and immature, in his personal *and* financial dealings. The only

168

thing he took seriously was the football field, and that was where he thrived. I didn't know if I could – or wanted to – do anything about his fucked up personal life, but I *could* keep his silly ass from going broke before he turned thirty.

If he listened.

"It doesn't even cost that much, man!"

I scowled. "Two hundred thousand dollars 'isn't that much'? Jordan, you have to be shitting me."

"That's like, a week of pay for me."

"And all it takes is a twisted knee, a surgery, and you're never on that field again. Your contract isn't guaranteed Jordan. Yes, it's ten million dollars over four years – that's impressive, yes. But you have to look at that ten million dollars like it's the only money you'll ever have.

Like these next four years are the last ones you'll get to play. Because they *just might be.* Be smart about this."

Jordan pushed out a heavy breath, then tossed his head back against the chair, staring up at the ceiling. "So no Maybach?"

"No Maybach. Get you an S-Class or something, man. It's a nice car."

He sat up, crossing his arms. "What do *you* drive?"

I grinned. "Why does that matter?"

"Just tell me, come on."

Shaking my head, I shrugged, then leaned back in my seat. "I drive a Range Rover."

"*See,*" Jordan said, standing up. "You're pushing a Range, but I'm supposed to get a little
Benz?"

"They cost the same," I argued, chuckling as Jordan started pacing in front of my desk.

"The swag isn't the same though."

"Okay so get a Range Rover."

Jordan sucked his teeth. "I can't drive the same thing as my *accountant*."

"*Accountant?*" I scowled, shaking my head. "I'm *not* an accountant."

I had to fight back a smile as I thought of Kora and old boy – the cheap cologne wearing accountant – who worked a couple of floors down. I mean-mugged him every time I saw him, and I wasn't even sure he knew why.

"I'm your *financial advisor*, not your accountant. *And*, I used to have your position young man, don't you forget it."

Jordan grinned. "Yeah, yeah old head, I know. Two championships and all that – that's why I came to you. You're supposed to get it."

"I *do* get it. Which is why... no Maybach. I'm looking at your accounts, your potential longevity in the NFL, all of that. At this point – a hundred thousand *max* on a damned car. You stay healthy and out of trouble through the playoffs, and we'll talk about an increase."

"And if we win the Super Bowl...?"

I stood. "You win the Super Bowl, your agent should be able to call Mercedes and convince them they *need* you to be seen in a Maybach. What are your endorsement prospects looking like? Got yourself an energy drink yet?"

"Nah, not yet," Jordan said, with a bit of a sigh. "But we *do* have UnderArmour and

GNC. You know, light work."

"Man, *hell yeah*." I stepped around the desk to slap hands with him before I pulled him into a quick one-armed embrace. "That's the kind of stuff I'm talking about. Stop all of this running around, fucking everything that moves before you get caught up with a baby. If you're smart about it you can live on your endorsement money, send your salary straight to your retirement savings. Invest more, let that money *make money* instead of spending it on flashy cars and child support. You understand?"

Jordan nodded. "Yeah, man. I get it."

"Okay." I clapped him on the shoulder, and then led him to the door. "Send me the numbers before you buy a car. I'm serious."

"Yeah..." Jordan bobbed his head like he was really hearing me, but his attention was elsewhere, across the reception area. I followed his gaze to see that Dawn had just appeared, and her face spread into a big smile when she saw me standing in the open doorway of my office.

"*Goddamit*, she is bad as fuck," Jordan murmured as she made her way over.

I clamped a hand on his shoulder again, gripping it hard enough to get him to look at me.

I met his eyes, and subtly shook my head. "I will *kill you*, you understand me?"

His eyes went wide. "Yo, that's *you*?"

I shoved him a little when I pulled my hand away. "She's my god daughter," I growled.

"And off limits like a mother fucker. You got me?"

Jordan pushed out a little sigh. "I guess."

"You need to do more than guess, you need – Dawn, hey baby girl."

I pulled Dawn into a hug as she made it to us, then shot Jordan a scowl over her shoulder.

He was too busy looking at Dawn to notice the death glare I was sending his way, and I grabbed the back of her sweater, trying to tug it lower to cover the shape of the unnecessarily tight jeans she was wearing.

"Will you *stop*," she scolded, swatting my hand away as she laughed. She turned to

Jordan, and then looked between us, apparently waiting on an introduction I wasn't about to give.

Jordan shook his head, then extended his hand to Dawn. "Jordan–"

"Johnson. Wide receiver for the Connecticut Kings. You've been the "man crush

Monday" pretty consistently for a few of my friends."

He smiled. "Just for your "friends", huh?" My stomach lurched over the way Dawn blushed, and I cleared my throat, loudly. Jordan looked up, and his eyes went wider at the look I gave him. He released his hold on Dawn's hand. "Aiight, well, I'll catch y'all later."

Dawn frowned as Jordan started across the floor. "You didn't even get my name!"

"He doesn't need it," I told her, grabbing her under the elbow to steer into my office. She gave me a playful roll of her eyes, then dropped into a seat in front of my desk. "What brings you by?" I asked, taking a seat in the chair next to her. "Show opens tomorrow, I'm surprised Kora isn't running you in the ground."

She sighed. "I had to get away, because you're right – she *is* running us into the ground.

She let us leave a little early though, so we could get some extra sleep before the show. She's *so* stressed. Have you talked to her?"

I nodded. "We've talked a bit, but she's busy right now."

"Not too busy for *Paul*." Her voice took on a mocking tone, and her lip curled in disgust when she mentioned his name. I'd been diligent in making sure that Dawn's disdain for Paul wasn't rooted in anything Kora or I needed to be concerned about, but a while ago, it became clear. She thought he was just corny at first, but then he divorced Kora, and she just plain didn't like him now.

"Anyway," Dawn continued, "She's still pissed at me. I wanted to take her out to dinner tonight or something, but I'm scared to ask."

"Well, that's what happens when you mess up. Your parents get pissed off about it."

"You didn't."

I lifted an eyebrow. "Says who? You must not have noticed that your monthly deposit wasn't – ah *shit*. That was supposed to be a surprise."

173

Dawn's eyes went wide. "*Seriously*? You're not depositing anything for me this month?"

"Hell no! So you can use it to get drunk and screw around with this little nigga that calls himself "Don Juan"? Nah. I send that money as a reward and incentive for you to act like you have some sense. And you obviously don't, so no trip to Gucci for you this month."

"I—*ugh*. What happened to good cop, bad cop?"

I chuckled, then leaned toward her to kiss her forehead. "Good cop realized his little princess needs to start facing some consequences. It's the least I can do. You're welcome."

"We weren't even doing anything," she complained. "We were minding our business both times, and those people wouldn't leave us alone because they recognized Donnie. They were *trying* to start trouble."

"So first off – your ass is only twenty, and you had a fake id so you could drink. You were doing something wrong. Second, sounds like you need to leave Donnie alone."

She gave me a deadpan look. "So you never drank until after you were twenty-one?"

"That's here nor there. *You* shouldn't. Cause I said so."

"Right. Parents reasons. But what about Donnie? What's wrong with him? He's smart, funny, we share the same passion, he has a really promising career, he—"

"Was photographed last week with his ex. And they were looking cozy as hell."

Dawn shrugged. "They're still friends. Just because they broke up doesn't mean they can't hang out with each and just be cool."

"You can't be…" I let out a heavy sigh, biting back the rest of that sentence. I wanted to tell her *you can't be that naïve,* but she was twenty years old, and yes, she actually could.

"Dawn, listen. I don't want to see you get hurt, but I know you're going to do what you want to do anyway, because whether or not I like it, you're a grown woman. All I can do it caution you, sweetheart, to be *very* careful. With men, period, but especially in the entertainment industry. And athletes. Anybody high profile, really. Those rumors about them being womanizers, having five and six different women… it's usually rooted in reality. And I don't want that for you. I don't want a man breaking your heart."

Dawn nodded, then propped her chin on her hand, resting her elbow on the arm of the chair. "But what if my heart isn't in it? What if I'm just having fun, like they are? Why does it have to be that because I'm a woman, it's assumed that I'm going to end up with hurt feelings?

What if all *I* want is sex?"

I just stared at her for a second, not quite sure of what to say. "I… *shit,*" I said, shaking my head as I dropped my gaze, then looked back up at her again. "The progressive part of me knows that the correct answer is: Be safe. Be discreet. Only deal with people who have your best interests at heart. Do what makes you happy. But the *other* part of me…" I chuckled. "Shit,

175

Dawn. I don't want to hear this. I don't want to know about this."

"Would you say that same thing if I was a man?"

"Probably not. No need to explain what's wrong with that, because I get it, but…" "Patriarchy." Dawn grinned.

I shrugged, then nodded. "But patriarchy. You know I love you though, right?"

"Of course. And to your original point, I *am* being careful. I'm not stupid – I know

Donovan is in love with Ariel. I don't have any delusions otherwise, so I'm not getting involved like that with him. Do you know how many times my mother has had the "industry men" talk with me?"

"With Kora? I can just imagine."

A gentle knock sounded at my door, and I frowned as I looked at the time. I didn't have another client for almost thirty minutes.

Dawn stood up when I did, explaining that she needed to head out anyway.

"Talk to your mother," I urged, with my hand on the door. "Yeah, she's pissed, but *you* messed up. So you make it right. Before the show. She has enough going on. Okay?"

She rolled her eyes, but pressed herself up on her toes to kiss my cheek. "Ok*aaay*."

I chuckled as the knock sounded again, then pulled the door open to see Julissa on the other side. I hadn't seen or spoken to her since the night before, so I was honestly a little surprised.

"I'm sorry," she said, shooting Dawn an apologetic smile before she looked back to me.

"I don't mean to interrupt. You told me before that you always keep this hour free, so I assumed you were in here alone."

"It's fine. Dawn was about to head out." I glanced over at Dawn, and my eyes went a little wider at the look of blatant disinterest she was giving Julissa.

"I don't think we've formally met," Julissa said, extending her hand to Dawn. "Julissa

Santos. Tariq and I are friends."

"Dawn Oliver."

Julissa smiled. "I *know*. I can't wait to see you open this show tomorrow. I was actually just coming down to confirm with Tariq if we were still attending together."

She looked at me and raised her eyebrow, locking her gaze with mine. I guess this was her way of letting me know she'd thought about everything from the night before, and wanted to move forward, so I nodded.

Over Julissa's shoulder, Dawn rolled her eyes and waved goodbye, not sticking around to hear any further conversation. I said goodbye to her again, then gave my attention back to Julissa, who was still pinning me with the same hopeful look.

"Yeah," I said, and watched her face light up. "Step in the office with me. Let's discuss the details."

twelve.

Kora

Breathe.
Breathe.
Breathe.
Whew.

I pushed out a deep breath and lifted my shoulders, doing a little shimmy to shake off my lingering anxiety. It was going to be fine. It *had* to be fine.

There was no turning back now.

In the mirror in my office, I checked my appearance one more time. I'd chosen all black for this opening night – black leather pants, suede booties for some texture, black lace corset, and an asymmetrically cut black blazer. My makeup was flawless, hair styled to perfection. Ears, fingers, and wrists all dripped with diamonds. I looked amazing, I had no problem admitting that to myself. But inside, I was a fucking wreck. I chuckled over that in my empty office, because really… beautiful exterior, chaotic interior was kind of a running theme in my life.

A knock sounded at the door, and I checked the time. It was still an hour before the show started, but people were already getting into their seats, the red carpet was booming, my actors were getting dressed, stage crew pulling everything together, and I… was hiding. The knock came again.

After yet another deep breath, I pulled myself away from the mirror to open the door.

Paul grinned at me from the other side, looking outright delicious in his beautifully tailored tux.

"Damn," he said, shaking his head as his eyes raked over me. "You look gorgeous tonight."

I blushed. "Thank you. You're coming to take me out there for pictures, aren't you?"

He nodded. "Yeah. You said you might need some convincing, so here I am: convincing. You're the director, Kora. You kinda *have* to do the red carpet." I pouted, and he chuckled a little as he reached for my hand. "Come on, woman. You look too good to *not* be photographed."

I accepted the hand he offered, and he gently pulled me out of the office, resting his hand on the small of my back as he led me down the hall. The weight of his hand set off little tingles at the point of contact, urging me to move closer to him, but I resisted. I still wasn't quite *there* with Paul.

We'd talked several times in the few weeks since he'd been back in my life. Had shared lunch on a couple of occasions. Although the fact that he'd dumped me always seemed to stick around somewhere in the back of my mind, I was starting to remember *why* I ever liked him.

I could talk to him about pretty much anything with minimal judgement – just like Tariq.

He texted me once or twice a day, with things that were often random, but never boring. Sometimes they made me laugh, and he *never* made me wait long on a response. – just like Tariq.

I never had to worry about a dull moment with him, even if things weren't necessarily exciting, but never tedious. – just like Tariq.

So it occurred to me, obviously, that I was just tagging Paul in as a substitute for the person I really wanted. But then I pushed that thought away, because what, exactly, did "tagging Paul in" mean? I wasn't *really* considering giving him another chance, and though he was clear that he wanted that, I was equally transparent that it wasn't an option.

There was nothing wrong with enjoying the attention though, right?

"So how are you feeling?" he asked, as we turned down yet another empty hall. The low rumble of voices from dressing rooms, and shouts from the paparazzi outside reached my ears at the same time, and a lump caught in my throat.

I swallowed. "Nervous as hell. This could be a disaster."

"It won't."

"But if the critics hate it—"

"They won't."

"Unless they *do.*"

"*Stop it.*" Paul turned me toward him, putting his hands on my shoulders. "I was there yesterday, for your final

181

run-through, remember? The show is beautifully performed, sexy, exciting, and emotional. You've done a great job. *Relax*. Everybody is going to love it."

I blew out a sigh. "You think so?"

"I know so. Now let's go take these pictures."

He didn't give me a chance to refuse before he pulled me around another corner, this one occupied with people rushing around for last minute fixes. We navigated down that hall, to the door, and with a reassuring smile, Paul opened the door and we stepped outside.

Because of the door we came out of, we easily blended into the crowd of people waiting to cross the carpet. By some measures, I was probably a little underdressed, but I would be on my feet, moving around, possibly fixing costumes, and who knew what else. I needed to be comfortable.

Paul pulled me through the crowd, cutting in line in front of several people – including

Pixie and her entourage, who I hoped wouldn't be showing up at the cast party afterward – to put me up next. I smiled and waved and vamped for the cameras, and even took a few pictures with Paul, even though I knew rumors would fly. He stood respectfully off to the side, not being

presumptuous, but I'd invited him as my date for the night. Why shouldn't we take pictures together?

I'd felt a little pang of guilt about it at first, knowing that Tariq wouldn't approve. But then last night, over her own version of a "make up" dinner, Dawn had dropped the bug in my ear that he was bringing Julissa. And if he had a date, why the hell shouldn't I?

When we finished with those pictures, we went back inside, making our way to the actual theatre. We climbed the short set of stairs that led to one of four VIP boxes, which I'd spent an unholy amount of money on to reserve half of the seats for my friends and family. Paul went off to speak to someone he recognized, and I took the opportunity to approach Nubia.

She was wearing a silver and white sequined romper, with a v-neckline that dipped to her belly button. With her signature big hair and red lips, and a luxurious white faux fur draped around her shoulders, Nubia was giving old Hollywood glamour in a major way.

The gorgeous young male model on her arm added to her vibe.

Nubia smiled when she saw me, unlooping her arm from her date to give me a hug. "You look *gooood*," she said, playfully swatting my butt before she stepped back. "I'm not going to ask you how you feel, because I already know the answer to *that*."

"Yeah, I'm sure." – I'd freaked out with her late last night on the phone, and she'd tried to talk me down with a similar speech to Paul's. – "What's with the boy toy?"

She shrugged, then glanced over her shoulder to her seats, where her date had already sat down. "Just a little eye candy for the evening."

"Uh-huh. Wouldn't have anything to do with you avoiding Stephen, would it?"

183

"Oh it has *everything* to do with avoiding Stephen Foster. Besides – he's here with a date anyway." She pointed across the room, where Steph stood with some pretty woman hanging on his arm like she thought he might get away. Tariq and Julissa stood beside them.

Tariq looked good, as usual, and Julissa was clearly dressed to impress. The liquidy gold fabric of her dress was beautifully draped over her body, cinched in the middle to show off her small waist. She had her hair pulled into an elegant knot, with simple, understated jewelry, and a black fur stole wrapped around her. She looked *amazing.*

I couldn't stand her ass.

I looked away, pretending I hadn't seen them, focusing instead on Tariq's grandparents as they came through the door. I exchanged hugs and kisses with them, and tried not to look too sick to my stomach when Tariq approached, and introduced them to Julissa. I didn't have time to dwell though – my own mother came in, and I distracted myself by going to speak to her. By the time I left everyone to get situated into their seats, there were only twenty minutes left before the show.

I snuck through the throngs of people in the theatre to make my way to the back. One wing of the back area housed the dressing rooms, and I went straight there.

I found Dawn in her private dressing room – one of the perks of being star of the show – and smiled at her when our eyes met in the mirror. Gently, I closed the door behind me, then leaned against it as I let out a heavy sigh.

"So here we are."

184

She nodded, and I could practically feel the emotions oozing from her. Fear, excitement, happiness… everything I would want or expect her to feel in a moment like this. "Here we are."

"You're supposed to be heading to the stage for the opening scene."

Dawn turned in her chair to face me. "But you knew I wouldn't be."

"Yeah," I nodded. "I did." I pushed away from the door and approached her chair, deftly adjusting a few loose curls before I met her gaze in the mirror again. "When I was twenty-three years old, I won a Tony award. *One* of my proudest achievements, and definitely the highlight of my career. I brought you with me to accept it. And you told me: Mommy, I want one."

Dawn smiled. "I remember that. I was six years old."

I nodded. "Yep. Six years old with these big brown eyes, and your hair in two big afro puffs. I always loved your hair like that, but your grandmother always wanted to slick it into a bun, or braids, or press it out. To tame it. But I liked it free, and wild, so I undid those braids, and put you in your puffs."

"I remember that too. Grandma fussed at you for a good month over the pictures from that night."

"Yes indeed," I laughed. "She did. But back to you – you looked at my trophy, and you spun that medallion, and you said to me, *mommy I want one.* I thought you were just being six years old. But you insisted on dance classes, so we put you in them. And you wanted to see any show your

185

grandmother and I would allow. Eventually, you wanted to go to acting classes, and voice classes, and it became abundantly clear that you were incredibly talented. Then I won another Tony award. You were eleven. And again, you said *mommy! I want one!*"

"And you haven't done another show since then." Dawn's eyes were glossy as she reached up, covering the hand I had propped on her shoulder with hers.

I smiled. "No, I haven't. Because I needed to do what I'd needed to do for a while. Focus on you. It was time to be mommy."

"You were *always* mommy."

"No." I shook my head. "Your grandma was mommy. I was out chasing a dream, from when *I* was a little girl, and I looked at *my* mother's awards, and said *I want one of those mommy.* I got one! And I got another. So it was time for me to step back from my dreams so I could be your mother full time, and help you find yours." I wrapped my arms around Dawn's shoulders and leaned down, pressing the side of my face to hers. "Look at where you are, sweetie. This is your time. All your hard work, all your dedication, listening to me cuss and fuss at you... this is the beginning of you reaching that dream. And I want you to understand, even though I'm hard on you – this feeling, this moment, about to watch you on stage... this is better than anything."

Dawn stared at me for a long time, and then shook her head, reaching to snatch a tissue from the box on the vanity. "Mama stop. You're gonna make me mess up my makeup, and you know you'll curse me out if I'm late getting on that stage."

We laughed, and then I hugged her a little tighter, closing my eyes when she brought her hands up to rub my arms. "I love you, Dawn."

She sniffled as she dabbed the corners of her eyes. "I love you too."

I nodded. "Okay. Now come on. It's show time."

~

"Ms. Oliver! Ms. Oliver! It's been said by many that you handed this role to your daughter as a family favor. Do you have anything to say in response to that?"

I pressed my lips together in a line, trying my best not to scowl at the young entertainment blogger holding a recorder up in front of her, waiting for my answer. "I," I took a deep breath, then allowed my mouth to spread into a smile. "I think Dawn's performance tonight spoke for itself. She did the show a favor by accepting the role. She – as the young people like to say – *slayed* the part of Raven, and I don't think those "many" that you mentioned can argue with that. Enjoy the party."

I walked away from the young woman with my head held high, ignoring the other media clamoring for attention. They quickly lost interest in me as Dawn herself appeared, freshly changed out of her last costume from the show. I was grateful Micah had convinced me of the value of extra security. Those big guys were doing a great job of keeping everyone at arm's length.

Seeing the way the crowd formed around her, people shoving recorders and cell phones at her, shouting and yelling to have their questions heard or ask for an autograph made anxiety rise in my chest. Still, when her eyes scanned the crowd and found mine, I kept my expression bright and happy, giving her a reassuring nod before she turned and began answering questions.

I couldn't wait for this portion of the "party" to be over. For about an hour, we were allowing press and fans to mingle with the cast, ask questions, etc, before the *real* party started. I looked around the crowd myself, searching for familiar faces, and grinned when I spotted Nubia. Stephen had finally cornered her, and from his confident stance, I could tell he probably thought he was in control of the conversation, and winning her over.

But I knew Nubia.

She wore the barest hint of a smile, and her eyes were lowered in an expression I knew well. I accepted a glass of champagne from a passing waiter, and watched as Nubia stepped a little closer to Steph, covering one of his hands with hers. She leaned into him, using the added height of her platform heels to speak into his ear. Steph's eyebrows went somewhere near his hairline in response to whatever she said, and then Nubia giggled, and reached up to wipe away the lipstick she'd "accidentally" left against his jaw.

Nubia must have felt my eyes on her, because she turned and looked right at me, and winked. She started to walk away from Steph, but he caught her by the hand, tugging her back toward him. She bit her lip, shook her head, and slipped away from him again, but this time, he didn't try to catch her. He simply watched, keeping his eyes glued to the bare view of her honeytoned skin, from where her romper dipped low in the back.

"What on earth did you say to him?" I asked, looping my arm through hers and leading her away. "He was looking at you like he wanted to spread you over a biscuit."

Nubia laughed. "That's exactly what he wants. He asked me to "just let him taste it."

I lifted an eyebrow. "And? Are you going to?"

"Hell no." Nubia shook her head, and grabbed some champagne for herself as the same server from earlier passed by. "Steph can't do anything for me. A face like that, a body like that, and that level of arrogance? Uh-uh. I know my limitations, and he would make me lose them *all.*

He can't get anywhere near my cookie."

"So what did you say to him?"

She smiled. "Well, he made the comment about tasting it, and I told him I couldn't let him do that. He asked why not, and I told him it was so good he'd be addicted from just that taste. That he'd feel like he had asthma, and my pussy was the only inhaler that could keep him alive."

"*What?*"

She shrugged. "I think it turned him on. Did you see how he grabbed me?"

"You're ridiculous," I laughed. "Why did you encourage him?"

"Because," she said, taking a big gulp of champagne. "Who am I to kill that man's hopes and dreams?"

I gave her a playful roll of my eyes, and shook my head. "*Anyway*. Dawn looks great."

"I'll toast to that." Nubia raised her glass, and I bumped it with mine as we found Dawn in the crowd. Nubia had been the one to outfit Dawn for tonight, in a short black and white dress with long sleeves, and a split neckline. It was perfect for her – designer without being over-thetop, age appropriate, but still sexy. "And now," Nubia continued, after draining the rest of her champagne, "I need to find my date."

I let out a little breath. "*Ditto.*"

Nubia left in search of her boy toy, and I looked around, trying to find Paul in the crowd.

I spotted him pretty quickly because of his height, with his arms crossed and a thoughtful expression as he talked to one of the show's producers. I knew *that* look too. He was almost definitely talking finance, which he managed to do everywhere he went. He'd be occupied for a while.

I answered a few more questions for the media, and then scanned the crowd for another waiter with champagne. Once I spotted one, I waved to get their attention, but they stepped away mid-wave, and my eyes connected with Julissa's. *Shit.*

I hurried to lower my hand, but the damage was already done. Her face brightened into a smile and she

190

headed my way. I considered the pros and cons of simply turning and walking in

the other direction, pretending I hadn't seen her, but in what seemed like no time, she was right in my face.

"*Hi!*" she exclaimed, pulling me into a hug that I dutifully returned, trying to keep my feelings from showing on my face. "The show was absolutely *amazing*, one of the best I've seen this year. And I love the theatre, so I've been to many."

Graciously, I smiled. "Well thank you, Julissa. That means a lot."

"How do you feel? I know you have to be incredibly proud of your daughter."

"I'm proud of the whole cast. They all worked hard to make this a success, and I think they fulfilled that goal."

"I agree." She nodded, and a couple of moments of awkward silence passed before she spoke again. "So, I don't believe Tariq has ever really introduced us, has he?"

My eyebrow twitched. "Um, no. I don't think there's been occasion to so far. But I've seen you and Tariq in pictures together," – *gag* – "And of course he told me about you."

"All good things, I hope!" She laid her hand over mine as she laughed way too hard for the non-joke, and my face froze in a smile.

"Yes, of course."

She bobbed her head, then glanced around a little before she pulled me over to the side of the crowd, to a quieter spot against the wall. I grabbed a glass of champagne

191

from that server as he finally passed again. I had a feeling I would need it.

"So," she started, still looking nervously around. "I understand that you and Tariq are really good friends, right?"

I blinked, then took a gulp of my champagne. "Uh, yes. I would say so."

"Right. And… you're a woman who has dated. You've been married. You know what it's like out here when you're single, and trying to pursue someone. So I'm sure you can understand my concern about the nature of your friendship with Tariq."

My eyebrow crept up my forehead. "I'm sorry, what? The "nature" of our friendship?"

She sighed. "Okay, maybe I should just be frank."

I swallowed another gulp of champagne. "Yes, maybe so."

"Are you and Tariq sleeping together?"

I narrowed my eyes and took a step back, tossing a scowl at the woefully low level of liquor in my flute. "Julissa, are you seriously pulling me aside at my cast party to ask me something you should be discussing with Tariq?"

"Is that a yes?" she asked, with a little more attitude than necessary, considering the fact that 1 – this wasn't the damned time, and 2 – I *wasn't* sleeping with Tariq. Our last time together had been over a month ago, when I was sick, and the next morning, he'd friend-zoned me for her. I couldn't believe she had the audacity to approach me at my event and be insolent.

I struggled to keep my face from pulling into a frown. If she was going to be with Tariq, and he and I were going to remain friends, it probably wasn't a good idea to have friction between us. "No, it's not a yes." – I left *you crazy bitch* off of my response. – "Aside from this being the absolutely wrong time and place, why ask me? This is something you should be talking about with Tariq."

"I did."

"And what did he tell you?"

She averted her gaze. "He said it wasn't my business if you two had slept together before, but that you aren't sleeping together now."

"Okay, so there's your answer. If he says we aren't sleeping together – we aren't." I drained the last of my champagne down my throat.

"Men lie."

I shrugged. "Everybody lies sometimes."

I turned to walk away, but heard, "I know he loves you." over my shoulder, and pivoted back in Julissa's direction. She had her arms crossed over her chest, and a look of fortitude on her face as she stared me down. "It's obvious. In the way he talks about you, looks at you, or avoids looking at you, like tonight. How am I supposed to trust that the minute I let down my guard, he's not going to go running to you?"

My lips parted, but it took my brain a few seconds to formulate an answer. "I don't know, Julissa. Maybe you can't." I shrugged. "You can't control what he – or any man, for that matter – does or doesn't feel for you. But I'm not the

193

one on his arm tonight, am I? I'm not the one he's going home with. I'm not the one he makes loves to. I don't know what you're looking for, especially from *me*, but I don't have an answer to give you."

"I'm looking for some assurance. Some sign that he's in this for the long haul. That he's serious about me. If you're supposedly his good friend, you would know."

I narrowed my eyes. "You've only been involved for a couple of months – he's not about to give you that, not anytime soon. Tariq moves slowly, and he's very careful with his feelings."

"What does that mean?"

"It means that if you want him, you're in for a marathon, not a forty yard dash. You aren't going to be engaged in six months. Hell, I've never seen it take less than six months for him to actually call someone his girlfriend."

Julissa met my eyes. "Almost like he's biding his time, waiting for someone else, right?"

I stared at her for a second, then shook my head, and started to walk away again, but changed my mind, halfway turning toward her again. "Let me give you a little piece of advice – Tariq isn't into insecure women. He might give you a little room to get stuff like this off your chest, but trust me when I tell you that it gets old, fast. Either you trust him, or you don't, but don't ask *me* shit else about him. Okay?"

Without giving her a chance to answer, I walked away, blindly weaving through the crowd, trying to hold back a sudden urge to burst into tears. Of course it was no

194

secret to me that they were together, but somehow having her in my face, having to explain him to her – defending our friendship to her… I didn't sign up for *that* shit. And somehow, I wasn't pissed at her. I was pissed at *him.*

I mean, he'd known me for goddamned thirty years! Surely he knew I didn't know what the hell I was talking about when I suggested that we be *just* friends. He wasn't supposed to go along with it, he was supposed to talk some sense into me, and… and… I sounded ridiculous.

I walked full force into a broad chest. Strong hands grabbed my arms to hold me steady on my sky-high heels, and familiarity swept over me before I could open my mouth to offer an apology. I swallowed hard before I looked up into Tariq's handsome face.

"Exciting night for you, isn't it?" he asked, releasing his hold on my arms. "I just talked to Dawn, and she is on cloud nine."

I nodded, taking a step back to put some space between us. "Yeah. Definitely exciting.

I'm just glad everything came together for a good show."

"A great show," he corrected with a smile. "Did you know the show was trending on social media?"

My eyes went wide. "No, I didn't. I've been so busy I haven't even touched my phone.

But that's amazing."

"Yeah, it is." My heart was already racing after that conversation with Julissa, but it started galloping in my chest when Tariq pulled me into a hug. "I'm proud of you," he murmured into my ear, then drew back just enough to press his lips to my forehead, with me still held tightly in his arms. I melted into him, more habit than anything, but also because I really needed this hug. Not *a* hug, *this* hug, from him, reassuring me that tonight had been a job well done.

But not just that either.

I was –irrationally, I could admit – angry with him, for actually choosing someone else this time. When I was finally past the silliness of not trying again to see what we could have, I had watch his pretty little girlfriend grin and smile while hanging on his arm.

It was a shitty situation.

But being in his arms reminded me that no matter what, we were connected. It was awkward between us right now, but our bond was unbreakable. I would get past the anger, and hurt, and Tariq would still be my best friend, the person who'd known me since I knew myself.

He'd cared for and protected me, been *everything*.

Just not right now.

"Hey, are you okay?" he asked, keeping his voice low as he looked around. I could practically feel Julissa's eyes burning into us from somewhere, so I took a step back, out of his arms.

"Yeah."

"Your eyes say something different." Tariq met my gaze, pinning me in place, and I chewed at the inside of my bottom lip.

I shook my head. "I'm *fine*. Just tired. Too much champagne, too much eye makeup, too many people. But I'm good."

"You're sure?"

"Yes," I insisted, straightening his lapel. "Your date is probably looking for you. And I have to go remind security to start getting the extra people out of here, so we can bring out the good liquor." I laughed, hoping it didn't ring false, and tore my gaze from his to scan the crowd.

"And there's Paul too, so have fun tonight, okay?"

He wasn't buying my false enthusiasm, but he nodded anyway. "Okay. We'll talk."

"Yes we will," I said, with a nod. "Later."

Much later, I thought to myself as I stepped away, heading *not* in Paul's direction. I beelined for the exit, and once I escaped, I went straight for my office and locked myself inside. I knew Micah and the other crew would handle the party, but I needed… something.

Peace and quiet was just the start of a long list.

thirteen.

Kora

They were already talking Broadway.

Of course, that was a long way off, and we still had to prove ourselves and raise money here at Warm Hues before taking it to *the* theatre was a realistic consideration, but the point was – the critics were talking *Broadway*.

And not just for the show either – they were raving about Dawn.

We'd gotten past the first week after opening with six amazingly performed shows. The critical reviews started rolling in, and I couldn't have been any happier. That ecstatic feeling was part of the reason I'd agreed to a dinner date with Paul. He caught me at the best possible time.

But now that I was here at the restaurant with him, I certainly had no regrets. As a matter of fact, my cheeks were hurting because a smile hadn't left my face since the moment he pulled up at the same romantic little pizza place he'd taken me on one of our first dates. Between us, we'd gone through one bottle of wine, and were working on a second.

"So it's the last night of the show, right? And I am as sick as a damned dog," I explained, taking another sip from my glass. "But the show had to go on, and my understudy was a complete bitch, so I wasn't doing her any favors. There was no way I was giving up closing night just because my throat was on fire and I had chills, and a fever, and a few tremors and body aches."

Paul threw his head back and laughed. "Of *course* not."

"Of *course not!*" I agreed, giggling. "But anyway, I'm mainlining cold medicine and hot tea so I can get on this stage and not sweat through my costume or faint. And somehow – had to be grace of God – I make it through the whole show, and I've actually done a decent job. We get to the final scene of the play, and I have this long, emotion-filled monologue to deliver, and I freeze."

"Oh, shit."

"Yeah, *oh shit!* So I'm staring at the audience, and they're staring at me, for like a full minute, and *then* I remember my lines. I'm giving it everything too, all my energy, but I can literally feel my brain turning to mush as I'm speaking. I'm slurring my words, I've taken my ass to a chair and sat down when I wasn't supposed to – it was a complete mess. And that's not even the kicker."

Paul's eyes went wide. "If that's not the worst part, I'm not sure I want to hear the rest…"

"Oh you definitely want to hear this. Do you know I never even said the last word? I passed out on stage, and had to be carried off once the curtains closed!"

"Are you serious?!"

I nodded, then ate another bite of pizza before I continued. "I should confess though, that my character was poisoned. So I was supposed to die in the scene anyway, but the slurring and the passing out? *Not* an act, and I got rave reviews for that night. I didn't even make curtain call after the performance. They couldn't get me to stand up."

"That is hilarious," Paul said, chuckling as he finished his glass. "How have I never heard that story before?"

I shrugged. "We were only together what, a little over two years? Between us, I'm sure we have a ton of stories that haven't been told yet."

Paul eyelids dipped low, and he let out a barely perceptible sigh as he nodded. "Yeah. Well," he picked up the bottle of wine and filled both our glasses, then handed mine to me. "I say this is a great moment to toast to."

I pushed my hair away from my face, and lifted an eyebrow. "I'm listening."

He grinned as he raised his glass. "To hearing those untold stories."

My breath hitched in my throat, and I swallowed hard to cover the sound before I raised my glass as well, tapping it against his. And right there, that was where the energy changed, from exes having dinner, to exes on a dinner *date*.

We laughed our way through sharing a wood-fired cinnamon roll, topped with *heavenly* brown sugar pecans, and a few more glasses of wine. Paul kept his hand tight around my waist, keeping me steady – as much as he could since *he* was nearly just as tipsy – as we made the walk to my building a block over.

When we reached my floor, I pressed my back against the wall beside my door. Paul settled against the wall opposite me, and for almost a full minute, we just looked at each other from across the hall. He'd always been sexy – undeniably so – but something about the way he was looking at me, with his eyelids a little low from the wine, lip pulled between his teeth, hands in his pockets like that was the only way he wasn't touching me right now… *dammit.*

"I should probably go now. It's pretty late."

I inhaled a deep breath through my nose, pushed it out through pursed lips. "Yeah. You probably should."

He nodded, then pushed himself away from the wall and walked toward me, making my heart race a little harder with every step. He stopped a few inches in front of me, just enough room that we weren't touching. "Good night."

I ran my tongue over my lips. "Good night."

He leaned in, pressing a kiss against my forehead, and then he stepped back and turned to head down the hall. I already had my keys in hand, so I pushed them into the door and unlocked it, but as soon as I pushed the door open to head inside – *alone* – something clicked in my mind.

Suddenly five weeks without sex felt like five months.

"Paul."

Half a second later, the footfalls of his heavy boots against the polished concrete floors stopped. "Yeah?" When I glanced down the hall, he hadn't yet turned around.

"Come here."

202

I didn't have to see his face to know his eyebrow shot up, but he tamed it before he turned around. His stride was purposeful as he approached, and he stopped just in front of me again, waiting for me to speak.

But I didn't.

I pushed myself up on my toes and grabbed his face, pulling him down to me. When our lips met, I melted into him, opening my mouth to accept his tongue. With one hand, he grabbed my waist, tugging me against his chest. The other hand gripped my chin, holding me steady as our tongues danced and tangled. The fruity remnants of our wine and the sweet cinnamony aftermath of dessert melded together for a kiss that did the last convincing I needed to make a decision.

When we finally pulled away from the kiss... I took him by the hand and led him inside.

~

I woke up to the sound of my doorbell being held down. My eyes snapped open, and I shot up, glancing warily in Paul's direction with a sigh. A sleepover had definitely not been the intention of us getting together for dinner the night before. Even though I'd been thinking about sleeping with Paul for weeks, I didn't plan for him to spend the night at my house.

This is what happens after two bottles of wine, I thought to myself, shaking my head. I flipped back the covers, groaned when I realized both of us were still completely nude, then climbed out of the bed. I was tying myself into a robe when the doorbell started up again, and Paul grunted, mumbling something under his breath.

I shoved my feet in my soft moccasins and went to my front door, flinging it open without bothering to look through the peephole first. "What the hell do you want?"

Nubia met my less-than-cheerful greeting with a big smile before she shouldered past me into the apartment, with two cups from Urban Grind in her hand. "Be nice to me, heifer, I brought you coffee. And you look like you could use it too."

"Thank you," I said, putting on a plastic grin before I accepted the cup from her. "Too much wine last night."

"Uh huh. You forgot to tell me how dinner went with Pa—"

"*Shh!*"

Her eyes went wide. "What?! Why are you shh— ohh!" I blew out a harsh breath as the sound of the toilet flushing in the distance gave away Paul's presence. Again, a huge smile spread over Nubia's face, and she sidled up close to me. "*What did I tell you?!*" she whispered, shaking her head. "He took you to the restaurant with the memories, and then it happened, didn't it? Finger in the ass, tongue in the kitty."

I leaned my head back, rolling my eyes toward the ceiling as I tried not to laugh. "No."

"*Stop lying!*"

"*I'm not lying!*"

"*Yes you are!*"

"*I'm not!*" I batted her away from me to take a sip from my coffee. Our eyes met, and I tried hard to suppress a smile as I lifted two fingers in the air and made a switching motion. "*It was the other way around, so shut up!*"

"*Aaaaah!*" Nubia shrieked, letting out a laugh that was so infectious I started laughing too, and had to put my coffee down before I spilled it. "*Lucky bitch! How do you always find the men willing to do the nas*—Oh hi Paul! Good morning!"

I took a big gulp of my warm drink before I turned to see Paul coming into the living room where we were. He was back in his clothes, clearly intending to leave, which was a relief. I really didn't want to have a conversation where I kicked him out, but I also didn't want to give him the wrong impression about what last night did or didn't mean.

"Good morning Nubia," he said, before he turned to me with a warm smile. "Good morning, Kora. I'm going to head out."

I nodded. "Okay. I'll see you later."

I tried not to roll my eyes at the look on Nubia's face as Paul kissed my forehead and then headed for the door, but she deftly switched it to a smile before he turned around. When he was gone, she looked right at me, eyebrow raised, and a wicked little grin.

"What, no *real* kiss goodbye between you and your salvaged man?"

I scowled at her. "Ha ha, very funny. Paul isn't my man."

"Does he know that?"

"Uh, *yeah*," I said, sucking my teeth. "Last night was mutual horniness, nothing more."

"To *you.*"

"What?"

Nubia shook her head. "I was correcting you. It was just mutual horniness *to you.* You don't know what Paul thinks happened."

"I know that Paul is crazy as hell if he thinks it was anything else."

"I'm just saying. *Anyway*… speaking of your love life—"

"Or we don't have to."

"Oh *hush*," Nubia said, waving her hand to brush away what I was saying. "Speaking of your love life, what in the world is going on with you and Tariq? Y'all used to be inseparable, and now…"

"And *now* he has a woman. You saw how they were at the opening together, she couldn't keep her damned hands off him. I can't be around him like that, especially when Julissa already swears we have something going on. I'm not trying to give anybody a reason to think I'm fooling with their man, okay?"

Nubia frowned. "Oh, so that's what sleeping with Paul was about. A little jealousy, some loneliness, some horniness. Never a good combination. But anyway… you're letting that girl chase you away from your friend?"

"No." I sucked my teeth, not bothering to refute her lonely, jealous, horny comment. It was indisputable. "I'm not letting her do anything. Tariq made his choice on what he wanted to do, and it *wasn't* begging me to stop being silly. I have to live with the consequences of that. One being that our friendship changes."

"Changes, or gets eliminated? Because from what *I* see, it looks like you're pushing him away. I mean, when is the last time you guys had a meal together, went and had drinks, watched movies? Y'all were doing stuff like that all the time, and now what, it just goes away?"

"It's not like that."

Nubia shrugged. "Okay, so explain how it *is*."

I pushed out a heavy sigh. "I need to get ready to go up to the theatre. Don't you need to get to set?"

"Um, no, little miss change the topic. My makeover subject got cold feet, so the producers are trying to talk to her and see what's going on. They're going to call when it's time for me to come back to set. In the meantime, explain to me how it is between you and Tariq."

Rolling my eyes, I went back to my room, with Nubia right behind me. "It's like nothing between me and Tariq. I saw him at the show. Dawn and I had brunch with him and his grandparents the next morning."

"And that's it? In the last two weeks, you've not been with him by yourself at all, which isn't normal for you two."

"We were together the night Dawn got in trouble."

She scowled at me. "Okay fine, so a week and half."

"Why are you pushing so damned hard about this Nubia?" I snatched off my robe and climbed into the shower, pulled the door closed behind me, and turned on the sprayer.

"Because I listened to you bitch and bitch about how you wouldn't try to be with Tariq because you didn't want to ruin your friendship. But it looks to me like you're ruining your damned friendship anyway, by distancing yourself because he got a damned girlfriend. I mean, wasn't Brooke one of his girlfriends a few years ago?"

I groaned quietly, scooping a handful of my shower smoothie into my hand. Brooke, someone I honestly considered my own friend now, was an artist Tariq dated almost six years ago. He knew her first, but their relationship hadn't lasted very long – Brooke wasn't one for monogamy, or staying in one place very long – but it ended on good terms, and she and I had

become somewhat close during that time. Through their relationship, I'd never felt a need to withdraw from Tariq, but I was careful to respect their time together.

Somehow though, this thing with Julissa was different. Maybe because she wasn't laid back like Brooke. Or maybe because now, I realized that my feelings for him weren't something I could just pretend away, no matter how hard I tried. Maybe because this time, it actually hurt to see him with someone else.

"It's more than I can explain," I said as I soaped my skin. "I just want everybody to be able to be happy, and if I'm getting in the way of his relationship, that's at least two unhappy people. I don't want that."

"I get that," Nubia called over the sound of the water. "But what about you? What about what makes *you* happy?"

I stopped, with my bath sponge clutched tight in my hand. "I... I'm happy."

"That sounds extremely convincing. You don't have to lie to me, Kora. You know that."

"I do." After a few long moments, I poked my head out the door, and looked my friend in the eyes. "I fucked up."

Nubia nodded. "I know."

"I don't know how to fix it."

"I know."

"I can't just break up his relationship. It's not fair to her, or to him, after he's been clear all this time that he was willing to give it another shot. What kind of person would it make me to go to him *now*, while he's trying to build a connection with someone, to tell him that I really do want to be with him?"

"An honest one." Nubia smiled. "Now, don't get me wrong, I *get* it. I'm certainly not recommending that you break them up, but I don't know. What's meant to be is going to be, and you know what I feel about you and Tariq."

"Right. Inevitable conclusion, I know."

"Mmmhmm. So, the thing is... *when* you get that chance again, please don't fuck it up, Kora."

I laughed, then closed the shower, stepping back underneath the hot water as the sound of her cell phone filled the bathroom. She answered it, and after a short conversation, called out to me. "That was my producer, so I have to go, but you remember what I said to you!"

"I will!"

Moments later, she was gone, leaving me alone with my thoughts as I finished my shower. I wasn't quite as confident as Nubia when it came to the whole "what's meant to be will be thing", and I wasn't even really holding out hope.

Truthfully… I was just confused.

fourteen.

Tariq

"Did his crazy ass *really* think we weren't going to figure out that he was hiding money, trying to leave it out of the merger? You heard him, didn't you? *"Oh, oh, I forgot."* How the hell do you "forget" twenty-eight million dollars in an offshore account? Money that belongs to the business, money they should be *taxed* on. I don't know if I should call the IRS or the FTC first." Julissa shook her head, letting out a dry chuckle as she pressed her forehead into her hands.

I sat back in my chair, swaying back and forth. "It's a mess, definitely."

"A mess isn't nearly strong enough to describe this. More like a disaster. But," she smiled as she lifted her head. "At least I do have dinner tonight to look forward to, right?"

I returned her smile. "Right."

It was beyond a relief that I was actually looking forward to it too. In the almost two weeks since we last had one of "those" conversations, Julissa had been different. Back to the confident, independent woman I'd first become interested in. We'd been out a couple of times since then, and not once had she brought up anything about Kora, or pushed me to put any official designations on what we were doing.

211

I'd even grabbed a bite with Dawn after one of her performances one night, and seen Julissa out on what was *clearly* a date based on how cozy they

looked. I even asked about it, so I wasn't making an assumption, and she confirmed that she'd been asked out, and accepted.

She seemed a little nervous about telling me the real deal, but I wasn't mad – I was relieved. As much as I truly did like Julissa, when she was being the fun, sexy woman I first met, a couple of our interactions gave me pause, and I knew it would take time for us to settle into something serious. If she wanted to date other people – like I suggested – and make sure she wasn't passing up somebody better to settle on me... *hell yeah.* It helped me not feel like I was being an asshole for keeping things slow.

And as far as her asking me about Kora, well... there was nothing to tell. I hadn't seen her since the day after the opening of the show, and that was honestly that was on both of us. Kora was definitely good for ignoring calls and avoiding me, but the thing was that this time – I hadn't called.

I was more annoyed than I wanted to be – more annoyed than was probably fair – about her continued attention to Paul. *He* was having lunch with her, *he* was at those important preshow rehearsals with her, *he* was on her arm opening night, *he* took her home. *He* had been smug as fuck when I saw him the other morning coming out of her building, way too early to have stopped by for breakfast, and still smelling like her.

Not that I knew what he smelled like, because I was just driving past. And maybe he wasn't looking necessarily *smug*... maybe just happy. Maybe my imagination was getting the best of me. It had been going wild, ever since his stupid ass came back into the picture.

But I shouldn't care.

I was dating someone.

So why the hell was I so envious?

For all of our talking about not wanting to go back to that place of jealousy and lost friendship, it seemed like exactly what was happening. What were we supposed to do about it?

How the hell did we fix this?

"This will be our last chance to be together before your trip, right?"

Julissa's voice broke me out of my thoughts, and I nodded. "Yeah. Flight leaves tomorrow morning."

"Do you need a ride to the airport or anything?"

"Nah. Already covered, but thank you."

Julissa smiled. "You're welcome. I hope you have a good time – you don't exactly seem *excited* about it."

"Yeah," I sighed. "This trip isn't exactly for pleasure."

She nodded. "Ah, I see. Well I'm going to let you get back to work. Thanks for letting me vent about this fool. I need to go make some calls about this, now that I've calmed down some." "Are you really going to call the law on him?" I chuckled.

"Hell *yes*!" She stood up, laughing as she grabbed her bag. "That man isn't about to have me out of my job, or worse – in *jail* – because of his antics."

"Well I can definitely understand that. Do what you have to do Ms. Santos."

She grinned. "Will do. I'll see you tonight."

"See you."

I watched the sexy sway of her hips as she left, closing the door behind her. When she was gone, I went back to what I was doing – poring one last time over the details of my trip.

Eventually I closed my computer and packed up, deciding to head home. My head wasn't on work today, so there was no point in sticking around here when I didn't have any meetings set anyway. This time tomorrow, I'd be sitting in front of my mother, and I wasn't sure how I felt about that. I hadn't yet shared the purpose of my trip with Julissa, for the simple fact that it was *so* deeply personal. I liked her, yes, but I wasn't anywhere near ready to let her in like *that* yet.

But how did I explain to myself why I hadn't yet told Kora?

The person who'd known me all my life, had *taken* these trips with me before, who knew exactly the toll it could take on me, who understood, and would listen without playing the role of judge… why hadn't I told *her*?

I couldn't really say that I had an answer.

～

My mother was an exceptionally beautiful woman. My whole life, I'd regarded her with a sense of reverence and awe. This strange, stunning person, to look at but never disturb, as if she were a queen, and I, her son, was unworthy to touch her garments. Thank God for my grandparents. They provided a sense of normalcy in a situation that wasn't. But back to my mother.

She was beautiful.

Smooth, deep brown skin that looked like it might be velvety to the touch. Sculpted cheekbones, regal features that were almost always pulled into an expression that made you feel like you were the center of her attention, the only person in the world in that moment. An easy, captivating smile. Big brown eyes that caught you and held, pierced through any little armor you had. You got to hide nothing. She hid everything.

These were the thoughts I had, the inventory that ran through my mind as I sat in front of my mother, watching her watch me with a hint of a smile on her face. She looked none of her almost sixty years old, and was dressed like she was heading out to brunch – cashmere sweater, diamonds, designer shoes. Her hair was pulled into an elegant knot on top of her head, and she touched it briefly, as if she were checking to make sure it was still there, and then leaned forward and grabbed my hand.

I didn't want to look her right in the eyes, but she tugged at my fingers, so I did. Those xrays of hers locked onto me, and with the dimples in her cheeks lending a deceiving amount of harmlessness to her face, she told me, "I'm glad you could come. Before… you know."

I lifted an eyebrow. "No, I don't."

"Oh, of course you do."

I closed my eyes, silently urging myself to be patient. "I don't. Can you explain?"

My question was met with a smile, and she stood so quickly that it didn't quite look right, like there was some disconnect in the signals between her limbs. She was a petite woman, but her short legs carried her quickly across the room to the double glass doors that led outside. Her

hand went to the handle, gripped it, pushed down on it, but it didn't turn. She didn't look back at me. Instead, she looked longingly at the lake on the other side of the glass.

"We should go for a swim."

"It's barely forty degrees outside."

"That didn't stop us before."

A vein throbbed at the side of my head, and I clenched my jaw. "And I spent a week in the hospital after that, remember?"

Finally, she turned and looked at me, her expression filled with disdain. "But you have an interesting story to tell, don't you?" *Interesting.*

Wow.

As if I ever brought that shit up at parties.

"That's one way to look at it," I said, propping my elbow on the arm of the chair, and my chin in my hand.

Her annoyance turned into a triumphant smile. "Yes! Just one way, out of many, but somehow, you always think

216

of the wrong way. According to you, I'm always doing something wrong."

"That's not true."

"Yes it is."

"No it—"

"It is! And I'm done discussing that. Did you bring me a tape of Dawn's show?"

I swallowed hard. "Yes."

"I still say you should have been that girl's daddy. If it wasn't for that—"

"Mother," I interrupted, letting my voice take on a warning tone. "Kora was fifteen. We were teenagers."

She shrugged. "So? Didn't stop her from having the baby. She had one for him, she could have had one for you. How is Kora, by the way?"

I took a deep breath, willing myself not to get angry. "She's fine."

"Your grandmother told me you were dating someone else. Why?"

"Why not?"

My mother narrowed her eyes at me. "Why are you being so difficult? You didn't have to come if you were going to be like this."

I opened my mouth for a rebuttal, and then clamped it right back, because she was right. I was being short with her. I could be warmer, but we were approaching the end of a three-hour visit, and I was exhausted, in more ways than one.

My flight had been delayed for hours because of the weather, and then there was turbulence in the air. For some unclear reason, there was nearly an hour holdup in actually being

let off the flight, and by the time I got my bag and stepped out of the airport, I'd had to head straight to the huge restored mansion where my mother currently lived.

From there, I'd spent two hours listening to her random, disorganized chatter, which I didn't mind, because it was pleasant. Those were the times when she went from looking forward to what she'd eat at dinner, to talking about new shoes, to talking about growing up near a lake just like the one outside, to grilling me about my love life, and when she'd get grandbabies. That was the mother I could handle. I could deal with disorganized conversation, I could bob and weave with dropped thoughts and randomly picked up topics.

I could *not* deal with what was happening now.

I'd seen it happen enough times to recognize the microscopic little signs that she was reaching the end of lucidity. Asking me about Kora and Dawn again, like she hadn't already, three times. That longing stare at the lake, the compulsive attempt to get outside, the paranoia…

"Mr. Evans?" I glanced away from my mother to see a tall woman standing in the door, flanked on either side by large men in polos and khakis, as if that made their status as security less obvious. The woman met my eyes with a warm, motherly smile, and gave me a little nod.

"Visiting time is over."

I sighed heavily, then turned back to my mother, who'd come closer, with her hands clasped in front of her, and tears in her eyes. "I guess this is goodbye," she said,

218

averting her gaze to the floor. "Would it be okay if your mother hugged you? Can you stomach that today?"

"Of course," I said, biting back the anger that was my first response. Her daily presence – and delusions – through the first fifteen years of my life should have been preparation for things like this – accusations that I didn't want her touching me – but it wasn't something a child ever got used to from their parent. Not even at damned near forty years old. It was *always* jarring, it *always* hurt, it *always* made me wonder why the fuck I came in the first place, and if it really even mattered to her if I didn't.

But I made my way to Oak Hill Healing center at least ten times a year. I still bit my tongue and didn't say what I wanted to say in response sometimes. I brought my ass here and I sat down and endured it because this was my mother, and I loved her. What the hell else was I supposed to do?

She wrapped her arms around me and squeezed me tight, and I returned the embrace.

"Thank you," she whispered. "Thank you for coming before it's too late."

I stiffened. "Too late for what?"

"You *know* what."

"I don't. Can you tell me?"

She looked up and met my gaze with an intensity that seemed to shoot straight into my soul. Her eyes were wide in terror, and filled with a deep, intense sorrow that made my heart rate spike in fear. She got closer to me somehow, maybe up on her toes, still staring and whispered something that I'd heard more than once, in different variations but was always terrifying.

"I want to die. If I die, they'll leave me alone."

And then she went back to the door to stare out at that lake.

"Mr. Evans?"

Reluctantly, I tore my eyes away from my mother to turn to Dr. Laura Alexander. An attractive black woman about the same age as my mom, she had become a constant in my life over the last twenty years.

We first met when I was seventeen years old, and dealing with the emotional implications of my mother's eleventh hospitalization –since I was born – for her mental illness. I'd actually been sent to see her sister, Layla, for family therapy. During one session, she came in, and introduced herself as the person who was treating my mother. She'd served as my mother's doctor ever since.

Dr. Alexander had been the one to recommend residential treatment for my mother's diagnosis of schizophrenia. My grandparents acted shocked, but it wasn't the first time they'd heard it, or other various diagnoses she'd received over the years, evidenced by the stacks of prescription antidepressants and antipsychotics she refused to take.

One time, and only once, with alcohol and old age clouding her brain, my grandmother had sat with me and told me everything I could possibly want to know about my mother. Afterwards, she acted as if she had no idea what I was talking about, but I knew, in my heart and head, that she was relieved it was off her chest.

And *I* was relieved to have my lived experiences validated.

In her youth, her mental illness was written off as "eccentricity". Cherie Evans was just a young, beautiful girl who laughed at inappropriate things, was a little irrational sometimes, and had *very* vivid "daydreams". She was too much of a free spirit – a dreamer, even – to finish college and get a job, so she never moved out of the home she grew up in with her parents. It happened all the time. Nothing to be concerned about, not really.

But then she got pregnant when she was twenty-three, by a "boyfriend" who disappeared shortly after her belly started to swell. My grandparents never looked for him, but I did once I found his name. I got a sick satisfaction from finding out he'd perished in an accident shortly after he abandoned her.

Through the pregnancy, she was withdrawn. She isolated herself, and became more than a "little" irrational. After I was born, it got worse. For the first year of my life, my mother was convinced I was something sent to control her mind. After a passing comment that she was trying to figure out how to "terminate my ability to communicate with my leader", my grandparents stopped listening to the "old folks" who insisted they just needed to pray about it, and started to actually worry.

They went to doctor after doctor, got one diagnosis after another. Got droves and droves of pills that my mother mostly refused to take. Overall, I can never say that my childhood was

"bad", because my grandparents took excellent care of me, and I was nothing but grateful for that.

But.

It was, simultaneously, a childhood delicately stained with confusion and terror. For every instance of my mother taking me swimming in a lake in winter when I was eight, or us sharing a bottle of wine when I was twelve, I had *ten* stories of great experiences. But the shit with my mother stuck to me like static cling.

"I wanted to speak with you, if you have a moment before you leave," Dr. Alexander said, leading me out of a door while one of the security staff and a nurse led my mother out of the other.

I nodded to her, pushing my hands into the pockets of my sweater. "Of course. My grandmother mentioned that mom had been having a hard time with something lately."

"Yes, but before we get to that, I'd like to hear about you. I never seem to catch you when you're here."

I smiled. "You're usually off shrinking patients, and I try not to be a drag on your time, when we usually communicate via email."

"Right," she grinned. "But I can't ask you via email if you're past that commitment issue, can I?" She chuckled a little as she nudged me with her elbow, and I shook my head and laughed.

Years ago, in a combined session with both Dr. Alexanders, I'd admitted to having a hard time opening myself up romantically, and dedicating my feelings to one person. Monogamy wasn't the issue – the development of those deep, passionate emotions was – and they'd spent the rest of the hour connecting that to my feelings about my mother.

Maybe it made sense, in a roundabout way. That when someone I cared so deeply about was unpredictable, and draining, and just a lot to fucking handle, that I would have a hard time dedicating that kind of emotional energy to anyone else. But I wasn't broken. I'd had friends, I'd lived, I'd loved, more than once. And I mean come on… if the way I felt about Kora wasn't a sign that I could dedicate myself to someone, I didn't know what was.

"Come on, Dr. Alexander. What have I told you about trying to psychoanalyze me? I'm not the patient here," I laughed.

She patted me on the arm. "I know, I know. Just trying to lighten the mood before we get serious."

Uh oh.

Years ago, during one of her random long periods of lucidity, my mother had signed a directive allowing Dr. Alexander to discuss all aspects of her care with me and my grandparents.

It was something of a blessing and a curse, honestly. I did appreciate knowing exactly what was happening with her, but I really would have been content without some of the ugly details.

I was happy just knowing that the luxury facility took excellent care of her, kept her safe, and for the most part, comfortable. She'd made friends with other patients there, regularly went on – well supervised – trips to the grocery store, the park, and so on. Dr. Alexander focused on holistic, therapy-based treatment, with medication as a last option for severe episodes, so she wasn't walking around like a zombie, getting pills shoved down her throat. With reassurance from my grandparents, Dr. Alexander, Kora, and most importantly, in the clear moments, my mother herself, I believed that we were giving her the best life we could.

Unfortunately, that didn't mean complete healing, or a cure.

"Tell me what's going on."

Dr. Alexander sighed. "Well, for the last few weeks, Cherie has been having a very hard time communicating. She's been irritable, and very combative at times. I think she's ramping up into another psychotic break."

I let out a huff, then pulled a hand from my pocket to scratch the top of my head. "Okay.

Is there anything we can do to head it off? Is it time to pull out medication as an option?"

Dr. Alexander shook her head. "She doesn't seem to be in a panic or a depression quite yet, so I'm going to keep trying to talk to her. We have group therapy a little later today, and she usually responds well to that. And you know we've had a rainy few weeks, so she hasn't been able to go outside for walks as she likes. Maybe during tomorrow's visit, you can join her for that? I think that would do her a world of good."

I nodded. "Of course. Anything I can do."

"Good." She patted my shoulder again, and then headed off. "See you tomorrow."

~

One would think my mother had never been outside before.

She was positively giddy about being outside for this walk, and her energy was

infectious. I didn't bother trying to keep the smile off my face as she talked about looking forward to spring, and how she hoped fewer people would want to take advantage of gardening this year, so she could get a bigger space. Many times over the years, I'd received a carefully packed express mail package, filled with whatever she was growing that year.

I looked forward to those boxes – *loved* those boxes, because they were reminders of the mother that I sometimes knew, who would make fresh pickles and fried green tomatoes, and made the *best* squash casserole.

Often – too often – I wished those were the only memories of her I had. But that wasn't our life. I'd long battled the guilt of wishing my mother was someone she wasn't, someone whose brain didn't fire in a way that shut her off from reality, and told her that the people who loved her were out to hurt her, and that her family members were the enemy. I still felt that way – I just didn't fight the guilt anymore. I accepted it as a part of life.

225

"You remember the first time I put a purple tomato in front of you?" she asked, leaning into me. She had her arm looped through mine as we walked side by side, bundled in heavy coats and scarves against the weather. The temperature had dropped overnight, into the low thirties, so

her breath made a little cloud in the air as she spoke. I wasn't about to complain though. The grounds at this facility were beautiful, the sun was shining, and my mother was happy. I could handle being cold.

"Yes, I do." I nodded, then chuckled a bit as I thought about it. "I thought something was wrong with it, and I went and told Mama Tamille you were trying to make me eat a rotten tomato."

My mother laughed. "Mmhmm. And *she* thought something was wrong with it too.

Wouldn't believe me until I ate it myself, and showed her the picture from the package of seeds."

"Those were the best tomatoes I'd ever had in my life too."

"*See,*" she said, nudging me in the side. "Your mama knows a little something. I'm not *all* crazy."

I sighed. "Don't say stuff like that…"

"Why not?" She shrugged, then unhooked her arm from mine to reach down and adjust one of her boots before stuffing her gloved hands deep into the pockets of her coat. "It's the damned truth. The word *crazy* doesn't offend me, son. Everyone else says it about me, why can't

I accept it for myself? Hurts a lot less that way. Just don't call me ugly or stupid."

226

She let out a peal of laughter after that, and I couldn't help joining in, because damn, this was easily the best moment I'd with my mother all year. We rounded a grove of trees on the stone paved walkway that would lead us back to the facility – she'd been granted permission for an hour, and we were fifty minutes into that. As we kept walking, I noticed that her footsteps slowed, and assumed she was trying to prolong the return inside as long as she could. She was still talking about the garden, listing the things she would plant if she got the space she wanted.

And then she took off at a sprint across the yard.

It took me a second to get over my shock that she'd just started running out of nowhere, and my surprise that she was *so* fast. Part of her treatment was keeping herself in good shape at the gym, but damn. Even then, I didn't immediately react, because there was a huge fence surrounding the entire grounds. Where the hell was she going to go?

We should go for a swim.

Oh.

Shit.

She was heading for the lake.

I took off after her, only remembering once I heard heavy breathing and footfalls behind me that a guard had been with us, keeping his distance to give us some privacy. My mother had come out of her coat, hat, and gloves without slowing down, and I had to push myself in a way I hadn't since before my knee injury to catch up to her.

She was maybe twenty feet from the lake when I caught her, grabbing her around the waist and pulling her as

227

gently as I could to the ground. She struggled hard – kicking, punching, clawing to get away from me, screaming the whole time.

"*I just want to swim! I just want to fucking swim! I just want to swim!*"

She repeated that over and over, screaming herself hoarse as the guard came to take over, and at least five nurses came sprinting outside.

"*I just want to swim!*" she kept on, her throat audibly raw as she struggled. Our eyes met as one of the nurses put a sedative-filled needle in her arm, and the person I saw reflected, I… I had to look away.

Someone had already gathered her outerwear, and they wrapped her in a heavy blanket as they lifted her to take her inside. And she kept on repeating, "*I want to swim, I want to swim,*" until she couldn't anymore, as the sedative took over. But in my head, *swimming* wasn't what she wanted at all. My mind kept replaying the last words she'd said to me the day before, and how she'd kept staring out at that lake like it was paradise.

I watched, still frozen in shock as my mother was carried inside. Like always, her face reeked of an innocence that mostly felt, to me, like a blatant lie. And then I remembered that swimming trip when I was eight years old. A lake just like this, near trees just like this, in weather just like this had "swimming" ever really been the goal? With that on my mind, I decided to cut my trip short.

It was time for me to go home.

fifteen.

Kora

I couldn't sleep.

Wine wasn't working, a hot bath wasn't working, and mindless TV wasn't working either. So instead of fighting it, I sat down to do one of my most favorite things: reading a new script.

This one was for a much more serious subject matter: A publicly successful woman's struggle with continued sobriety as she tried to navigate running a stressful business, her relationship with her sister, and the difficulties of fully allowing romantic love into her life. It was a show I'd *love* to get my hands on.

Even though the material was definitely enthralling, I still found my mind slipping away, into thoughts of the night before. It had started off well, with a smash performance of *The Chase*.

Afterwards, when everyone was supposed to be gone from the theatre, I'd stumbled upon Dawn and Donnie on the practice stage.

At first, my heart soared, because although it had gone unnoticed by the audience, they'd made several mistakes in one particular scene. When I quietly snuck into the mostly darkened room after hearing their voices, I was happy to see that they were – without being instructed to – running through the scene to practice where they'd messed up.

It was a rather steamy scene though, and right before my poor eyes, they went from rehearsing, to the opening stages of something no mother would *ever* want to see. I snuck my nosy self out of there before they noticed my presence.

I was busy trying to scrub the visual from my mind as I headed back to my office, when Paul caught up with me.

"Hey," he said, grabbing my hand. "I was looking for you."

I grinned. "Well, here I am."

I unlocked the door to my office and he followed me inside, where he wasted no time pressing me against the wall. A moment later, his tongue was in my mouth, and he was kissing me like a soldier fresh from overseas. He went to undo my pants, but I covered his hands with mine, stilling his movements.

"Wait a second. Condom?"

He groaned. "I don't... no, not on me right now. Don't you have an IUD anyway?"

I shook my head. "That trip to the doctor I mentioned, last week? Got it removed, and Dr. Morris wants to wait a week before she puts it back. So unless we're trying to make a baby..."

"Would that be so bad?"

Wait, WHAT?

Record scratch like whoa.

"Umm… we need to talk."

Paul lifted an eyebrow, and his shoulders dropped a little as he took a step back to give me some space. "Okay, what do we need to talk about?"

"Well, I'd like to know what you think is happening between us, so we can make sure we're on the same page. Because hell yes, a baby *would* "be so bad". We're divorced."

"Yeah, for now." He pushed his hands into his pockets. "I know you said that you weren't looking for anything right now. But, we've been getting to know each other again, having a good time together. You didn't rule out getting back together."

"I told you I wasn't really sure about it."

He smiled. "Right. *Not really sure.*"

"I don't think that means what you think it means, Paul. You know how when you were little, and you asked your mom for something, and she says "I'll think about it". But eventually you learned that "I'll think about" is actually just a postponed *"no"?*"

"Yeah… you're saying I should apply that here…"

I gave him a wry smile, and nodded. "I mean… I think you're a good guy, and we've always enjoyed time together. I think you'll make someone a really great husband one day, but… you divorced me. And it's," – I sighed – "it's really not even *just* that you divorced me, you didn't *try* to fight for me. I can't get that out of my head. What if we do all of this, I fall in love with you again, and here comes

231

something else. And instead of counseling, and talking, and compromise, you just go see a lawyer again? Us hanging out, having dinner, even sex… that was one thing. But if you're talking about getting back together, that's not something I can ever give you. I'm sorry."

Paul blew out a sigh, then scrubbed a hand over his face before he nodded. "I guess I can understand that. Every love story doesn't get a second chance, I know, I just…,"— he sighed again, and then lifted his gaze to mine, with a genuinely remorseful smile. "I hoped for one, with you. I'm sorry that I hurt you."

I nodded, then smiled as he cupped my face in his hands, softly brushing his lips against mine. "And I'm sorry that I hurt you too."

We parted ways a few minutes after that.

Now, a day had passed since then, and I needed to not dwell on it. Shaking my head, I tried again to focus on the script. It had reached a pivotal moment, where the main character was faced with an almost overwhelming urge to take another drink. I was inhaling the story, line by line, and the main character was raising a glass to her face, inhaling the bouquet of a freshly opened bottle of red when my doorbell rang.

I glanced at the time.

Three in the morning.

With a heavy sigh, I pulled myself out of bed and checked my phone for missed calls. There were only three people in the world who could show up at my place at this time of the morning, and all of them could get cursed out, without a second thought.

I padded across my newly polished wood floors with bare feet, praying I didn't slip and fall on my ass on the way to the front door. Once there, I looked through the peephole, and stifled a little gasp.

What the hell is he doing here?!

I tightened the belt of my short silk robe around my waist, not wanting to give an impression that would contradict my words to him. With a deep breath, I unlocked the door and pulled it open. There was a long moment where neither of us spoke, each just staring at the other, as if we hadn't seen each other in forever.

And really, it felt like we hadn't.

The last time I'd been alone with Tariq was weeks ago, right before the show opened. I'd only seen him a few times after that, and none within the last two weeks. Our normally constant correspondence had dwindled to nothing, and seeing him now, I had to swallow past a lump, and clear my throat before I spoke.

"Hey."

"Hey."

His locs were neat, and pulled back from his face, into a ponytail at the base of his neck.

He looked tired, like he hadn't been sleeping well, but still handsome as ever, even in sweatpants and a hoodie.

"You know what time it is?" I asked, dropping my gaze as my eyelids began to sting with tears.

"Three twenty-six."

233

Still looking at the deep purple polish coating my bare toes, I nodded. "Right. You shouldn't be here. What would your girlfr—what would Julissa think, about you being here at three-twenty-six, instead of wherever she is?"

"To be frank, I don't care."

His shoulders were drooped in a type of defeat that I'd seen on very few occasions from Tariq, a man who exuded the type of confidence that made women weak in the knees. He had his hands in his pockets, trying to appear casual, but everything about him, from the way he was slumped in my doorframe, to his red-tinged eyes, screamed that he was hurting for some reason.

That made it even harder to keep tears from escaping my eyes.

"What's wrong?" I asked, swallowing hard as I tried to hold my composure.

Tariq let out a heavy, deep sigh, then looked up at the ceiling as he spoke. "Got back from a trip a few hours ago, took a shower, had a drink, and now I can't sleep."

"A trip? What, a little getaway for you and Julissa?" That petty jab dropped from my lips before I could help it. My hand circled the doorknob, ready to slam the door in his face if he'd come to me to discuss his problems with his insecure girlfriend. Instead, he brought his glossyeyed gaze to mine, and shook his head.

"No. Oak Hill."

The air rushed out of my lungs, and I swayed a little on my feet. "*Oh.* I didn't know you... why didn't you tell me?"

234

He offered a shrug. "Didn't seem right to burden you, when we were in weird space. Can

I come in?"

"*Yes,* of course."

I opened the door a little wider for him to step through, closing my eyes for a brief moment as his scent wrapped around me. He didn't venture far into the apartment, and when I turned around after closing and locking the door, he was right behind me. For another long moment, we just stared. I had no idea what was going through *his* mind, but I had no idea what to say.

Through the years, Tariq and I had joked often about our shared "mommy issues", one of many facets of our bond. It wasn't the normal overbearing attitude, or absentee issues that most people faced though. No, ours was the type of dysfunctional shit that you laughed about so you wouldn't cry.

I'd refused to go to school so I could sit by his side in the hospital for a week, when his mother decided near-freezing temperatures were ideal for a swim. I'd walked to his house from mine, taken care of him until his grandmother got home when he called me in a panic because his mother had gotten him drunk on what she'd sworn was just "special juice". There were *so* many moments where his mother had hurt him, physically or otherwise that I'd lost count, but I'd always been there, whenever I could. And even then, I couldn't possibly ever make up for what he'd done for me when my own mother wouldn't. At least *his* mother couldn't help hurting him.

In any case, words had always failed me when it came to this subject. Well... not *always*.

Once upon a time, I had a "normal" baseline I could approach things from, could give him words of encouragement that actually held some value. Not just platitudes, but words that actually meant something. When you believe that a mother, as a rule, is your ultimate protector, that she would do anything for you, that she loves you more than she loves herself, it's easy to champion that mindset for someone else. But when you know different... what then?

So my approach changed. For the last twenty years, instead of assuring Tariq that his mother meant no harm, I focused instead on one thing.

"Tell me what you need from me right now."

The words weren't even completely out of my mouth before Tariq's lips were on mine. The kiss caught me off guard, and took my breath away. As his tongue invaded my mouth,

slipping and sliding against mine, a little voice nagged at me, admonishing that this wasn't okay.

This was *so far* from okay, but what was I supposed to do? Push him away?

Yes.

Right.

But, no. This was Tariq. My best friend. The man that I loved was telling me, right now, what he needed from me when he was hurting, and the one thing I was absolutely not about to do was push him away.

I didn't realize he'd been moving me backwards until I felt the cool surface of the wall against my skin. Tariq's mouth dropped to my neck, and one of his hands eased between my legs, pushing my thighs apart. I opened for him, and he let out a low groan when his fingers met bare flesh, unrestricted by underwear. A moment later, his fingers were inside me.

Shamelessly, I rode his hand, panting and moaning as he kept kissing my neck. With what seemed like one tug, he had my robe open, and then his hands were everywhere. Squeezing my ass, caressing my thighs and stomach, cupping my breasts, teasing my nipples. I pushed away any logical thoughts. In the moment, none of them really mattered. The only thing I cared about was Tariq kissing his way down my body, sucking and nibbling my nipples, licking a trail from my belly button to my clit as he settled on his knees with his head between my legs.

He covered me with his mouth, propping my leg up on his shoulder as he licked me. My lips parted, back arched as he devoured me with fervor. I buried my hands in his locs as he moved his head, nibbling, licking, and sucking until I could barely hold myself upright. He licked me harder when I came, moving his tongue in firm strokes over my sensitive clit as my nectar spread over his face. My legs were still shaking, open robe just barely hanging onto to my body when he stood, and in a few deft motions, picked me up and pushed himself inside of me.

Different tears than before sprang to my eyes as my body stretched to welcome a familiar old friend. He felt so

237

good, so *perfect* that I had to close my eyes as moisture dripped down my

face. Sex with Paul was fine, but it was just sex. Not matter how much I wished it weren't the case, *this* was something different. Sex with Tariq was *bliss*.

He wrapped my legs around his waist and balanced me against the wall so he could yank off his hoodie and tee shirt. Once he'd tossed it to the floor, he pulled me closer, pressing my sensitive nipples into the hard, warm plane of his chest. Tariq buried his face in my neck as he thrust into me, over, and over, driving away the hurt and powerlessness he felt. I draped my arms around him, pushing my nails into his shoulders as another orgasm began to crest.

Tariq burrowed himself in me hard, practically growling into my neck as he came. The force of that last thrust brought me with him, and my body pulsed around him, coaxing his release into me. Our chests heaved in unison, making it even harder to breath as we fought for the same space to exhale. He chuckled a little, and then altered his position so that we were taking turns instead, still wrapped tightly in each other's arms. And then reality set in, and I got mad.

I wiggled around until he pulled out of me, and let my feet back on the floor. Grabbing the ends of my now sweaty, wrinkled robe, I wrapped it tight around me, and belted it. Unaware of the fury growing in my head, Tariq tried to touch my face – grab my chin, to kiss me, but I pulled away.

238

"It's late," I said, not meeting his eyes. "You got what you needed, right?"

He scowled as he pulled up his boxers and sweatpants. "What?"

"The sex. That's what you came here, to me for, right? You got what you needed from me, and it's late, so…" I glanced toward the door, then bit the inside of my lip, trying my best not to let a fresh round of tears free, but I had low hopes of success. I felt like shit, in this moment, in more ways than one.

I wasn't even surprised when Tariq grabbed me by the arm as I tried to get away, foiling my attempt to escape into my bedroom. His grip wasn't tight, but it was firm, and his fingers curled under my chin, tipping my head to make me face him. "Kora, explain yourself. *Now.*"

"I get it," I said, my voice broken with badly restrained emotion as he pinned me with his gaze. "You needed me. You couldn't go to Julissa, because you probably haven't told her about Cherie yet. *I get it.*" I licked my trembling bottom lip to wet it, then continued. "If you need to stay and talk about your trip, you can. I won't withhold my friendship from you. But what we just did… when you *needed* somebody, you came to my door, because she can't do it for you. But she's the one that everybody sees on your arm. It isn't fair for you to come here and use me to make yourself feel better, when tomorrow, you're going back to *her.* It's not okay."

Tariq's lips parted halfway through what I was saying, but he was silent until I finished speaking. Then, he

239

moved his hands to both sides of my face, holding me still as he lowered himself to eye level with me. "Kora, are you fucking crazy?"

I blinked several times, then shook my head as much as I could while he was still holding my face. "What?"

"I asked if you were crazy. But I'm not sure why, because you have to be, if you're actually implying that you think I would ever choose Julissa over you."

I shoved his hands away from me, and stepped back. "How so, Tariq? Who are you getting photographed with? It's certainly not *me* you're taking to premieres, holding hands with and shit."

"You had bitch ass *Paul* with you on your opening night, at your rehearsals. You gave *his* ass a lunch date you *never* would have given me right before a show!"

"Because you friend zoned me for your little sexy lawyer! So tell me again how you didn't choose her over me!"

"I was doing what you fucking *asked me to do*. The shit was *your* idea, Kora!"

"Yeah, well, you should have known better!" I screamed, jabbing a finger in his face. My throat was starting to get raw, snotty nose, tears streaming down my face, and I didn't care about any of it. "One of us is supposed to have some goddamned sense, and I was hoping it would be you, but look at us! I lobbied so hard for us to not be together because we almost ruined our friendship last time. We're bonded too tightly, you've done too much for me, you mean *everything* to me, and I don't know if I could survive losing that."

Tariq sighed, scrubbing a hand over his face. "We're losing it *now*."

"I know," I sniffled, wrapping my arms around myself as I nodded. "It's like, we're damned if we do, damned if we don't. But as soon as I decided I wanted you too much, loved you too much, to not give it a try, you tell me you want to see where it could go with *her*."

Tariq sucked his teeth. "Man, fuck *her*."

"You and I both know you don't mean that."

He blew out a breath, threading his fingers behind his head. "You're right. I don't. But goddammit, Kora... if you're telling me I actually have a choice, I choose *you*."

A gasp caught in my throat, and I tried to swallow it as yet another round of tears sprang to my eyes. I shook my head. "What about Julissa?"

He shrugged. "What about Paul?"

"Paul isn't a problem."

"You married him."

"Because I couldn't marry you."

Tariq's eyes went wide, and his hands dropped to his sides as he tilted his head. "What?"

I lowered my eyes. "I've loved you as more than a friend for a long time, Tariq. Way before that night we celebrated your first big win, and it led to... more. But you weren't available to me. Even when we *were* together, I understood that with you, a ring was going to take a long

241

time, if it ever happened at all. But I was okay with that, because it was *you*. We

didn't work out, but I met Paul. He wasn't you, but he had so many of the same qualities that I love about you, that when he asked me out, it was a no-brainer. When he asked me to marry him, it was like I was getting something I never expected I *would* get, because I loved *you*."

Tariq's eyes narrowed in confusion, and he shook his head. "So what does that mean?"

I laughed a little through the tears still streaming down my face, and let my mouth spread into a smile. "It means Paul was right to divorce me. I deserved it, because it was never him. It was always *you*."

He just looked at me a little longer, biting his lip as he sorted what I was saying in his head. Suddenly, he broke into a grin, and nodded. "Okay. So Paul isn't a problem."

"But Julissa is."

Tariq shook his head again. "Nah. It's been two and a half months. We're still casual."

"She doesn't know that."

He lifted an eyebrow. "Yeah, she does. We've talked about it, more than once. She knows I don't rush things, knows we're still getting to know each other. We're not even near a discussion on being official."

I let out a little sigh, and then approached him, this time cupping his face in my hands. "Listen to me. *Trust* me, as someone who is a woman, and therefore knows them better than you do. To Julissa, you are her man." He started to argue, but I shook my head. "*Seriously*, Tariq."

242

"Okay," he said, closing his eyes, exasperated. "But still. Paul isn't a problem. Julissa isn't a problem. I will talk to her tomorrow, pay her off, whatever, but I'm done with me and you not being together." He brought his hands to my face, wiping away tears before he kissed my cheeks. "We'll make it work, and if it doesn't, we'll still make it work. I *love* you."

I pulled my top lip between my teeth, then nodded. "I love you too."

I closed my eyes as he pressed his lips to mine, then pulled me to his chest. He wrapped me in his arms tight, kissing my forehead before he dropped his mouth to my ear. "You're mine,

Kora. Nothing is getting in the way of that anymore."

sixteen.

Tariq

The very last thing I wanted to do was let Kora out of bed. I'd waited so long to be able to call her mine, it felt like the only *right* thing to do was to keep her close to me all day.

Especially after the night – morning – we'd had.

Eventually, marathon lovemaking had given way to us talking about why I'd actually come to her in the first place. I told her the whole story about the visit with my mother, and after scolding me for not telling her about the trip before it happened, she'd cried more than enough tears for both of us.

At some point, we'd passed out, naked and tangled together in Kora's deep purple sheets. When I opened my eyes, her place on the bed was empty, the air was scented with her body wash, and she was standing in front of her mirror, putting diamond studs in her ears.

I groaned a little, propping myself up on my elbow as I watched her zip her feet into dark red boots. "Don't tell me you're going to the theater."

Kora turned around, with a little grin on her face as she sauntered toward the bed, stopping right in front of me. She leaned down, and pressed her lips – painted a color that matched her boots – to my forehead. "Unfortunately, I can't do that."

She shrieked with laughter when I grabbed her around the thighs, pulling her down to the bed. I climbed on top of her, positioning myself between her legs. "Why not?"

"*Because*," she giggled, batting my hands away as they crept up her sweater. "We still have rehearsals, lighting changes, new costumes… my work isn't done yet."

"You can't go."

Kora grinned, pulling her lip between her teeth as I groped her ass through her jeans. "I have to. We'll have tonight though."

"Not good enough."

She laughed again, grabbing my face, and leaning up to press a closed-mouth kiss to my lips. "I'm sorry, my love, but it has to be."

I groaned, then squeezed her ass again. "Say that one more time."

"What?" she asked, in a sensual, breathy little voice. "*My. Love?*" She shrieked again as I pressed myself against her, mimicking the motion of a stroke. "Tariq stop!"

"*You* stop," I laughed, grabbing her thighs and propping them around my waist. "You're about to make me tear these pants off of you."

With another one of those sexy little giggles, she tried to maneuver herself out of my grasp. "*Stoppp*. You're getting dick germs on me!"

"Dick germs?"

She nodded. "Yes. You haven't showered yet, so there's no telling what you're spreading on my clean clothes, negro."

"Are you calling me dirty?"

"Yes."

I scoffed. "Well, I was in *your* pussy, so…"

"Oh whatever!" She sucked her teeth, then playfully shoved at my arms, but I didn't budge. I let her push for a few moments before I rolled over to the side, letting her free. A few seconds later, a pillow hit me in the face. "That's for making me late!"

Before I could recover, she'd dashed out of the room, and there wasn't much I could do except laugh as I heard the front door close in the distance. I laid there thinking about how different I felt now, compared to just twenty-four hours ago, and smiled. I'd gone from – possibly – realizing that my mother may have tried to harm me when I was just a child, to finally

being able to call the woman I'd long thought to be my soul mate, mine. Obviously, it didn't erase the trauma of the experience at Oak Hill, or do anything to heal those negative memories, but it certainly did a helluva job of improving my mood, and giving me something else to think about.

I climbed out of bed, and used Kora's shower to clean up before I opened the bottom drawer of her dresser to retrieve some fresh clothes. I knew if I went in her closet, I would find several suits hanging up near the back, but for today, I just needed fresh boxers and sweats. I was going back home.

I turned on my phone, which had been off since I left Oak Hill, and called Fletch to come and pick me up. He'd dropped me off at Kora's place last night since I had a few drinks, and probably wasn't fit to drive. While I was waiting on him, I took the opportunity to check my messages and emails, which I'd been ignoring while I focused on the trip to see my mom.

They were mostly work-related, but there were a couple that made me frown. Reporters. Asking me about Dawn, asking me about Kora, wanting to know my connection to them, requesting interviews, all of which I simply deleted, instead of even bothering to politely decline.

When I was done with that, I went into my text messages, and my stomach flipped at the last message received.

"Hope you're enjoying your trip! <3 – J. Santos" sent last night, at 8:39pm.

I took a deep breath, and then typed out a reply, deleting and retyping several times before I finally sent something that seemed right.

"Hey, thank you. Sorry for the delayed response, my cell was turned off. I actually came back to town early. Do you think you could meet me for an early dinner tonight?" She responded right back.

"Sure, but dinner on a Tuesday? Is something going on? – J. Santos."

"We can talk over dinner. I'll send you the details, and see you then."

By the time I hit send, Fletch was calling to let me know he was downstairs, and I stuck the phone in my pocket. I *really* didn't want to have this meal with her, but what kind of asshole would I be if we had this conversation via phone, or text? I felt like I owed it to her to talk with her in person, but if past experience was any indication, there was no way it would go well.

But it had to be handled.

ASAP.

When I climbed into the back of the Range Rover, I sat back, and asked Fletch to make a dinner reservation somewhere nice. "And private," I added, after he nodded. "Very, *very* private, and with minimal extra items on the table."

From what I could tell, Julissa seemed like the type that might start throwing shit.

~

"I come bearing gifts, bruh."

I grinned, then slapped hands with Stephen as he came through the front door of my condo, with his hands full of bags that smelled good as hell. "Goddamned hero is what you are

Steph," I said as I closed the door behind him, then followed him to the kitchen.

"You actually have *Mama* Foster to thank for this. She dropped it off at the office for me on her way to the church, and it was more than enough, so since I *need* to hear the details behind that cryptic ass text you sent me, I decided to be generous."

"What text?" I was already digging through bags he'd put down on the counter, pulling out and opening containers of traditional Argentine food. Asado, and a little dish of chimichurri, beef empanadas, a bowl of carbonado, and a platter of alfajores… "Your father's people must have been for a recent visit. I see your mom is flexing, proving she can do any cuisine."

Steph chuckled. "You already know. The fuck you mean, *what text*? Nigga *this* text."

He whipped out his phone, holding it up in front of me as I stuffed a spoonful of hearty stew in my mouth, then bit into one of the empanadas.

"MOTHERFUCKING FINALLY. – T. Evans"

"You ready to explain what that's about, or…?"

As soon as I swallowed, I shot him a grin, then said one word. "Kora."

He narrowed his eyes in confusion at first, but then slowly, recognition spread across his face in the form of a smile. Steph raised his fist, and I bumped it with mine before he slapped me on the shoulder. "*Motherfucking finally* indeed," he chuckled, sitting down at the counter. "I wish you'd explained that earlier, I would have grabbed a bottle of champagne. This shit deserves a celebration!"

"Man, whatever Steph."

"I'm serious," he laughed, throwing his head back. "Man, how long have you been trying to convince her to take your ass back? Twenty years?"

"It hasn't been twenty years, stop playing."

He laughed harder. "Alright, alright. Less than twenty, but at least ten."

"Man, whatever. I would kick you out, but you brought your mother's cooking."

"I'll make sure to pass along the compliment. But what about Julissa, man?"

I groaned, then took a swig from a bottle of water I'd grabbed. "I have to call it quits."

"With fine ass Julissa?"

"For fine ass Kora. Yes."

Steph sat back, popping an empanada in his mouth as he shook his head. "You do have a point there," he said. "You think maybe now you can make that Nubia thing happen, or…?"

"I don't think Jesus himself can make the Nubia thing happen, Steph," I laughed. "Why are you sweating her so hard?"

"Have you *seen* her?"

"Obviously."

"Then why the fuck do you have to ask? Nubia is *put a ring on it* fine. *Tell your other chicks it's over* fine. *Eat the booty like –*"

"I get it, *damn.*"

"Then stop asking stupid ass questions. I want a piece of that, and she won't give it to me, that's why I want

251

it so bad. She told me it was good, and I believe her too. She *walks* like she tastes good."

I almost choked on a mouthful of food laughing. "Dude, you do realize that Nubia hasn't even let you hold her damned hand, and she already has you wrapped around her finger. She has your head gone, man. Talking about putting a ring on it, telling other chicks it's over…"

"Hey, let's be clear. I said she was that fine—not that I would actually *do* it."

I scoffed. "Yeah, right. I've known Nubia for years – don't underestimate that woman.

It's a chess game to her."

"I know how to play chess."

"Yeah, but Nubia is a grandmaster."

Stephen sat back, with a sigh that was damned near dreamy. "I know, man. And I fucking *love* it. Worthy opponent."

"I don't want to hear your whining when she hurts your feelings, cause I warned you!"

A knock at the door interrupted Stephen's response. I pulled myself away from the counter, wondering who it could be. *Hoping* that it was Kora, so I could kick Steph out, and spend some time with my lady.

I smiled.

My lady.

I peered through the peephole to see who was on the other side of my door, and the smile dropped from my face.

What the fuck...

I turned around to see Steph standing at the end of the kitchen for a view of the door.

"Who is it?" he asked, munching on one of the dulce de leche cookies.

"Julissa," I mouthed, then rubbed my forehead, trying to ease my sudden headache. And Steph... that asshole started laughing as I moved away from the door.

"I'm about to get out of here. Julissa is Dominican, and you're gonna break up with her *here*? She's about fuck *all* this fancy shit in here up. Knock your framed jerseys off the wall, put your championship rings down the toilet. I hope you have insurance."

"That's not funny."

"The hell it isn't. Why would Fletch let her up here?"

I groaned as the knock sounded again, a little firmer this time. "I didn't tell him yet, man.

Shit." I swallowed hard, then took a deep breath as I headed back for the door.

"Wait!"

I turned to look at Stephen, eyebrow raised in confusion. "What, fool?"

"Hey, let me grab one of these pillows real quick for cover before you open that door."

I sucked my teeth, then shook my head as I pulled the door open to see Julissa standing on the other side with her phone up to her ear.

"Hey," she said, smiling as she pulled it away, then pressed a button to turn it off. "I was just about to try calling. I knew I heard voices. Hi Stephen," she waved, and when I glanced over my shoulder, Steph was waving back as he headed back to the kitchen.

"Don't mind me," he called. "I'm going to take this food into the TV room, give you two some privacy."

"So!" I turned back to Julissa at the sound of her voice, and flinched as she pressed herself against me. "I was hoping to stop by and ask you on a surprise lunch date, but it smells like you've already had it. What Latina do you have cooking for you, hmm?"

I stepped away from her, crossing my arms over my chest so she wouldn't try it again.

"Uh, Steph's father is Argentinian, his mother is black. She cooked the food."

"Ah, I see." She smiled again. "So you want to tell me why you asked me to dinner in the middle of the week? That's new." She took a step toward me again, and I casually took another back, then played it off by heading into the kitchen.

"Well, we need to talk."

She drew her head back, and the smile faded from her face. "Oh. Okay. *We need to talk* is never good. So what is it?"

"Do you want to maybe sit down?" I asked, gesturing toward the bar stools. "A bottle of water or something?"

She lifted an eyebrow. "No. I don't want to sit, and I don't want water, I want you to tell me what the hell is going on —wait. Wait a minute, this is it, isn't it?"

I frowned. "This is what?"

"This is where you finally come out and tell me the truth, after you've strung me along for almost three months. Right? This, this *we need to talk*, the reservations at Bar Sapphire… you're dumping me, aren't you? And I bet it's for goddamned Kora Oliver, isn't it?"

Her eyes were filled with something incredibly close to hatred as they met mine and I nodded. "Yes."

"You piece of shit. I asked you if you were screwing her, and you made it seem like it was nothing to worry about, like it was your past! Come to find out, after I've invested time and energy with you, after you've fucked me, that you're dumping me for her. Were you screwing her this whole time? Why drag me along with you, while you paraded her in my face, under the guise that she was your *friend*? I fucking *knew* better!"

I opened my mouth, but nothing came out except a heavy sigh as I leaned back against the counter. Obviously I wanted to defend myself against the things she was saying. I hadn't "strung her along", and I hadn't been sleeping with Kora. But Julissa's feelings were hurt – *I* – had hurt her feelings, so she wasn't trying to hear any of that. Instead, she could say her piece, curse me out, whatever. And then everybody could move on.

I swallowed hard, trying to figure out what to say, but the only thing that seemed even remotely right was, "I'm sorry, Julissa. It wasn't my intention to hurt you. I'm sorry that I did."

She narrowed her eyes, staring right at me for several long seconds before she shook her head. "Fuck you. And

255

your apology. You're not sorry. Or wait. Yeah, you are. You are sorry as hell, you lying sonofabitch." *Whoa.*

"Okay, hold up. I understand you're upset, and I truly am sorry that I caused that. I know that I've hurt your feelings, and I'll let you say what you feel like you need to say... *except* that."

She sucked her teeth. "Except *what?*"

""Lying sonofabitch". I haven't lied to you, and you don't know my mother, so keep that shit out of your mouth."

"You're *not* a liar?" she scoffed, shaking her head. "You actually believe that?"

"Uh, yeah," I said, eyebrow lifted. "What have I lied to you about? *You* said you were fine with us taking things slow. *You* said you could deal with my friendship with Kora. Hell, initially, you swore all you wanted was sex from me. Is any of that shit true, Julissa? No, it's not. So you tell me who the liar is."

"Fuck you!" I cast a wary eye at Julissa's hands as she used them to emphasize her words. "Men think they can just play with women's emotions, and then when they're done, throw them away. But guess what? Karma always comes back and bites you in the ass for the shit you do. I just hope I get to see it."

I bit the inside of my lip to keep from telling her to get the fuck out, since she was stomping toward the door anyway. She flung it open, and turned to me with an expression that would have had me writhing on the floor if looks could kill.

"And your sex *isn't* that damned good."

I chuckled. "Yeah, okay."

She narrowed her eyes, and her face wrinkled into a snarl as she stepped out, slamming my door as hard she could – which was hard enough that it echoed loudly, and the reverberation made the frames and trophies on the shelves shake.

"*Daaaamn,*" Steph said, laughing as he came into the room, then jogged in a little circle. "I have *got* to open a window in here to let out some of this tension, it's so thick!"

"Yeah, go open one, so I can push your stupid ass out."

He chuckled. "*Aww*, man!" he clapped me on the shoulder. "Seriously though, you good?

That shit was intense!"

"You were listening?"

He sucked his teeth. "What? Hell yes. I was listening. You didn't *really* think I wouldn't, did you?"

"Not really."

"Good," he grinned. "I may have had to wonder if you really knew me at all. So what's next? You calling your girl to let her know you're a completely free man now?"

I nodded. "Yessir. But first…" – I grabbed my phone – "I'm calling Fletch to tell him not to *ever* let Julissa up here again."

seventeen.

Kora

"Officially no longer involved with Julissa. All yours. – T. Evans."

I smiled at my phone as I read the message from Tariq once again. As a matter of fact, my cheeks were starting to ache, because it I hadn't stopped smiling since I woke up.

Maybe that's just the kind of thing love does to you.

It was like someone had flipped a switch, and instead of the state of loneliness and confused feelings I'd been operating from before, my heart was just *full*. I couldn't be happier.

"So what do you think, Kora? Yes? No?"

I looked up from my perch on the vanity to see Nubia gesturing toward Dawn. She'd dressed her in mustard yellow pants, a navy and white sweater, and cranberry-toned booties that gave her at least four more inches of height. Her hair was free, hanging around her shoulders in her signature wild curls.

She looked amazing.

"Um, it's a yes from me," I said, climbing down from the counter. "It's always a yes from me, isn't it? You're the fashionista around here."

Nubia smiled. "I am, aren't I? But still, Girl Gab is one of the biggest internet talk shows out right now. We have to make sure *our* girl is flawless for this interview, right?"

"Right," Dawn and I said in unison, then laughed.

"You ready sweetheart?" I asked, repositioning a few of her curls.

She grinned at me, then nodded. "Yeah. I want to get it over with, so I can go try to catch a nap before the show."

"Well, go ahead and get out there then. Good luck."

I gave her a little hug before she headed out to where the interview was being held. The host, Gabriella, liked to interview people in their comfort zone, and for Dawn, that was Warm Hues Theatre. I declined the offer to sit in on the conversation, because Girl Gab was known for honest, but drama-free interviews, and it was a perfect opportunity for Dawn to experience handling it by herself.

Soon though – *very* soon – it was going to be time to get an agent for her.

There was only so much that I could do when it came to her career, without seeming like a stage parent. I wanted to be very careful with that, and let Dawn manage her own success. I

also didn't want people thinking of her as "Kora Oliver's daughter". With her talent, she could stand on her own.

Already, only about a month into the show's run, Dawn was receiving major attention. Rave reviews from important critics, interviews like the one that was about to start, trending

topics on social media. It was amazing. It wasn't anything like how it was when I first started, where you were lucky if your name got mentioned in an article at all. Dawn was getting headlines, having to turn down offers and interviews, and as *awesome* as that was for her career, it came with some ugliness too.

She was very quickly seeing how any little thing she did or said was met with a level of scrutiny she hadn't experienced before. Thank *God,* for Officer Wiley having our backs that night she and Donnie almost got in trouble, because that would have undoubtedly been dug up and spread around by now.

There was already talk about her time at Juilliard – apparently there had been an affair

with a white boy who'd become a breakout star as the lead in one of those teenaged dystopia movies. There was talk about the clothes she wore, the luxury building she lived in – seemingly, there was a made up sugar daddy funding her lifestyle, since the boring answer of a celebrity mother and celebrity godfather didn't fit the scandalous narrative. And, what made me most sick to my stomach – the speculation about who Dawn's father was.

Which meant they were talking about *me.*

I'd endured my share of media attention back when I was a "big" star, and still got a little bit now. Usually it was only when I wanted the attention though, like if I was promoting something. Which, in a way, applied to now, but still. I wanted people to stop talking about, stop wondering about *that*. It was completely private, no one's business except mine, his, and

Dawn's,
and even *she*
didn't know the
whole story. I
really wished it
could be left
alone.

Instead, they dug harder. They'd scraped up every boyfriend I ever had, and one major asshole had gone so far as to put their faces on a big screen, comparing features. I hated the name Wesley David with a passion now, and this all started because he was pissed that Dawn had cancelled her interview with him to accept a last-minute offer to do Good Morning America with the other main cast.

Who Tha Daddy Is? was now a daily segment on his thirty minute gossip show, which played on cable TV, and attracted millions of viewers. Paul, Tariq, and even Stephen had all been named as possible fathers, and all ruled out – as *everybody* he could possibly think to drag onto his show would be.

But whatever.

I was happy.

I wouldn't – *couldn't* – let silly gossip phase me. The interview, a meeting with the theatre's board of directors, and another run of the show passed, and by the time I could leave, I was exhausted. Tariq had offered to come by, but I was so busy that I wouldn't have been able to enjoy his presence, so I passed. Now though, it was time to go home, and I had to take a second to calm myself down when I realized how easy it was to think of "home" and have my mind fill that space with Tariq's place instead of mine.

So that's where I went.

I didn't even bother knocking – I used my key, because I was coming home, and I dared him to say different. I found him in his office, elbow propped on the desk, his head in his hand. When he looked up and saw me in the door, the tired, stressed expression he wore spread into a smile, and he stood, crossing the room in what seemed like just two steps to reach me.

He didn't even say anything. One hand went around my waist to pull me close, the other got buried in my hair, tugging my face to his for him to kiss me. I sank against him, relishing the new, but somehow still incredibly familiar, reality that he was mine, I was his. I'd felt it forever, that sense of ownership that came when you knew somebody was the one you were supposed to be with. But feeling it and living it were two different things.

"How was your day?" he asked, when he finally stopped kissing me long enough to let me catch my breath. He cupped my face in his hands, using his thumbs to stroke my cheeks, looking at me like he couldn't *possibly* look at me enough.

"Long. Tiresome. I missed you."

263

He pulled his lip between his teeth, and nodded. "I missed you too." I closed my eyes as his lips touched mine again. "And ditto, on the long, tiresome day. Add stressful to that."

My eyes popped open, and I grinned. "Oh yeah, you had to break up with someone today, didn't you?"

"Don't remind me."

I laughed as he threaded his fingers through mine, leading me into his bedroom. "No sir, I have to, because I've got to hear this. Tell me what happened."

Tariq groaned, then plopped down on the end of his bed. He let himself fall backwards onto the covers, then hooked his hands behind his head, and told me the story of his "breakup" with Julissa.

"So seriously," he asked, sitting up after he was done. "Tell me if I'm wrong here. And tell the truth."

I scoffed. "Oh you know I'll gleefully tell you when you're wrong about something. But in all honesty, this situation is complicated."

He lifted an eyebrow. "Explain."

"Well," – I bent to unzip my boots – "*I* don't think you're in the wrong, technically. But in Julissa's eyes, you are. And if *I* were in her place, I'd probably think you were wrong too, because you hurt my – her – feelings, and that's really all it takes."

Tariq frowned. "So it doesn't matter if I *did* anything wrong. I hurt her feelings, so I'm wrong regardless?"

I shrugged, then stood to put my shoes in the closet. "Yep. Basically." I laughed at the look on his face, then pulled my sweater over my head. "Everyone plays the bad guy at least once or twice in their lifetime. It's your turn."

"But I didn't *do* anything."

"You hurt her feelings. You broke up with her. You wouldn't make her your official girlfriend. That's at least *three* things."

Tariq's eyes went wide. "Kora, are you serious?!"

I unbuttoned, unzipped, kicked off my jeans. "Um, yeah. I'm *dead* serious. Listen, my love, I know you think that you did your part by being transparent with what you wanted from the relationship, where things between you and her stood, all of that. But you have to understand that men and women communicate differently."

He groaned, then flopped back on the bed. "Here you go…"

"No," I giggled, storing my discarded clothes with the rest of the things to be drycleaned. "Just hear me out okay?"

"I'm listening."

"Good. So when women speak to men, you guys take us at our word. And I'm not talking about like, street harassment and shit, where men can't take no for an answer. I mean like… A woman says she wants a marriage and kids, and a man will hear "marry me *right* now, and put a baby in me *yesterday*." You know? As a general rule – which means there are always exceptions

– you take us really literally, so when we say, for example… let's just have sex, no strings attached, that's what you expect, nothing more, nothing less."

265

Tariq sat up. "I can see that. So like, when a woman tells you multiple times that she

wants to just be platonic, no more "friends with benefits" –"

"Shut your ass up." He smirked, then flopped back on the bed again, and I rolled my eyes. "*Anyway.* For a lot of women, we're kind of the opposite. We hear you say "sex with no strings", and it's like a challenge to make you love us because you love our pussy. We hear "my female best friend isn't going anywhere", and it's like you're daring us to get her out of here. "I move slow in relationships" gets interpreted as "I need you to love me harder and be around me more and get a little nastier during sex so I can tell if I like you.""

"That's crazy."

"That's life. You did what you were supposed to do – what a lot of men *won't* do – by being transparent and honest. Julissa knew what it was, she just wanted it to be something else.

She had the opportunity to drop your ass at any time, and she didn't."

Tariq blew out a heavy sigh as he stared toward the ceiling. "Isn't there like a color wheel or something for feelings? I should send her some "I'm sorry" flowers. What color is that?"

"*No!*" I stalked over to the bed and stood over him, making sure he met my eyes.

"Seriously. *No.* The only thing you could do to make her feel better is fall off a cliff. And since I'd rather you not,

266

maybe just leave her alone? She needs liquor, ice cream, and home girls to talk her out of trying to catch uncatchable men. She does *not* need your damn sympathy flowers.

She's a grown woman, I'm sure she's dealt with a breakup before."

"You know, I wondered if something was going on between her and one of the partners at her firm. This one dude has been looking at me sideways in the elevator since she and I first got involved. But he just got engaged like two months ago…"

I smirked. "Hmm, so right around the time Julissa suddenly wanted to be more than sex buddies, and got stage-five clingy?"

Tariq sat up, eyes wide. "You think maybe…?"

"Mmmhmm. He suddenly gets engaged, she's left out, and now she wants to steamroll you into something you aren't ready for. Purely speculation, but…"

He shook his head. "No, it makes sense. Damn."

"Right. She can't seem to catch a break. Maybe I should introduce her to Paul." Tariq let out a loud laugh, bending forward to clutch his stomach. "What's so damn funny?"

"Paul always getting the girl after me."

I sucked my teeth. "Negro, are you calling me leftovers?!"

Tariq stopped laughing to look at me and shrug. "I mean, technically… *wait!*" he called out, chuckling as he caught my arm to stop me from stomping into the bathroom. "You know I'm playing with you. If you're leftovers, you're

267

like, second-day sweet potato pie. Better than the first, cause now all the flavors have matured and soaked in."

"That is the corniest shit I have ever heard in my life," I quipped, fighting a smile. "Get the hell out of my face so I can take a shower."

"Second day spaghetti?"

"Tariq…"

"I mean, you *could* be second day fried catfish, from the microwave at work. I'm trying to compliment you, damn." I burst into laughter as he wrapped his arms around me, pulling me close. "Seriously, baby. You're fresh catfish, hot out of the grease, on a piece of white bread, with some hot sauce."

"Shut *uppp!*" I laughed, nuzzling my face against the soft fabric of his tee shirt, not caring that I was probably getting makeup on it.

"No, stop hating. I'm on a roll here," he said, lowering his hands to grip my ass. "We've got a nice little Georgia peach right here," – he moved them up to my breasts, squeezing them through my bra – "Some good sized grapefruits—" – he tugged down the lacy cups, ran his thumbs over my nipples – "and some juicy blackberries."

Still giggling, I batted his hands away, then darted into the bathroom and closed the door.

"Let me shower in peace, please!" I shouted through the door, grinning when he yelled back.

"Fine, since you want to act like my comparisons weren't romantic as hell!"

268

I did take my shower in peace, and then pulled my box of things from under his counter to clean my face, brush my teeth, moisturize my skin, and tie up my hair. When I came out of the bathroom, he was in bed, looking freshly showered himself, with ESPN on the TV, and the remote in his hand.

I didn't say anything as I went into the closet and found a pretty blue negligee in my drawer. I pulled it over my head, smiling at how the soft, silky fabric felt on my skin as I climbed into bed. It took me a few minutes to realize Tariq's eyes were on me, and when I turned to him, he didn't look away.

"What is it?" I asked, briefly closing my hands when his hand ran up my thigh.

He shrugged. "Not sure. It's just being here with you like this... we never really got to do *this* you know? Me waiting for you to come to bed. Seeing you with your hair tied up, you having the whole room smelling good. I like this."

I nodded as he eased toward me, then balanced himself on top of me. "Yeah. Me too. It's nice." I bit my lip as he pressed his mouth to my neck, drawing a moan from me when he flicked out his tongue. He brought his lips to mine, kissing me there before he ventured lower, over my jaw and collarbone, down to my breasts.

Through the fabric of my gown, he tugged my nipples – gently at first, then harder – between his teeth, nibbling and biting and then soothing the sting with his tongue. I squirmed underneath him, pressing myself up and

269

against his mouth until my nipples were hard peaks to his touch, pleasantly sensitive as he pushed his hands under the negligee and flicked them with his thumbs.

Tariq's mouth kept moving lower, kissing trails along the undersides of my breasts, down to my bellybutton and then back up, pulling the gown over my head to taste my nipples again. He cupped and squeezed handfuls of my ass cheeks, kneading and massaging as he kissed a path down to the apex of my thighs.

He spread my legs wide, and then he spread me open with his fingers. When he first put his mouth on me, it was just soft kisses over my lips, gentle bites on my butt cheeks and the insides of my thighs. He avoided my clit, slowly licking me everywhere else, pushing his tongue inside me, kissing me above and below, but not where I needed it.

Until suddenly, he did.

I arched off the bed when he covered me with his mouth, sucking and licking and slurping me up. My fingers tangled in handfuls of his locs as he pushed my legs toward my head, opening me up to him more. He stiffened his tongue, licked me everywhere he could reach and some places he couldn't, but at least tried.

It was... amazing. An overpowering tightness built in the pit of my stomach, and I tried to pull away, but Tariq locked his arms around my thighs and caught me by the wrists, holding me firmly in place as he devoured me. There wasn't much I could do except throw my head back into the pillows and scream as the orgasm wracked my body, leaving me with trembling legs and static in my ears.

I hadn't even caught my breath before Tariq was inside me, filling me up, with my legs hooked over his shoulders. He took me with deep, powerful strokes, pulling my bottom lip between his teeth and sucked it hard as he plunged into me and just stayed there. Instead of moving in and out, he circled his hips as he devoured my mouth. He was in me as deep as he could go, and each time he moved, sweet friction swept across my clit, making me jerk with pleasure with every touch. Inside, he was right against my sweet spot, and he knew it, from the way he looked me right in the eyes, grinning as he pressed against it again.

"Is this good for you, gorgeous?"

I moaned, closing my eyes as he pressed so deep my toes curled. "You know it is."

"If I ask you whose pussy this is…?"

"It's yours," I answered immediately, shamelessly as I maneuvered my hands up to his face. "It's all yours."

"Tell me again." I whimpered as he suddenly started stroking me again, hard, fast strokes that made it hard to catch my breath. He moved back, wrapping my legs around his waist instead of over his shoulders, and pressed his thumb firmly against my clit, rocking it back and forth. 'I said tell me again."

"It yours!" I screamed, using the short amount of breath I had as he moved us again, pressing one of my thighs against the bed to spread me wide as he plunged into me. He pinched my clit between his thumb and forefinger, just hard enough to skirt the line between pleasure and pain, and I came unglued.

271

My fingers went to his hips, digging my fingernails into his cheeks to urge him closer, deeper, and he obliged. He leaned forward at an angle, using the leverage to drive into me. This time, he swallowed my scream with a kiss as I came. My world went black, and silent. I needlessly closed my eyes, and heard nothing, saw nothing, felt *everything*, electric tingles all over my body while I floated away.

When I opened my eyes again, a few moments later, Tariq was panting beside me. We were both covered in sweat, and if he felt anything like I felt, we *both* felt amazing. After another minute or so had passed, Tariq sat up some, turning my seemingly boneless body toward his.

"You okay?" he asked, with a cocky smirk that he absolutely deserved to wear.

In response, all I could do was grunt, close my eyes, and listen to him chuckle. I felt him climb out of the bed, then heard him in the bathroom. He cleaned himself up, then me, while I lay uselessly across the bed, still waiting for the feeling to return to my legs.

I flinched, then grinned when he came back to bed, and gently smacked my ass. I felt his lips on my shoulder, then my neck, then my ear before he murmured, "That's what you get for coming to bed smelling all good like that."

After that, he pulled me close, and I drifted off to sleep wearing a smile.

eighteen.

Tariq

"But you *have* to go back."

I leaned back in my chair and put down my fork, taking a long drink from my sweet tea

before I looked at my grandmother. I'd flown to see them before they took off for another long trip, this time to Italy for a few weeks. I was stuffed full – greens, macaroni and cheese, and fried pork chops. If nothing else, the food was worth the trip. My grandparents were the only black multi-millionaires I knew who would actually get in the kitchen and cook *real* food, the type of stuff that I – and by extension, Kora – grew up on.

But there was a tradeoff for seeing my grandparents and getting this home cooked meal.

Since I walked through their front door, they'd been trying to convince me that I needed to go see my mother again, soon, and simply put, I wasn't interested. Two weeks had gone by since that visit, and I was finally starting to put it out of my mind again, focusing instead on the fact that I was in a great place with Kora. I couldn't understand why they insisted on dragging me back.

They'd suggested, hinted, demanded, threatened, and now, because I wasn't moved by any of the previous methods, my grandmother had resorted to begging.

"Tariq, *please*. We all know that it's a difficult situation, but your mother loves you. Dr.

Alexander says she's been completely distraught since that awful day. She didn't even know what she was doing. She doesn't *want* to die."

"Okay, so why does she keep saying it, then?" I asked, frustrated that we were still stuck in this circular conversation. ""I want to die" sounds like the words of somehow saying exactly what they mean, if you ask me."

"It's the illness speaking. She would never *actually* hurt herself, or anyone else," my grandmother said, putting a hand on my arm.

I scoffed. "Is that right?"

"Yes, of course."

"So tell me what really happened at the lake that day, huh? I didn't really remember until that little incident two weeks ago, but why, when we were leaving the house, did we have to write notes to grandma and grandpa? Hmm? We left the house walking together all the time, and never wrote "I love you, goodbye," notes. So, why then? Why *that* day, when she was taking me to get in freezing cold water knowing I could barely swim? Why'd she fight so hard when those men happened along and pulled us out? Why the vacant look in her eyes afterward, if she would never harm herself or anybody else?"

"Tariq."

I stopped talking to take a deep breath, then turned to look at Kora, who'd intertwined her fingers with mine. She squeezed my hand, not scolding or supporting, just reminding me that she was there.

"She's sick, Tariq." Across from me, my grandfather met my eyes, his expression weary.

"Try not to hold it against her. Those voices, whatever is haunting her… that's not *her*."

"I know that," I said, squeezing Kora's hand. "I'm not holding it against her either, I'm just… I prefer to not subject myself to it. Let's be honest here – we all know why she tried to get into that lake, whether it was her illness driving her or not. I don't think it's selfish of me to feel like I need some room to breathe after that."

After a deep sigh, my grandmother nodded. "I suppose I understand. I just hate thinking about her needing us, and we aren't there. No matter, that's my child."

"And no matter what, that's my mom. I love her, I do. All of my memories of her aren't bad, but many of them are. It's hard to balance that, when those trips leave me emotionally drained. At some point I'm sure I'll go back, but for now it's off the table."

My grandfather nodded, then grabbed my grandmother's hand. "I guess we understand. We have to. You've done the best you could by your mother, considering everything. So we understand."

I nodded, and a somewhat uncomfortable silence accompanied us for the rest of the meal.

Later – much later – Kora and I found ourselves back at home. Her place, for the night.

We hadn't yet figured out a living arrangement, or even talked about it really. We were honestly still figuring out a lot.

Anyway, we were in her living room, wrapped together in a blanket under the fire. She had the drapes that covered her big floor-to-ceiling window open since it was snowing, and we sat there watching the flakes pile up against the window as we talked.

"So you see Donovan got back with Pixie, right?" Kora asked, turning her face up toward me. She was sideways in my lap, with her legs draped across mine.

I ran my fingers up the side of her thigh. "I didn't, actually. Dawn hasn't mentioned it to me. How is she taking it?"

Kora laughed. "Like any young girl would take getting her heart a little broken – even though she *swore* it wasn't like that. You know that scene in the show where they fight, and Raven slaps Kyle? Well Dawn has been smacking the *shit* out of Donovan lately. He actually complained, so I asked her to lighten up. I think she may have hit him harder though."

"That's my girl."

She sucked her teeth. "Don't you encourage that! Especially not when Julissa probably wishes she'd gotten a chance to smack *you* for getting back with your ex. You see how karma is working out? Came for your god daughter. Are you proud of yourself?"

"That's not funny."

"The hell it isn't," she giggled. "But Dawn was destined to get her heart broken over Donovan anyway. Blind people could see he and Pixie aren't done with each other, but Dawn had to learn that lesson on her own."

I slid my hand up to her ass and squeezed. "You think I should pay him a visit?"

"*No.*" Kora scowled at me. "Let those kids live." She reached up, running her fingers over the coily hairs of my beard. "But I really can't thank you enough for the way you've been there for her. For treating her like she's yours."

I smiled. "According to her, I am. Eleven months old, looked me right in the face and called me *daddy.*"

"Because you taught her that, fool."

"But she recognized that quality in me, and responded accordingly."

Kora rolled her eyes. "Tariq, you were seventeen years old. You had no business teaching a baby that wasn't yours to call you daddy."

"See that's where you're mistaken," I said, squeezing her ass a little harder. "Who got in trouble for skipping school to sit with you and rubbed your back on the days you were too nauseated to get out of bed?"

Kora pulled her lip between her teeth. "You."

"And who got in touch with their dad's relatives in Ghana to get you the *finest* shea butter to rub on your belly so you wouldn't get stretch marks?"

She laughed. "You did. And bonus points for your belly rubbing skills."

277

"Okay then, now we're talking," I chuckled. "Come on, Kora. I helped you pick a name with a meaning for you, I went and got you those disgusting pickles in the plastic pouch, you almost ruined my football career before it started, damn near broke my hand squeezing when you went into labor. After you held her first, who did you hand her to? Who talked to their grandmother to figure out you needed cabbage leaves to help soothe your breasts when your milk came in? And who went and *got* the cabbage?"

"You did, my love."

"Damn right I did, trying to tell me whose daddy I'm not. On paper, in public, yeah, I'm her "godfather", but we know what it really is."

Kora giggled, then sat up a little more, straddling my lap. I groaned as she sank down against me, suddenly pissed that either of us had on clothes. "Why did you do all that for me?

We were kids, Tariq. None of that was your responsibility."

"Because you needed somebody to do it for you, and your mom was... your mom. I even talked to my grandparents about it, explained that I intended to be there for whatever you needed.

They supported that. They supported *you*. They loved you. I loved you. That's why."

She tipped her head to the side. "But we were just friends. And you... super handsome, super popular, star football player and you weren't even a senior yet. There was so much other stuff you could have been doing, but instead, you were saddled down with little miss teen mom."

I smiled, then raised my hands to bury in her hair, bringing her forehead down to mine. "I was just repaying the friendship you showed me. You think I took it lightly when you would sing to my mother to calm her down? Or let me hide at your house when my grandparents were gone, and she would fly off the handle, breaking shit, and screaming?"

She shook her head. "No, but you *did* get mad when I told your grandparents their trips out of town weren't going as smoothly as you made them seem. You didn't speak to me for like a week. And we were what, twelve? A week without speaking was forever to us back then."

I chuckled. "A week without speaking to you is *still* forever, gorgeous. But yeah, I was pretty mad."

Unfortunately, I remembered that vividly. My mother had been drinking a bottle of wine – which she wasn't supposed to mix with her meds anyway – and offered some to me in a cup.

I'd never drunk before, and knew it was only for grown ups, but I was twelve. It was my mother, someone who I saw every day, but was still a mystery to me. I was desperate for a connection to her, so I accepted that cup, and then another, and before I knew it, I was dialing the number to

Kora's house in a panic. I was sick to my stomach, my head was spinning, and my mother was on the floor in a puddle of her own drool, in a dead sleep.

Kora had left her house – no need to sneak because her mother was rarely there anyway – and come to me, helping me through the ugliness of being drunk at twelve years old. I later learned that she knew what to do from watching and caring for her own mother, but that was beside the point.

When my grandparents returned from their trip, eleven-year-old Kora had somehow gotten them alone, and told them what happened. My grandparents thought my mother was on her meds consistently, which was why they left me in her care while they worked and took business trips. After all, ill or not, she was still my mother. She was supposed to keep me safe, but apparently, it wasn't until the wine episode that they determined that wasn't the case.

A lot of screaming happened in the house that night, and it ended with my mother mad at me. I took that hurt and anger of being banished by her out on Kora. When Cherie stopped being mad at me, I stopped being mad at Kora, and that was just the first example of the fucked up emotional co-dependency I was avoiding like the plague.

My reluctance to spend extended time around my mother wasn't just because I was angry. It was largely due to a need to manage my own mental health. I was protecting my sanity.

"I'm sorry about that, still," I told Kora, raking my fingers over her scalp. She closed her eyes, then dropped her head down to my shoulder, moving until she had her face pressed up against my neck.

"We were babies, Tariq. I hope you don't think I'm still upset about that." "Still."

She nodded against my chest. "I know, I know. You hate being the bad guy."

"Here you go with *this* shit again…"

"Oh whatever," she laughed. "You know it's the truth." She squealed when I smacked her ass, squeezing after to pull her a little closer. "Can you believe it's been a whole two weeks, and we haven't killed each other? I haven't even wanted to. Isn't that crazy? When we were together before, I thought about killing you at least five times a day."

I pretended to gasp. "Wow, imagine that. Who would have thought we would grow and mature from the bullshit we were on in our early twenties?"

"Shut up."

"You shut up."

"*You* shut—*mmmmm.*"

"Yeah," I said, grinning as I moved my fingers deeper inside of her. "*You* shut up."

"This isn't fair," she murmured. "I'm trying to have a conversation with you." "So talk."

She rolled her hips against my hand, shaking her head. "Uh-uh. This first. Talk later."

~

281

Kora

I was about to be late.

I cursed myself under my breath for letting Tariq and his dick keep me awake half the night. Even though I'd enjoyed every second, I'd woken up late – after turning off my alarm and falling back asleep – to an empty apartment. Tariq had already left to get to his office, so I couldn't even blame him in person that I was about to be late for an important meeting.

The other script I'd been reading, *Trouble Don't Last*, had turned out to be fabulous. I would love to take it on as my second project – *if* I could get my ass out of the door, and to the theatre within the next thirty minutes.

I still had the glass of water from swallowing my daily vitamin in my hand, and was grabbing the remote to turn off the TV when I heard Dawn's name. That was the whole reason the TV was on the entertainment news channel – to catch news bites about Dawn, or the show in general as I got ready to start my day.

I rolled my eyes when I realized Wesley David's stupid ass was on my screen, but when I looked at the images on the screen beside him, my heart slammed to the front of my chest, and stopped.

"Well, well, well. It looks like we may have finally done it. As always, Wes has come through for you ladies and

282

gentleman, with the tea, and it is piping hot! *If you look to the left of*

my handsome face, you'll see Dawn Oliver. To the left of her, you'll see the incredibly handsome, former black Hollywood heart throb Remy Toussard. And just for poops and giggles, let's put up a picture of dear old mom, Kora Oliver too.

As you can see, the more mature Ms. Oliver is a chocolate sister. Dark skin, dark eyes… so where did Dawn get the caramel skin and hazel eyes and that head full of pretty creole hair?

I'll tell you. She got it from her daddy – Remy!

Now wait, wait, wait! I know you're sitting at home saying "what the hell is Wes talking about? That man is twenty years older than Kora, and it's a well-known fact that she was a young teen mother. How in the world would a fifteen year old girl be in personal *touch with Mr.*

Black Hollywood himself?

You know I'm going to tell you!

My team is tireless, okay? All it took was a little simple math, and some digging through old news and photo archives to discover that one Kathryn Oliver – Kora's mother, former Broadway and Hollywood herself, still *got it going on – used to date fine ass Remy Toussard.*

And according to all *sources, it was hot and heavy.*

At least, until her little vixen of a daughter came along and snatched his attention away. Hmmm, something to think about right? Like mother like daughter, since Kathryn

283

Oliver was well known to snatch somebody's husband. Looks like she reaped what she sowed.

We reached out to the oldest Ms. Oliver for comment months ago, and she declined to speak... but the little check she tried to slide us told us everything *we needed to know – that there was something to find out. And listen y'all, I was* not *expecting* this.

It's long been wondered what happened to Remy Toussard, before he passed away a few years back. Why he suddenly dropped out of the stratosphere, followed closely by Kathryn

Oliver. And then a few years later, the poster child for "making it out" as a teen mom, Kora, is suddenly a rising star?

MmmMmmMmm. There's a whole lot in this milk that ain't clean, and you can just call me a filter, because Wesley David will *sort it out.*

So what do you think? Tweet us, Facebook us, comment on Instagram, call into the show.

Let's talk about it! Do you think Remy is Dawn's father. Did Kora Oliver screw her way to the top? We've all heard about how teenage girls are these *days, but looks like they were just as scandalous back in* the *day. Let's talk!"*

The glass of water and the remote slipped out of my hands. I swayed on my feet, suddenly feeling lightheaded as shards of glass splintered everywhere across the floor, mixed in with batteries, shattered pieces of the remote, and droplets of water. My stomach lurched as I stared at the picture of Remy Toussard, one of many images I avoided with a

284

passion. It rolled and flipped as my phone started ringing, and once it started, it didn't stop.

My head was swimming, eyes suddenly wouldn't focus, and I was going to be sick.

I sprinted to the bathroom and emptied my meager breakfast into the toilet, not pulling my head up again until my throat was raw. After I cleaned up, I stood in the mirror simply looking at myself for a long time, and I didn't like what I saw.

With my face scrubbed free of makeup and my hair pulled into a ponytail at the back of my head, I looked too young, I looked too fifteen years old. Too gullible, too vulnerable, too powerless to do anything to help myself.

Not important enough to my mother, not more important than chasing another Tony, or a Grammy, or a man, or a drink, or whatever other stupid shit she wanted that never should have held more value than being available for your daughter.

My doorbell started ringing and I cringed, hoping and praying that I wasn't already losing my privacy thanks to this "news" story. I washed my mouth out one more time, then flipped off the light and went to the door.

I checked the peephole first, and was relieved to see Dawn on the other side. I opened the door and quickly pulled her in, slamming the door shut behind her, and locking it.

"Mom, did you see what everybody is talking about?" she asked, frowning at the broken glass on the floor as she headed for the TV. "I was on my way over here, trying to catch you at home, when my phone just started blowing up.

Why are there pictures of me all over social media, side by side with Remy Toussard? Why am I a *meme* now?"

My lips parted to speak, but nothing came out. I just shook my head, searching my mind for what I could possibly say to my daughter about something like this.

Dawn's eyes were mired in confusion as she looked away from me, and back to the screen, where Wesley was recapping his story for anybody who may have missed it before, as if it weren't all over the internet by now. I watched her watch the TV, saw each little emotion – bewilderment, disgust, anger – play over her face. When he was done, Dawn turned to me, her expression twisted into … *something*, and she asked me, "Mama, is this *true*? A man I studied in film class? *This* is my father?"

"Tariq is the only thing even close to a father you've ever had, *not* that bastard."

Her eyes went wide. "So it *is* true? One of grandma's boyfriends? Mama, really?"

My stomach did another flip flop, and I held up a finger in her direction as I rushed to the bathroom again, erupting in dry heaves before my fingers touched the switch to flip the light on. I had nothing more to give, so after a few moments, I rinsed my mouth again and went back out to my living room to find it empty.

Dawn was gone.

Shit.

Shit, shit, shit.

I grabbed my phone, ignoring the missed calls and texts to call the theatre and cancel my meeting. When asked what reason I wanted to give, I said I was sick, which was true. The next call was to Dawn, but the line went straight to voicemail. She'd probably turned her phone off. *Shit.*

My stomach wouldn't stop turning and flipping, and after staring at my phone for a long moment, I concluded that I needed to call either Nubia, or Tariq.

Before I could decide, the phone started ringing again, and I lifted an eyebrow at the words displayed on the caller ID. My finger hovered over the answer button for a few seconds before I pressed it down, sliding it to the side to accept the call.

"H-hello?" I asked, hoping someone wasn't looking for something to sell for TMZ.

"Hi, is this Kora Oliver?"

I immediately recognized the voice, and perked up in response. "Yes, this is she."

"Hey Kora, this Dr. Morris, your OB. I'm calling personally to first of all, *sincerely* apologize, because the office had a major IT issue a couple of weeks ago that we *thought* was corrected, but apparently some of our appointments and recent patient information got wiped from the system. We've been going through our patient files calling everyone, trying to get back on track, and I see that you never came back in for your IUD replacement."

My stomach lurched again, and my mouth went dry. "I... *what?*"

"Your IUD, Kora. Your birth control? You didn't forget that you weren't protected right now?"

"I... yes."

I closed my eyes, thinking about how quick I'd been to ensure the presence of a condom with Paul. Protection was a must with anybody I was intimate with... except Tariq. I knew he was diligent about his sexual health, just as I was with mine, and I was on semi-permanent birth control. I didn't have to remember protection to not end up with a baby... until I did. Like now.

With the running of the show, excitement of being back with Tariq, reading new scripts,

serving as Dawn's manager until she hired one, etc, etc... that damned IUD hadn't crossed my mind at all.

Dr. Morris sucked in a sharp breath. "Okay. So would I be correct in assuming that there might a chance of pregnancy?"

Tears built behind my eyelids as I closed my eyes, nodding like she could see me. "Yes."

"Alright. Well, we aren't going to panic, okay? Let's get an appointment set up for you, for this afternoon. We can do a blood test, and see what's happening, and then depending on those results, in a few weeks – after we've tested you again – we can get your new IUD put in. Okay?"

"Okay. I'll see you later today."

"Okay. See you then."

There was silence on the line for a moment, and then my phone chimed to let me know

the call had ended as tears dripped down my face. I sank down onto my couch, with Wesley's voice still droning in the background, and my beautiful hardwood floors covered in glass. My heart was racing, and my chest was so tight I could barely breathe.

I dropped my head between my legs, trying my best to breathe deep. While I sucked in air, my eyes fell on my shoes. My gorgeous, *amazing* shoes. Beautiful black glitter Jimmy Choos, with satin ribbon ties at the ankles that reminded me of one of my first professional stage roles, as a ballerina. Tariq probably thought so too, and that was probably why he'd bought them, and left the pretty cream gift box on my bed. No note, just those great shoes, because today was supposed to be a great day.

But today was fucking *awful*.

I started sobbing, even though I could barely breathe, which obviously made it a little harder. My head was aching – swimming, practically, and I was just thinking that maybe it wouldn't be so bad to simply pass out when I heard my name.

I felt a hand on my back, rubbing in circles, and when I opened my eyes, Nubia was beside me. Instead of saying anything, she just held my hand, and kept rubbing my back while I worked through that round of tears. Afterwards, she pulled me into my bedroom and sat me down in front of the vanity. She stepped into the bathroom for a hot towel and then sat down beside me, using it to clean my face.

"Okay," she said, when my face was dry, and my breathing was as normal as it seemed like it was going to get. "Talk to me Kora. Tell me what's happening."

I pulled in a breath through my nose, then let it out as a sigh, shaking my head. I knew

289

she wasn't asking me to explain about Remy, because she already knew that story. She wanted to know how I was feeling, what I wanted her to do, what were the next steps, but there were no easy answers for *any* of that. I was just as lost as she was.

"I might be pregnant."

That was what came out of my mouth instead answering her question, and Nubia's eyes stretched wide. "Kora, what did you just say to me?"

"Preg-nant," I repeated, closing my eyes as I propped my elbows on the vanity, and dropped my head into my hands. "As in, with child. Knocked up. A bun in the oven. Expecting."

"Heifer I know what pregnant means. I'm saying *how*?"

Not looking up, I explained about the phone call from the doctor, and Nubia let out a

string of curse words. "You oughta sue that doctor's office. Is she even serious? Like, they market the thing with these happily *not* pregnant heifers talking about they can forget their birth control, which is fine until you need to remember the fucking birth control!"

"Same thing I thought," I mumbled.

I looked up as Nubia let out a grunt of disapproval. Her face was pulled into a frown, but as I watched, it softened into a more thoughtful expression. "I mean if you *were* pregnant would that really be that bad? You and Tariq love the hell out of each other, you're finally together now. You can certainly *afford* a child. Dawn is grown, and about to have her own money. It's really not the worst thing that could have happened."

I lifted an eyebrow at her. "A possible pregnancy in the midst of a paternity scandal where half the country is probably calling me a whore right now? You're really trying to figure out how to turn this into a positive?"

"Would you prefer a negative?"

"I'd prefer reality. Come on, Nubia. Can you imagine me telling Tariq, hey, we've been fucking willy nilly without protection because I was on great birth control. Only *oops!* I'm actually not! Surprise! You might be a daddy – biologically this time."

Nubia sucked her teeth. "Seriously? You know Tariq would step up."

"I don't want him to step up, I want him to *want* to have a baby, if we have a baby. You know how Tariq is. Progression in relationships is hard for him, period. I mean, it took him a year to warm up to you, and another what, two years for you guys to *really* be friends? And yes, we're together now, but I'm not expecting things with me to be much different. A title, a ring, a baby… I got into this knowing I may never get those things from him. I mean, of course I want them, but I know how he feels about me whether or not they happen. I've made my peace with it a long time ago, because I want *him*. And now this happens." I shook my head, then met Nubia's eyes in the mirror. "And I don't know what to do."

"That's what we're here for."

I expected a statement like that to come from Nubia, but the voice belonged to Tariq. We whipped around to see him standing in the doorway, and I practically tripped over myself getting up from the bench to get to him.

He pulled me into a warm embrace, rocking me back and forth. His lips pressed to my forehead, then the top of my head, before he spoke into my hair. "Why didn't you call me?" he asked. He drew back, tipping up my chin. "I had reporters showing up at my office, asking me for comment, and I had to google. And you're not answering your phone."

"I'm sorry, it's just been a little hectic."

He nodded, then kissed my forehead again before he turned to Nubia. "Thank you for coming to her."

I couldn't see her, but I heard Nubia scoff. "Nobody could have kept me away."

"I know," Tariq said, and I snuggled closer to him, soothed by the rumble of his voice. "So you hear that?" he asked, obviously directing the question at me. "Between me and Nubia, and we'll round up Stephen, and the Drakes. We'll take care of this. I overheard you telling her you don't know what to do, but you don't have to do anything. Tell us what you need."

If he'd overheard about the baby, I was sure he would have mentioned it. So that was a relief in itself, that one of these potential disasters could be put off until I had more information.

"Just find Dawn, please. Talk to her, make sure she's okay."

"Okay." He smiled at me, then swept his thumbs over my cheeks to wipe away the fresh round of tears that had started. "I've got you. *We've* got you. Okay?" I nodded, then dipped my head to lay against his chest again, and he wrapped his arms around me. "Nubia, call Gabi Lucas-Whitaker and find out what legal action we can take against Wesley David. Slander, harassment, whatever sticks. And call Chloe McKenna for me too please."

"The publicist?"

"Yeah. We have to figure out how to get ahead of this, before the lie festers into the accepted truth. Kora, baby?"

I raised my head again to meet his gaze, and he smiled me again. "I'm going to go find

Dawn. You stay here. Don't answer the phone unless it's me, Nubia, Steph, Chloe, Gabi, Dawn... you get it. Don't talk to any reporters, or anyone. Don't answer the door unless it's one of us either. I already have Fletch arranging some security, so you shouldn't be bothered. Later tonight, I want you to come to my place."

"Okay."

He kissed my forehead again. "Okay. We've got you. Remember that."

I nodded, and then he was gone, and Nubia was beside me, reaching to squeeze my hand.

"You didn't tell him about the appointment."

"Yeah. I don't want to give him something else to worry about."

She nodded. "I think you did the right thing." She leaned over, kissed my cheek, then pulled me into a hug. "I want you to lay down. You're shaking, and you look exhausted."

"Because I am. Late night, and then this *mess*."

"I'm getting on the phone. You lay down. I'll wake you for your appointment, and make sure you can get there safe, okay?"

I agreed, then sat down on the edge of the bed to take off my shoes. My head was swimming, mind running with the complications and problems, and possibilities of everything unfolding today.

My stomach lurched and flipped again, and I made myself push those thoughts away. I undressed while Nubia got my lawyer on the phone, and then crawled underneath the covers, closed my eyes, and willed myself to sleep.

nineteen.

Tariq

"Listen, I'm really not above breaking this dude's legs."

On the other end of the line, Steph chuckled. "T, come on. Didn't you almost get tossed in jail for fucking somebody up over Kora before?"

"Damn near fifteen years ago. It might be time to get physical again, cause I'm not letting this shit slide."

I'd done the best job I could of holding it together and appearing calm in front of Kora so I wouldn't add to the stress she had to be feeling already. But honestly? I wanted to do much worse to Wesley David than break his fucking legs. I wanted to rip his stupid ass in half for the shit he'd said about her.

"Just *chill*." That was Braxton Drake, who was on this phone call as an old friend, instead of the usual capacity of business. His twin brother, Lincoln, and our other friend, Dexter, were both on the line as well. We'd known each other since high school, and while all of us weren't as close as me and Steph, I knew these dudes had my back. That meant, by extension, that they had

Kora's back too.

"Yeah, Tariq," Dex spoke up, clearing his throat. "You know I'm not shy about laying hands when necessary," – Dex worked in personal security, the kind where his clients needed him for actual protection, and not just keeping paparazzi away – "But this involves Kora. It's a public spectacle, so we have to expect that any action we take against the little shrimpy white boy is going to be public knowledge."

Lincoln chimed in. "Exactly. You said her lawyer is Gabi Lucas-Whitaker, right? We know her. Brax and I had dinner with her and her husband last year about a hotel investment in

Atlanta. They're good people, great lawyers. Let them handle it. Hit this dude in his pockets, get that little bullshit show of his tossed off the air. Keep your angry ass out of jail, man."

With a heavy sigh, I leaned into the soft leather of my back seat, glad that I had Fletch available to drive, so I could focus on the million phone calls I needed to make. This was a damned nightmare.

"Yo, Tariq? Where you at, man? You're not on your way to old boy's house or anything are you?" Steph asked.

I clenched my hand into a fist. "Unfortunately no, but I wish. I'm trying to find Dawn. She's not at her apartment or the theatre, and she's not answering her phone. I've got one more place to look, and then after that I don't know."

Braxton groaned. "Okay, what about her friends?"

"Called them all that I could think of and had numbers for. I'm trying not to call Kora.

296

Nubia said she was sleeping, and I want to let her do that."

"Right, but why not ask Nubia? She could get Kora's phone, see if she has numbers for some of the ones you don't?"

I glanced out the window as the car slowed to a stop, and unclipped my seatbelt. "I need one of you to do that for me. Steph, I'm going to give you... wait, no. Braxton, I'm... shit, not you either. Lincoln or Dex, I'm going to give you Nubia's number. I need you to call her for me and get that information while I go talk to someone."

Lincoln and Dexter both confirmed, but Steph and Brax protested over them.

"Wait a damned minute," Steph said. "This is an emergency, and you're still not going to give me the girl's number?"

"Fuck no."

"And what about me? I've never even had the pleasure of meeting Nubia's fine caramel ass," Braxton added.

"Bye."

I hung up the phone and climbed out of the car, sending Lincoln and Dex Nubia's information in a group text between just the three of us as I walked to the front door. Fletch had successfully gotten us past the news vans and paparazzi at the front security gate which was normally wide open, but was closed today.

Before I could knock, the door swung open and Kathryn Oliver swept me with a steely gaze. Her eyes were bloodshot like she'd been crying, and though it was barely ten-thirty in the morning now, I could distinctly smell bourbon on her breath.

"I'm guessing you've heard what's happening on the news?" she asked, wrapping the long, thick sweater she wore around herself a little tighter, and *not* inviting me in.

I nodded. "That's why I'm here."

She narrowed her eyes at me. "It's not a good time, obviously, Mr. Evans. What can I do for you?"

"You can't do shit for me." She flinched, and I almost regretted snapping at her, and then I remembered that this was her fault in the first place. "I'm not here for you to do anything for me. I want – I *expect*—you to do something for Kora."

Her eyes narrowed a little further, and I caught the subtle movement as her hand tightened around the doorknob. "Something like what? The truth is out. I can't do anything about it anymore."

"The truth?" My face pulled into a disgusted scowl. "You and I both know the story that man spun for millions of people to see is *not* the truth."

Kathryn huffed. "The man is dead, Tariq! He has children, and a widow. You don't speak ill of the dead, and tarnish their lega—"

"I don't give a damn about that piece of shit's legacy!"

She started to swing the door shut in my face, but I stepped forward, blocking it with my arm. Kathryn stumbled backwards, catching herself on the table just inside the foyer. I took the opportunity to invite myself inside.

"I hoped," I started, "that when I came here, you would be contrite. That you would, for once in your pitiful fucking life, put your daughter ahead of yourself."

"Get out of my house!"

"Gladly. *After* you hear me. Kora came to you and told you that motherfucker was touching her after you moved him into your house with her. I know she told you because I was in her room, hiding in her closet after convincing her to tell you. She was scared. Thought you'd be mad at her, thought you'd be depressed because maybe it meant your goddamned boyfriend was going away, but no, that's not what I heard. I heard you tell your fifteen year old to stop being a slut, stop making up stories, stop *flirting* with Remy and it wouldn't happen, as if your *teenaged little girl* had any control over that grown assed man! And what happened? He did it again. She called me, from that very same closet, fucking crying and sobbing, because he'd taken it further, and she was hiding from him."

"I *know* what happened."

"Obviously not, since you said Wesley told the "truth"! Instead of being protected by the person that brought her into this world, she had to call the teenaged boy next door to save her. *I* broke your front door down. *I* pulled that motherfucker off of her. *I* tried to stomp his damn head in the ground. *I* protected her! And what the fuck did *you* do?"

"I made it so that she could live with the aftermath!" Kathryn screamed, jabbing a finger in my direction. "Yes, I
299

messed up! I didn't do right by my daughter at first, because I didn't *get* what she was saying to me! She called me into her room after I'd just gotten in from a party, and you know what those parties were like in the nineties, and I was... I wasn't myself." Kathryn's voice trembled as she spoke, and right in front of me, she began to shake, but I didn't feel a single ounce of sympathy for her. "The next day... I thought she had to have made it up. Or I imagined it, because she didn't say anything about it again."

"Because you accused her first of lying, then just being a whore. So maybe *that's* why your daughter wouldn't want to bring it up to again."

"I know that! I know. I messed up. But I didn't think Remy would *do* something like that, he was such a good man, and—"

"Good men don't molest people. Good men keep their fucking hands to themselves."

"I *know*." Kathryn sank against the wall, shaking her head. "When I realized what was really happening though, when it couldn't be denied, I tried my best to make it right. I got rid of him, I supported Kora's decision to keep the baby—"

"That's not true," I interrupted, shaking my head. "Can you just tell the fucking truth, *please*? You didn't want Kora to have that baby because you knew how it would look, that your teenager was pregnant. You were worried about your fucking image, which is why you did whatever you did to make that assault charge against me disappear, and Remy ended up in

300

Europe somewhere, across the damned planet."

"I wanted what was best for her."

"You wanted what was best for *you*. When you couldn't make her get rid of it, you let the public believe Kora's pregnancy was just youthful indiscretion, and made yourself look like mother of the year for being so supportive while Kora started a career. Taking care of the baby while she went rehearsals, paying for classes, such a goddamned humanitarian. You were covering your own ass."

"I was doing what I could!"

I scoffed. "You didn't do *enough*. You can't make up for not believing your daughter, not supporting her when she needed you. Why do you think she can't even be in the same room with you for long periods? Why do you think she barely talks to you, tells you nothing about her

personal life?" I took a step closer, bent a little so that I was at eye level with her. "Kathryn... why do you think she stepped away from her career when you got married and started bringing your ex-husband around her daughter? She didn't trust you to protect her little girl because you didn't protect *her*. She only tolerates you because she feels like you did at least *try* to make up for what you didn't do. But that easy love, that friendship that you see between Kora and Dawn?

You'll never have that with her. And it's because of *you*."

Kathryn swallowed hard, and fixed me with a glare. "What is your point, Mr. Evans?"

"To make you understand that you haven't done nearly enough to cite Remy Toussard's 'legacy' as a reason to not speak up for your daughter. But you know what? Just the fact that bullshit like that came out of your mouth lets me know you're a lost cause." I turned to leave, then thought better of it. "Do you know where Dawn is?"

Kathryn's eyes went wide. "What?"

"Your granddaughter. Dawn. Do you know where she is?"

Kathryn slowly shook her head, then stopped. "Actually, yes. Maybe. She had an interview today."

"An interview?"

"Yes," Kathryn nodded. "Another one of those internet things. She sent me the link, and the time she was going to be on last night."

"When is it?"

"Ten-thirty." *Shit.*

"Where is your computer?" Kathryn looked confused, so I asked her again. "Your computer, where you were going to watch the interview. It's after eleven, so the interview started a while ago. Where is it?"

"Oh! The kitchen. It's set up in the kitchen."

I darted into her kitchen, with her right behind me. Her laptop was open, and already on the website where Dawn's interview was taking place. The volume was turned down, but Dawn was already on the screen, along with the duo who ran the popular blog – Arnez and Arizona.

Dawn looked subdued. Her eyes were normally bright, sparkling with energy, but today, she was visibly deflated. She was smiling though, and as I turned up the volume, her voice sounded clear, and even. Even with things crumbling around her, she was poised, and polished.

"So, Ms. Oliver," Arnez, the male half of the duo said, leaning towards her. "We're at the end of our time here. We are fans of yours here at Arnez and Arizona, and have seen *The Chase* about five times between the two of us. Your interview with us has been scheduled for about a

month prior to today's filming, and we can't thank you enough for agreeing to do it, and for following through. But we also have a duty to *our* fans. Now, you can tell us to shut the fuck up and mind our business chile, and we won't be mad, but we *do* have to ask… did you see the news report on that *show that must not be named* this morning?"

Dawn swallowed hard, then nodded. "Unfortunately, I did. And I have to say that I'm disappointed and disgusted by it. And a little confused as to why something that's so incredibly personal, and happened so long ago would become the headlining news on that show. It's gross."

"Agreed," Arizona chimed in, flipping her hair over her shoulder. "I wanted to reach in my screen and snatch his ass."

"Honey you and me both." Arnez shook his head. "So can you tell us how you feel about the allegations that the acclaimed "Mr. Black Hollywood" is your father?"

Dawn ran her tongue over her lips. "Well I have no comment about the allegations themselves, because I have no facts as it comes to that. But looking at the information Wesley gave on his show, I'm a little grossed out that my

303

mother, who was a young teenager at the time, is being portrayed as the villain here. She was *fifteen*. He was damn near forty. Now, Mr.

Toussard is no longer alive, and I don't feel comfortable commenting on him directly. But to me – and maybe I'm wrong, but I don't think I am – a forty year old man who does anything of a sexual nature to his girlfriend's daughter is disgusting, and a criminal. And that young girl is a victim, not a *vixen*, or the villain. The adults in that – hypothetical—situation failed her, and I think it's beyond gross that the scrutiny is falling on her."

Dawn had been easing forward in her chair as she spoke, the natural motion that came with impassioned words. When she was done speaking, she sat back, looking a little unsure of herself, but Arnez and Arizona broke into applause.

"*Yaaassss,* girl! Come through with the clapback for your – hypothetical – mama!" Arnez exclaimed, waving a hand in the air. "Dawn Oliver, honey you are fine, you are talented, you are sweet, and look at *Gawd*, your common sense is on fleek!"

Dawn laughed, but Arizona nodded. "I know that's right, because among your age group, common sense is seeming less and less common. So guess who wins our "You Better *Werk* Bitch!" award? That's right, little miss Dawn!'

"And I *know* you don't have to ask who wins the "Ugh! Bitch Why Are You So Damned

Wack?" award!" Arnez added. "Boom! You guessed it. You was right! None other than Wesley

David. I mean, we're all out here trying to be taken seriously, your little mediocre ass gets a show on major television, and *that's* what you do with it? I mean, we may not have degrees, but there *is* a little something called journalistic integrity, and you need to find it." "He tried it." Arizona pursed her lips, shaking her head.

"Tried the fuck out of it." Arnez let out a heavy sigh, then turned to face the camera and began their final comments for the show.

I turned the volume down, then turned to Kathryn, who was clutching a glass half full of dark brown liquid in her hand, even though she was already looking a little wavy on her feet.

"You see that," I asked, taking a step toward her. "That twenty year old girl understands this shit better than you. I hope you have enough decency to be ashamed of yourself."

I didn't say shit else to Kathryn, or even look her way again as I left. I climbed into the back of the Range Rover as I checked my phone for new information. I ignored the stuff from social media, then navigated to my texts to send Dawn a message.

"Proud of you. Thank you for being on your mother's side."
She texted me back almost immediately.

"Who else's side would I be on? Is that stuff true? Mama was a wreck this morning,
I couldn't deal... - Princess D."

"Everything YOU said was true. For now, if you have questions, you can ask me. Let's give your mother some space with the details on this topic."

"I don't have any questions. I can pretty much put it together, and I know enough.

That man has nothing to do with me. I have a daddy ☺ -- Princess D."

I grinned, then texted her back. *"Damn right, let these people know. And go see your mother. She NEEDS to see you. I'll be there later."*

"Going now. – Princess D."

~

It was starting to get a little late when I arrived at Kora's building. I was relieved to see that thanks to the security I'd arranged through Fletch – who'd reached out to Dex – there weren't any photographers or reporters waiting outside.

Kora's apartment was mostly dark when I stepped into it, but I easily found her in her room, curled up in the bed. Her eyes were open and the TV was on, streaming *Chicago!* but I doubted she was watching. She sat up when she saw me in the door, and I took a seat beside her on the bed.

"Where's Dawn?" I asked, glancing at the empty space on the other side of her. I'd have expected a bed full of candy wrappers and ice cream between the two of them.

306

"Guest bedroom. She went in there to sleep. Said I was "probably going to want be with her *real* father, and she didn't want to see or hear us being nasty." Exact words."

I laughed, then pulled Kora toward me, and she curled into my lap. "How are you feeling?"

"Better. It still feels surreal, honestly. Doesn't even seem like this only started this morning, but I don't want to jump out of the window anymore, so there's that."

"Good."

There was a short moment of silence before Kora sighed, then turned her face up toward mine. "I talked to my mother. She called me, drunk, crying. Swore you nearly killed her."

"I didn't—"

"I *know*." She shook her head, and laughed. "That woman is… something. She says she's going to release a statement. Remy's estate did."

My eyes went wide. "Seriously? Saying *what*?"

"Well Remy's family distanced themselves, as expected. Some stuff about past mistakes. And they released donation records, showing that they've been making sizable contributions to charities that offer resources for abused teenagers, ever since Remy died a few years ago. So… somebody in that family knew."

"Definitely. Maybe that "natural causes" death wasn't so natural."

Kora gave a dreamy sigh. "Oh, if only. A girl can dream, right?"

I chuckled. "And what about your mother?"

307

She sucked her teeth. "Oh please. I'm not holding my breath for that. Kathryn is as selfish as they come, and I doubt she'll be making a statement until she can convince the world *she* is the victim in this. But whatever. You heard my baby's interview, right?"

She had such a big smile on her face that I couldn't help smiling back if I wanted to. "Yeah. She sounded like somebody raised her right."

"Didn't she? And not just the scandal. The whole interview was amazing."

I raised a hand to stroke her face. "Well, she has an amazing mother. How could she be anything but amazing herself?"

Something about my words made the smile drop from Kora's face, and she sat up, sliding into the space beside me instead of my lap. "I went and got a blood test done today. Nubia snuck me out, and back in afterwards."

I lifted an eyebrow. "Why did you need a blood test?"

Kora scraped her teeth over her bottom lip, then met my gaze with glossy eyes. "To see if

I was pregnant."

It took me a second to process those words, and even after that, I shook my head, confused. "Pregnant… why would you be pregnant? You've had an IUD for the longest time." She took a deep breath, and then explained what had occurred, but I was still baffled. "It's only been two weeks, don't you need longer than that to find out?"

"Not with a blood test. With those, they can tell as soon as eight days."

"Oh. Okay. So…?"

"No. But I have to get tested again in two weeks just to be sure, and then we'll get the IUD put back in. I don't think I'm pregnant though. At least I didn't feel like it. It's just precautionary."

I nodded. "Okay. Okay. Um… That's good, right? I mean you didn't *want* to be pregnant, did you?"

She tipped her head to the side at me. "Uhh, hell no," she laughed. "I've been thinking about it all day, and I do *not* need a baby. I'm 36, with a grown daughter, extremely busy, and I like to drink. I don't think a baby is a good idea. But if that test had been positive, I…" – she sighed. "When that test *wasn't* positive. I was a little sad. I'm still a little sad, because while I would love to make a baby with you, it's really not ideal anymore. And when I think about the time we wasted, it's sad. And besides that, do you even *want* kids?"

I let out a breath. "I don't *not* want kids. I've only ever really considered the possibility with one person, who I've loved for a long time. But then I think about my mother, and the chances of mental illness being hereditary, and I stop considering it. But it's a small chance. It's just a *tiny* chance, and if the love of my life wants me to start considering it again, before it's too late to consider it—"

"No." Kora covered my hands with hers, and leaned into me, resting her head on my shoulder. "I do *not* want a child bad enough to put you through that kind of worry for the rest of your life. We *have* a child. A great child." She raised her mouth, planted a kiss against my jaw. "Condoms, until I get my IUD back in."

"And what if you're pregnant now? What if it's just too early to tell?"

Kora sighed again. "Then we'll have to figure it out. I am *so* sorry."

"Stop it," I said, pulling her back into my lap to straddle my legs. "If you're pregnant, then I guess we're having a baby. And more than likely, it's going to be fine."

"You're only saying that because you love me."

"You are absolutely right," I chuckled. "Because I came over here thinking I was going to be consoling you, and now I'm fucking terrified. We're almost forty, Kora. We don't have any business with a baby."

She smiled. "That's true."

"But it'll still be fine."

"Cause you say so?"

"Damn right." I brought my hands up to cup her ass, and squeezed. "So aside from possible pregnancy, how are you feeling?"

"You asked me that already."

"I'm asking again."

She smiled. "Exhausted. Angry. Embarrassed. Grateful. Horny."

"Uh-uh," I scolded, shaking my head. "I don't want to hear about your horniness when we can't get down."

"Yes we can," she laughed. "I *need* to get down. Somebody just has to get condoms."

310

"I'm not using a condom with you. Are you crazy? I'll pull out."

She sucked her teeth. "I do *not* trust you to pull out."

"You shouldn't."

"Y'all, *ugggh!*" I pulled my eyes away from Kora to see Dawn standing in the open doorway, arms crossed, face pulled into a scowl. "I come to check on mama, and this is the conversation I walk up on?"

Kora smirked. "Learn how to knock then little girl."

"The door was open!"

"Then close your eyes and ears," I said, fighting not to laugh. "And you may want to move on, unless you want to hear me remind your mama that we have fingers and mouths we can use to—"

"*Ewwwww!*"

Dawn tossed us one last grossed-out look, then reached in to grab the doorknob to pull it closed. When she was gone, Kora and I looked at each other and broke into a laugh, which lasted until she grabbed the sides of my face, holding me still.

"Now that we have some privacy, tell me more about what you plan to do to me with your mouth."

twenty.

Kora

We need to speak with you regarding your future with
Warm Hues theatre.

Out of all the lines in the email from the board of
directors, that one stood out.

A blur of a week had gone by since that completely
shitty day, where Wesley David had decided to take his
pettiness to a whole new level. Those seven days had passed
by in a blur or avoided calls, dodged paparazzi, and a nice
little lawsuit for harassment and slander, which honestly, I
should have done before.

But hey, no time like the present, right?

When the story first broke, I was shocked. It seemed
crazy to me that Wesley and his team could have figured it
out on their own, so I searched my mind for the people who
could

have possibly said something. My mother, Tariq's
grandparents, Tariq, Nubia, or Remy himself. Remy was too
dead to divulge any secrets, and whoever in his family had
made that statement and those donations... I somehow
doubted they would have shared the information in the first
place. I even briefly considered Paul as the culprit, but I'd

313

never shared even a little bit of that story with him. No one else who knew would have said anything, I was sure.

And, then I realized the obvious.

In simply *looking* at Dawn, and comparing her to Remy, she honestly did look like him. Not enough that I saw him when I looked at her – because I tried very hard not to think of him at all – but enough that some dogged journalist looking for a break in a story could have pretty easily laid out those facts. And when I thought about it like that, it was kind of amazing that it hadn't been figured out before.

But it was out *now*. And it was out in a big, big way. The scandal – if I could call it that – was driving ticket sales, trending topics, and a lot of debate, despite the fact that everyone was working on speculation, because I had not, and would not, publicly address it. The problem with that was that while a lot of people were talking about me and Dawn, they were *not* talking about *The Chase*.

The furor surrounding Dawn's parentage and my teenaged feminine wiles – or lack thereof – was overshadowing the show, and the theatre. And the board of directors wanted to talk about it.

I wasn't stupid.

That email meant my job was in jeopardy.

I showed up to the meeting in brand new shoes, because new shoes made me feel good. Jeweled Miu Miu pumps made me feel *great*. I walked in with my head held high, sat down in the appointed chair. I crossed my legs, squared my shoulders, and looked around, smiling at the members of the board I personally knew.

314

This job, as head director of the theatre, had been good to me. I really couldn't imagine losing it over something that happened *to* me more than twenty years ago, but I understood that

above everything, this was a business. They had to protect the theatre's interests, even if that meant getting rid of me.

I felt eyes burning into me, as my gaze continued around the table, but I didn't rush. I wanted to appear cool, collected, whatever little advantage I could get that would contribute to my worth as head director. Finally, I got to the other side of the table.

My heart slammed to the front of my chest when my gaze landed on Julissa.

Her lips were painted a deep purple, and with her dark hair falling around her shoulders in waves, she looked distinctly witchy. Or maybe it was the evil smirk she wore as she raked her eyes over me, then cut them away like she was bored.

I kept my expression pleasant.

No matter how hard I wanted to roll my eyes, or flip her off, it wouldn't be good for the reason I was here, so I kept myself composed. A few moments later, the meeting was called to order.

"First of all, I want to thank everyone for coming," Nashira Haley spoke up from her seat near the other end of the table. She served as speaker, and coordinated most of these meetings.

Not to mention, she was Braxton and Lincoln Drake's married baby sister. She smiled in my direction, and gave me a subtle nod that warmed my heart. If nobody else was on my side, I knew Nash was.

"We have a special guest with us today, Ms. Julissa Santos, who is filling in for Adam North while he's on an international vacation. Adam and Julissa work together at the same law firm, and share a love of theater, so he has asked her to sit in."

Well isn't this some bullshit...

"In any case," Nashira said, casting a smile around the table, "We don't want to be here very long, so I will get straight to the point. As we all know, there has been some recent controversy in the news surrounding our incredibly talented head show director," – she gestured toward me, and Julissa rolled her eyes – "And that controversy has bled over into the press about *The Chase*, and into the reputation of our theatre. Now, while *I* don't see it becoming an issue, and think this is a waste of our, and Ms. Oliver's time... per our bylaws, this is an occasion where we have to consider whether or not to retain her as a valuable resource to Warm Hues

Theatre."

That declaration hit me like a sledgehammer to the chest, even though I was expecting it.

I did my very best to keep my expression impassive, but inside, I wanted to burst into tears.

"What exactly does that mean?" one of the other members asked, and Nashira gave a little sigh.

316

"It means that we will – at a later date, a week from now – be voting on whether or not

Kora will remain as our head director."

Julissa's hand shot up in the air like a kindergartner, and Nashira narrowed her eyes at her a little before she motioned for her to ask her question.

"Why do we have to wait until next week? Can't we just get this over with now? I already know my vote."

Nashira chewed at her lip as she looked at Julissa, then pressed her hand to her temple and rubbed. "Um... the whole point of this is to go through proper channels. If it wasn't for that, we wouldn't be having this meeting at all."

"You mean if it were up to you?"

That question was posed from yet another member of the board, a woman I didn't really know, but also, for some reason, had never really liked. Now I knew why.

Bitch.

"Yes, that's *exactly* what I mean, because this is ridiculous. Kora has been invaluable to us, and has served us well. There's no reason for this beyond politics and paperwork." "And fairness," yet another Debbie Downer chimed in.

Lord, I'm going to get voted out because these people don't like Nashira.

"Okay." Nashira smacked her palms together, clasping them in front of her as she pressed her lips into a tight line. "I think we're done for the day here. Unless... Kora, do you have something you'd like to say to us, that we need to take into consideration for our votes?"

My eyes went wide. "I… uh… just that I hope that the work I've done, and would like to keep doing, will be the determining factor in whether I'm allowed to retain my position or not. When I took this job, I anticipated a long tenure here, putting forth a lot of great shows, and helping Warm Hues create new trends, and expand the level of artistry that we're known for. Please don't allow something from my past that was incredibly… that I worked hard to put behind me… I don't want to continue to be affected by that. Please."

Nashira gave me a supportive smile, and nodded. "Very well said. Thank you. We'll be in touch."

~

Tariq

"I keep on trying to tell you to leave those young ass girls alone, Steph. They're trouble."

"And perky titties."

I chuckled as Stephen and I stepped off the elevator on my floor, heading toward my office. We'd just left a business lunch with the Drakes, and on the walk back to the building, he'd been sharing the details of his latest "dating" adventure.

"No titties are perky enough for *that*," I teased, gesturing toward the deep purple bruise around his eye, spreading across his dark golden-brown skin.

Steph scoffed. "Oh the titties weren't, but the head definitely was. Probably why her boyfriend was so pissed, I'd be stingy with a mouth like that too. I almost felt bad kicking his ass after he got that sucker punch off on me."

"See there? Young girls. Trouble."

"Hell, the ones our age are too," Steph said. "Speaking of, here comes Julissa, and she looks *mad*."

"What?" I stopped in my tracks. "Where?"

Instead of answering the question, he busted out laughing, causing several people to look in our direction. "I'm just fucking with you man, but that was a good response. Never know where she might pop up, got to always be ready."

"Whatever Steph," I chuckled, nodding at the receptionist as we stepped through the door of Evans Foster, our personal and business finance firm. "That shit wasn't funny. I'm out here trying not to catch a sucker punch like you did, and you're making jokes."

I walked to the door of my office and pulled the handle, but it wouldn't budge.

"Did I lock this when we left?" I asked Steph, fishing my keys out of my pocket.

He shrugged. "I don't remember."

I looked thoughtfully at my keys, trying to recall, then brushed it off. I rarely remembered to do it since we had a receptionist, and I didn't keep anything sensitive in the office anyway. I was *trying* to turn it into a habit though, so maybe I'd actually done it today.

In any case, I unlocked the door and stepped in. It was still the middle of the day, right after lunch, so light streamed in through the sheer window coverings, saturating my office in warm sun. The handle of my laptop case slipped out of my hand, and my mouth dropped open.

My eyes went wide, taking in the sight of toned legs spread open right on top of my desk. Graceful, manicured fingers gripped the hem of her dress, pulling it up inch by inch, giving me a perfect view of missing panties and—

"Daaamn, Kora!"

Shit.

I'd been so enthralled by the sight in front of me that I forgot Steph was with me. I turned around and shoved him out of the office, closing the frosted glass door behind him and turning the lock. When I turned towards Kora, several little plastic packets hit me in the face and chest, and in a husky voice that immediately made my dick hard, she said, "Get over here. Now."

I glanced down at the packets on the floor, chuckling when I realized they were condoms.

"So that's how you're feeling today, huh?" I left the wrappers on the floor and sauntered over to stand between her legs.

Her hands immediately went to my belt, deftly opening it before she attacked my pants.

"After that meeting, yes. This is how I'm feeling."

"So it didn't go well?"

Kora opened my pants, then immediately slid her hands into my boxer briefs to palm my ass. "Don't want to discuss it right now." Her eyes were a little glossy when I met her gaze, but she shook her head. "Less talking, more of you getting undressed."

"I have a meeting in forty minutes."

"Then I guess you'd better be careful not to wrinkle your clothes."

My eyebrow hiked up at those words, and I stepped back, smirking as I undressed – carefully – and draped my clothes across the chair in front of the desk. Kora seemed much less concerned than I did – she snatched her dress over her head and tossed it across the floor, along with her bra.

"*Come onnnn,*" she groaned, arching her back up in a way that made her breasts bob in the air. She ran her tongue over her lips as her eyes landed on my dick, but I took my time getting back to her. I touched her knee first, then ran one finger over her soft skin, trailing it up her thigh.

I planted one hand on the desk beside her, then slid the other up her stomach, squeezing her breast before I continued upward. My fingers went to the back of her neck, while my thumb grazed her throat. She gasped a little when I tightened my grip, then leaned into me.

"This is how you want it?" I asked, smirking when I felt the pulse of her throat under my thumb as she swallowed hard.

"Yes."

"Right here on the desk?"

"Yes. *Please.*"

321

I moved my free hand from the desk, then pushed her thighs to spread her a little wider.

The sadness that I'd seen in her eyes before was gone, replaced by heated desire as I slipped my fingers between her legs. She held my gaze as I moved them inside her, and bit down on her bottom lip. I pressed my thumb to her clit, but didn't move it, letting the simple pressure make her throb around me. A little shiver wracked her body as I plunged my fingers deep, hooking them towards the front of her body.

Her legs were already starting to tremble when I lowered my head, trailing my tongue from her collarbone up to her ear. She whimpered as I pulled her earlobe between my teeth, sucking on it before I let it free.

"You don't think this is a little inappropriate, gorgeous?" I murmured into her ear, using my hold on her neck to pull her closer to me. "Coming to my office, showing my pussy to

Stephen..."

"I couldn't wait." She squirmed against me as I pushed another finger into her, and I moved to check the expression on her face before I responded.

Pure bliss.

"Couldn't wait for what?"

"*You.*"

Her chest was starting to heave, breath coming in short pants as tension built in her body. She closed her eyes, letting her head fall backwards as her legs began to jerk and she arched into me. She vocalized her pleasure in high

322

pitched little moans that got louder and louder until I had to cover her mouth with mine, swallowing her scream as she came all over my fingers.

I was inside her before she even opened her eyes, buried deep enough to let out a yelp I knew people outside had to have heard, but I didn't care. That was one of the perks of working for your damned self.

"Tariq," she said, breathlessly, digging her nails into my biceps. "We're supposed to be using a—"

"Don't worry about it. I've got you." I started stroking her harder. Fast, deep strokes to help her clear her head. Before I knew it, she was giving it right back to me, rocking and rotating her hips to fit my rhythm as I moved.

I dipped my head, tasting and teasing her nipples, tugging them between my teeth, flicking them with my tongue. Her hands went to my head, tangling in my locs as I sucked her breasts, relishing the taste and smell of her skin as we made love.

I brought my mouth back to hers, and she moved her hands to my face, slipping her tongue between my lips. She kissed me like she was marking her territory, nibbling and licking and sucking and I loved every second of it, because hell yes, I *was* hers. I'd been waiting a long time for this.

"Thank you," she whispered against my lips, then moaned as I hooked her legs around my waist to get deeper. "You have no idea how bad I needed this."

I grinned, and smacked her ass before I squeezed a handful on each side. "*Any* time."

She buried her face in my neck, and I felt the change in her body as she neared an orgasm. I held out just long enough to feel her melt in ecstasy around me before I plunged into her one last time, then pulled out, spilling the results of my climax over her pretty brown skin.

When she caught her breath long enough to realize what I'd done, she rolled her eyes at me, even though I could tell she was fighting a smile. She leaned back on her elbows on the desk, lifting her eyebrow at her stomach and legs. "My love, you don't think *this* is a little inappropriate?"

Before I could make a smart response, she ran her fingers through it and then licked her hand, looking me right in the eyes while she did it. My dick sprang back into attention, and she smirked as I reached for her, quickly maneuvering herself away from me and off the desk.

"Don't you have a meeting in like ten minutes?"

Shit.

A second round would take way longer than that.

I scowled as I followed her into the private bathroom to clean up, and then back into the office to get dressed again. Kora pulled a little silver can from her purse, and sprayed it in the air before she put her bra back on.

"What the hell is that?" I asked, sniffing as I pulled on my pants and boxers.

"Room spray." I watched her ass cheeks move as she took a few steps to get to her dress. "Nubia's idea when I told her what I was coming to do. To get the sex smell out of the air." "And what about the ass print on the desk?"

She stopped pulling her dress on to roll her eyes. Once it was on, and she'd smoothed it out a little, she walked back to her purse, digging around for a second before she tossed me a pack of antibacterial disinfectant wipes that I had to stop tucking in my shirt to catch.

"I came prepared, baby."

I laughed as she stepped back into her shoes, which had come off at some point during our little escapade. "I see. Meeting must have been pretty rough."

She cut her eyes at me, then pulled her purse up on her shoulder and crossed her arms. "It honestly wasn't the worst meeting I've ever been in, but I'm really, really concerned about the aftermath. They're talking about firing me because of this Remy thing, when I didn't do anything wrong, and it was twenty years ago."

"That's fucking stupid," I said, stepping into my shoes. "You've done big things for Warm Hues, they can't let you go because of this. The board knows better. I don't think they're going to do something like that."

Kora shook her head. "I'm not so sure. For one, it seems like all the female members of the board suddenly hate Nashira. They might vote against me just to avoid voting *with* her."

"Why don't they like Nash? She's cool as hell."

"Tariq, take a wild guess."

I picked up my tie, and just looked at her for a second, confused, before realization dawned on me. "Ohhh. Braxton."

"I'm sure. He was at the theatre opening for sure, and Nubia said she saw at least *one* of these women all over him, so, sucks for me."

"I'm sure they won't be that petty."

Kora sucked her teeth. "Oh *please*. Are you kidding? Women – and *men* for that matter – will absolutely be that petty when they feel played. And uh, speaking of scorned women, your little bitter ass hot tamale got herself a temporary place on the board, and has voting privileges.

So, again, sucks for me."

My eyes went wide, and my hands paused over the knot to my tie. "Julissa?"

She nodded. "Julissa. And if I lose my job? I'm dragging *her* ass first, because she was super eager to vote, and I know it will be against me, even though *I* didn't do anything to her."

"Baby, I'm sor—"

Kora waved her hand, brushing me off. "Whatever. I don't want to think about it anymore, or I'm going to lose my *amazing* sex high. I just want to focus on that, okay? And when you get home tonight…"

My dick jumped as she ran her tongue over her lips again, and I released my hold on my tie to cross the room and pull her against me. My hands went down to her ass, cupping and squeezing again as a knock sounded at the door.

"Looks like time is up," she whispered, pulling her lip between her teeth.

I groaned. "Yeah. Hey, you're not wearing any panties right now are you?" I asked, running my hands over her ass again to confirm.

"Well, I was wearing them when I snuck past your receptionist and got in here."

The knock sounded again, and I ignored it. "And where are they now?"

Kora pulled herself out of my arms to walk to the door. She glanced meaningfully around my office, then smiled as she pulled the door open.

"Let me know when you find them."

twenty-one.

Kora

Tariq's place was perfect for an intimate event.

Easily twice the size of mine – for no good reason – his gorgeous downtown condo, with big windows and a beautiful view of the city was the perfect backdrop for a celebration.

My baby girl's birthday.

It honestly felt like it had come out of nowhere, but with everything going on, it had been the last thing on any of our minds, including Dawn. She seemed surprised when I asked her about her plans, and *I* was surprised when she told me she didn't have any. I was almost certain her lack of enthusiasm was related to Donovan.

She was, to my delight, taking the news about her father in stride. I think a lot of that could be attributed to Tariq's presence in her life, filling that role so she'd never felt it was something she lacked. And that was just one more thing to thank him for.

I, on the other hand, was still pretty rattled.

Luckily for me, now that *The Chase* had been running smoothly for almost two months, my responsibilities as director were drastically scaled back. And anything that needed to be done, Micah could handle it, which meant that I

329

could avoid going to the theatre at all. I preferred staying at home, and hiding myself away from the paparazzi. I was sure most members of the board preferred that too, since I'd not yet received an answer on the status of my employment. Two days.

That's all that was left before they put my fate to a vote, and my head was still swimming with the choices surrounding that. Did I even *want* to stay at a place that would hold such a thing against me? If I got fired, what would that mean for my reputation? Would this one thing blackball me from the world of theatre?

I *had* to not think about that though. It made me feel a little better to focus on the positive

things that had happened since then, like the amazing support I'd received from my old friends and colleagues. So many of them, on being asked about the scandal, had lent their voices to a much needed conversation about the vilification of victims of sexual assault, and the completely ridiculous idea that teenagers were actually capable of seducing grown ass non-pedophile men.

Even Paul, who I didn't believe was mad at me, but certainly wasn't expected to come to my defense, had verbally destroyed a nasty reporter who tracked him down and insinuated that I had, since a teenager, "gone after" men with money.

And the support wasn't the only thing. The ferocity and speed that Gabi Lucas-Whitaker had let loose on Wesley David had him running scared. Not only had the episode of the show been removed from the air and scrubbed from his

330

social media accounts, I had it on good authority that the network was strongly considering a complete removal of his show, after the backlash they'd received from allowing it to air. His team reached out to us with a formal apology, and even posted it online, but I didn't give a shit, and neither did Dawn. She and I were in agreement regarding his bullshit apology: we didn't accept.

Dawn had doubled down on her statement of support from the show she'd done with Arnez and Arizona. She took a moment to speak for me in a roundabout way – when asked how I was feeling, she replied with "upset and disgusted", which was accurate. And, it was the only little bit they'd ever get from me, because I still refused to offer a public response. Chloe – the publicist – wasn't thrilled about it, but she understood. I had no desire to be prodded and questioned about something I wanted to forget. If she wanted to do things to "guide the conversation", fine. I just wanted to move forward in the peace I'd finally found. With things like this dinner party.

When I stepped into his condo, an hour before the party was due to start, it was swirling with activity. An attractive woman in jeans, casual blazer, and a white tee-shirt with *Posh Petals* emblazoned across the front smiled at me, and approached with her hand extended and a beautifully styled tray of white roses and purple dahlias under her arm.

"Simone Taylor," she said, as I accepted her hand. "From the flower boutique."

"Nice to meet you. Kora Oliver."

Her face spread into a big smile. "I know. I'm a *huge* fan." Internally, I cringed, but she held up a hand in a soothing manner. "Don't worry though, I'm not about get all weird on you, I just I think you and your daughter are both amazing, and my husband and I have seen *The Chase* twice, and so have our friends." *Whew.*

I smiled back, and nodded. "Thank you so much."

"You are *beyond* welcome. Now if you'll follow me, we're almost done setting the dining room up for your approval. You got here at the perfect time!"

I lifted an eyebrow. "*My* approval?"

"Yes," she nodded. "Mr. Evans said the lady of the house would have to approve of everything before we left. That's you, right?"

My lips parted, and I stammered a little before I finally just said, "Yes. I guess so."

She led me through the condo to Tariq's huge dining room, which led out to the pool. The sun was going down, which helped provide some contrast for the flickering candles that lined the middle of a sixteen-seat table, separated by large flower arrangements like the one Simone had in her hands.

Lighted branches lined the room, projecting purple and white stars onto the textured black wallpaper, and larger arrangements of the roses and dahlias were strategically placed. A huge white cake sat in the corner, decorated with purple and silver feathers made of sugar, and surrounded by matching cupcakes. Over the table, her name was posted in purple lights, and I could already imagine the way Dawn would scream when she saw this.

I gave Simone my approval and thanks, then headed back into the main area, taking a closer look at the full bar as I passed. Tariq had – apparently – hired a bartender for the night, and Dawn had a signature cocktail – a spiked blueberry lavender lemonade, served in a glass with a purple-sugared rim.

Shaking my head, at how he was overdoing it – I spotted the head chef of *Honeybee*, another of our favorite restaurants in his kitchen – I made my way into the bedroom to change. I took a quick shower, and when I stepped out, moisturized, flat ironed, and made up, Tariq was there, pacing the room while he spoke on the phone. Even though he *always* looked good, I did a little double-take as I looked him over. A simple grey Henley, charcoal blazer, dark jeans, and black suede Bottega Veneta sneakers... understated was completely sophisticated on him.

He caught me looking at him, and winked when I met his gaze. I rolled my eyes at him as I moved toward the closet, giggling when he copped a feel as I passed him.

I hadn't intended to match Tariq, and contemplated a last minute change to my outfit. Then, I smiled. Who cared if it was corny or not? Tonight, I was coordinating with my man.

My man.

I smiled a little harder. *Loved* that those words still gave me tingles. We'd been together for just under a month now, and while things hadn't been perfect between us all the time, most times, they were pretty damned blissful. So far, the only things we really argued about were dinner, and where we would be spending the night. It concerned me a little at first, because *all* couples argued, it was just part of being human. Then, I remembered that I'd known this man for nearly all my life. We'd learned each other's communication styles, preferences, and ideals so long ago that we were already adjusted to them, knew how to interact with each other. There wasn't much to argue about anymore.

We definitely still got on each other's nerves though.

But even with that, there was a marked difference in how we were as a couple now versus how we were before. When I walked into his apartment and saw pretty-assed Simone, not even a stitch of jealousy entered my mind. If we were out to dinner and women stared at him, flirted right in front of me, or looked me up and down, I felt none of the murderous rage I remembered from before, and one night during pillow talk, Tariq had revealed a similar sentiment. After loving, protecting, caring for, supporting, and making love to each other this long, neither of us was going anywhere.

No need for jealousy anymore. We were good and grown.

I slipped into wide legged jeans and cable-knit sweater, and smoothed the soft gray wool over my skin. I was getting ready to step into my shoes when Tariq grabbed me from behind, pulling me against him. The off-shoulder style of my sweater gave him easy access to my bare skin, and he peppered me with kisses from my arm up to my jaw.

334

"You had that appointment today, right?" he asked, sliding his hand down to my belly.

I turned in his arms and nodded, tipping my head back to meet his eyes. "Yes. I did, and..." I shook my head. "No baby."

I didn't expect him to start jumping up and down with joy at the news that I wasn't pregnant, but I did expect shoulders sinking in relief, or a smile. Instead, his expression was almost somber, as he ran his tongue over his lips, and gave me a subtle nod. "Okay."

I raised an eyebrow. "... Okay? That's it? No, well it was probably for the best? No *yesss*? Tariq, are you sad about there not being a baby?"

"I..." He left out a heavy sigh, then tightened his arms around my waist. "Sad isn't the right word. Maybe a little disappointed. I *might* have been thinking about how cute you were with Dawn, and started thinking about seeing you like that again. It was just a thought though.

You're right. We talked about this already anyway, and decided not to. You got your new IUD put in?"

Dropping my gaze from his, I shook my head, then looked up at him again, trying my best not to smile. "No. I didn't. I um... I went with pills, for now. I thought we might want a little more time to think about it, before we committed to being baby-free for another five years."

When *those* words left my mouth, I got the smile I was expecting before, with a little
extra. "I like that. I like it a lot."

"I thought you might. It's just, with the lawsuit, and all of that, I didn't want to make a hasty decision. We can talk to some doctors, talk to Dr. Alexander and discuss your fears. And maybe even talk to your mother. If we can get a clear moment, I think she'd not necessarily have advice, but at least some good insight. And your grandparents too. Let's evaluate everything *together*, and then we can make an informed decision. Right?"

Tariq didn't say anything, just stared at me for a long moment before he dipped his head down to mine, and captured my lips. He brought his hands to my face, pulling me deeper into the passion of his kiss, and when he drew back, he met my gaze and smiled. "I love you so much."

I gave him a little nod, and smiled back. "I love you too. We have a good three years until I'm forty, and closing down shop. We've got a little time." The doorbell chimed, and I laughed at the timing of it. "Or not. That's probably Nubia or Steph or somebody. Let me put on my shoes."

I slipped on my shoes and followed Tariq to the door, frowning when I saw him with his ear pressed to the front door. When he saw me, he raised a finger to his lips, then waved me over, motioning for me to listen.

"—don't understand what *you* don't understand about me telling you no." – That was Nubia speaking, her voice muffled by the thick barrier of the door.

"You're telling me you're not interested, but your hand is still on my chest, and your eyes are practically begging me to touch you."

I clapped a hand over my mouth, eyes wide as I looked to Tariq. She was talking to Steph!

"You know how that sounds, right?"

Steph chuckled. "Yeah, I know how it sounds, but we both know what it is. You want me. I want you. What's wrong with saying yes?"

"Because a yes means you win, game over. And I greatly enjoy playing with you."

"See what I mean? Saying shit like that while you're tugging on my belt buckle? You need to quit playing with me, girl."

Nubia giggled. "You aren't gonna do shit." A second later, we heard a muffled *smack*, and Nubia let out a little "*Oh!*" before she broke into a peal of laughter. "See what I mean?" she asked, before one of them pushed the doorbell again. "If I told you yes, we wouldn't be able to keep having fun like this."

Shaking his head, Tariq opened the door. Nubia was in front, smirking, and Stephen was behind her, his eyes trained on her ass.

"Hey Tariq," Nubia said, sidling past him to get to me. She looped her arm around my waist for a hug, then leaned in to speak into my ear. "Girl, do you see how good Steph looks tonight? I need a damned drink."

Steph *was* looking quite handsome as he stepped in, slapping hands with Tariq. He wore designer sneakers, jeans, and a luxuriously thick sweater in an oxblood color that looked amazing on his pecan-toned skin. He still had his rugby body, tall and well-built, with powerful biceps and muscled thighs. Though he'd suffered some beatings on the field, his chiseled features, sensual lips, and dark hazel eyes made for a – quite frankly – gorgeous face. Even *with* the crooked nose from multiple breaks.

He and Nubia were both about thirty minutes early, supposedly to help set up the party, but actually to talk to me and Tariq about each other. Luckily, Tariq's overzealous ass had enough staff – including the ones he'd hired just for the party – to take care of everything without us. An hour later, the party was in full swing, and the house was full of people.

Dawn would go out for her *real* twenty-one year old fun with her friends later – this party was for us grown folks to celebrate her. She did bring an entourage with her when she arrived, but most of the people were ones who'd watched her grow up from a baby.

Tariq's grandparents – who he'd been on the phone with while I was getting ready – were overseas, and my mother had declined the invitation she was only extended to not seem rude. I didn't really want her there, and neither did Dawn.

The cake was cut, food devoured, happy birthday horribly sang, and many birthday cards of cash were slipped into Dawn's hands. She gave us a couple hours of her time before she took off with friends to do young stuff, and the grown folks hung around for the drinks and conversation.

"If it wasn't for Braxton, you know we wouldn't be voting for shit." Nashira said, taking a sip from her martini as she shot an ugly look at her brother. "You know I found out he's slept with half the board, right?"

"Yeah, I heard." I shook my head, then downed my margarita. "Thanks a lot Brax."

"You know," Nash continued, "If I go to this vote in two days and these bitches act up, I think Brax should replace your salary. He has money to be building hotels all willy nilly, shouldn't be a problem, right?"

Braxton sucked his teeth. "Those women knew what it was, and none of them can claim dissatisfaction. I won't be funding any salaries – sorry Kora. You know Tariq is going to lock you down in a few months anyway now that he finally caught you."

"Oh please," I laughed, glancing at Tariq. "We *all* know this man barely wants to call somebody a *friend* inside of a year. It'll be a miracle if I get a ring at all."

Tariq rolled his eyes at me, but he laughed with everybody else, cause we knew it was true. Everybody here had known Tariq at least ten years, and couldn't claim any different. Still… from the way he was looking at me for the rest of the night, I had a feeling I'd stumbled upon one of those arguments we supposedly "didn't have."

As everybody left, snow started, and I stepped out onto the huge balcony and sat down on a chaise to watch it fall. Tariq was inside, directing the clean up, and I sat out there thinking about how much – just in the last six months – our lives had changed. When I went back inside, we'd get ready for bed, maybe argue, probably make love, and I'd go to sleep in his arms, not as his "friend". As *his*. And though it felt exciting, and new, and *amazing*, it didn't feel strange at all. It felt right, and organic, like we were finally doing what

339

we should have in the first place. It felt like one of those inevitable conclusions Nubia was talking about, that Tariq and I were simply *supposed* to be.

We just needed to get out of our own way.

"You *have* to be freezing out here."

I looked behind me to see Tariq standing in the doorway, with a thick blanket in his hands. He walked out, sitting down behind me with his legs on either side, then wrapped the blanket around us and pulled me close.

"Dawn was born at the very end of a night like this, remember? Clear, and beautiful, snow coming down."

I felt, rather than saw him nod. "Yep. I remember. Born just before dawn."

"A new day," I murmured. "My baby girl that changed my life. I almost can't believe she's all grown up now."

"Yep. You're getting *old* as hell, gorgeous."

I sucked my teeth, playfully jabbing my elbow into him. "If you're old, I'm old."

"Nothing wrong with getting old. I'm aging like good liquor."

"Mmhmm. And what about me?"

"Like a wise investment."

I broke into giggles, turning to look at him over my shoulder. "That's a *much* better compliment than leftover spaghetti."

He grinned. "I try." We were quiet for a long moment, and then he tightened his arms around me, and grabbed my hands, warming them with his. "So about that shit you said earlier…" – *damn!* – "You really think I'm never going to give you a ring?"

"I was just being silly," I said. "It's not a big deal."

"Was it a big deal when you were talking about it with Nubia that day in your bathroom?"

I tipped my head to the side, trying to think of what he could be referring to. A moment later, it hit me. He was talking about the day Wesley David had turned my life upside down, and

I'd nearly – or definitely – had a panic attack. "You overheard all of that?"

"I don't know what "all of that" is, but I heard you telling her you got with me knowing you may never get a baby or a ring. I guess I'm just not sure why you would think that."

I let out a little sigh as he pulled his hands from mine, leaving them exposed to the cold.

He moved his arms from around me too, and I didn't dare look back to see his face. "Because it's how you are, Tariq. Cautious, and slow. You're not quick to let people in, or get too attached.

You're like that with everybody."

"But *you* aren't *everybody*." His arms came back around me, and when he didn't say anything for a long moment, something told me to look down. When I did, I gasped.

He was holding a ring – not just any ring, but a fucking *ring* – between his forefinger and thumb. Beautifully set diamonds surrounded a larger stone in the middle, and pave-set diamonds covered the entire platinum band.

"For the record," he said, taking me by the hand, and sliding the ring onto my finger, "I was already going to do this, just not tonight. Nubia and Dawn helped me pick this ring out, and I was going to take you to a quiet dinner after you found out the results of the vote from the board. Either make a good day a great one, or make a shitty day better. *But* since apparently I've been unclear about how I feel about you somewhere along the way, I'm doing it now."

I turned around to face him, grinning back when I realized he had a smile on his face.

"Kora Oliver, I have waited too long to take any chances on you getting away from me. I love you, with everything I have to give. I want you to be my wife. I want you to have the wedding you've probably dreamed about, but thought that if you chose me, you'd never get. *Anything* that you want, if it's in my power, gorgeous, it's yours. You have all of me, Kora. It's yours."

He stopped for a second to scrub a hand over his face, and it took every bit of self-control

I had to not burst into sobs when I realized he was trying to control his emotions. "So," he continued, meeting my eyes after he'd cleared his throat. "Will you marry me, and keep on the engagement ring that I presumptuously put on your finger, and keep the "*I didn't say yes, why'd you put this on me*" to yourself?"

I laughed, nuzzling my face against his hand as he reached up to wipe away the tears that had sprang free. "But

I *didn't* say yes, while you're putty rings on people all willy-nilly."

"Kora..."

"Yes."

He lifted an eyebrow, and the corners of his mouth twitched. "Yes, as in...?"

"As in yes, I'll marry you."

Tariq let his mouth spread into another full smile, then pulled me into a kiss that snatched my breath away. "And so we're clear," he said, after he pulled back, "that ring isn't just for play, or just to put you off. We can go to the courthouse *tomorrow* if that's what you want to do. I just want you to know I'm serious about us, and I'm serious about you."

"Yeah. But I knew that before you put a ring on my hand."

"I know you say you were fine with it, and that it wasn't a thing for you, but I didn't want to take that chance."

I smiled, and nodded. "I appreciate that. Now can we go inside? I want to make love to my fiancé."

Tariq scoffed. "Hell yeah. I thought you'd never ask."

We got up from the chaise, giddy like teenagers. As we went back inside, something occurred to me, and I turned to Tariq with a playful scowl. "So tell the truth. Is there any little part of you that wants to marry me just because Paul did?"

He lifted an eyebrow. "A little part? Nah, that's a good five percent of the reason."

"Tariq!" I gasped, then broke into a laugh. "I cannot believe you. Well I can, but still."

He shrugged, reaching down to palm my ass. "What? I couldn't let his bitch ass be the only one to put a ring on your hand."

"Tariq…"

"And mine is better than the one he gave you too."

"Tariq!!"

"*What*?"

I scowled at him a little longer, then shook my head as I smiled, and wrapped my arms around his shoulders. "I love your stupid ass."

He pressed a kiss against my lips. "I love your stu—"

"Don't even try it."

~

My heels tapped a stilted, choppy rhythm as I strode down the hall, in an unnecessary hurry to get to my destination. I stopped in front of the bank of elevators, mostly alone because of the odd time of day, and waited for one of the six to come down from the top floor.

The closest one was still twelve floors away when the hairs raised on the back of my neck. I lifted an eyebrow, then turned around, looking into the eyes of someone I honestly should have already expected to see.

Julissa.

It was petty of me, maybe, but in that moment, I kind of didn't care. I felt great, so I let my face spread into a smile before I turned back around to wait.

"I guess you're here to share the good news," she said, taking a few steps to put herself in line with, but not quite beside me.

I nodded. "Yes."

The elevator arrived, and I stepped on. To my dismay, she followed, and hit the button for the floor right above Tariq. I let out – what I hoped was – an inaudible sigh as I put my back against one side of the elevator. Julissa took the opposite side.

Silence lingered between us.

Well, this should be a fun forty-three story ride.

"You know it really wasn't personal, right?"

I rolled my eyes, then ran my tongue over my teeth, forcing myself not to react badly.

"No. It definitely was. But whatever."

"It's not whatever. I'm telling you, it wasn't personal."

"And I'm telling *you* that it was. You see as much as you may want to believe that you really do think my little controversy was a negative distraction for the theatre – even if you *do*

believe it, you voting against my job wasn't business. It was as personal as it gets, and you did it because you were trying to hurt Tariq by hurting me. Unless you were fucking Braxton too, that's the only way it makes sense to me, that as

345

a woman, you would vote in favor of my molestation and *rape* as a teenager being held against me."

Julissa's nostrils flared in anger, but she kept her ass against that wall. "Whatever."

"Yeah, that's what I already said. You'd just better be glad it didn't work, because an "anonymous" source told me that an "anonymous" member of the board questioned whether Dawn's presence was a detriment as well. I swear to God that your day, and this trip in this elevator would be very different if your bullshit had worked."

She crossed her arms. "Are you saying you would *do* something to me? Like I wouldn't tell the world, and ruin this little good girl rep your publicist is trying to build for you now."

"Girl, don't let the Tony award fool you. I'm saying I would *drag* your ass if you'd affected my daughter's career. But you didn't." I gave her a bright smile, and raised a hand to move my hair away from my face. I caught the exact moment her eyes caught the brilliant glint of my engagement ring, and her face twisted into an even uglier scowl. I turned back to the front of the elevator, ignoring her.

She scoffed. "You have a lot of nerve acting like that man of yours is a catch."

"You have a lot of nerve acting like he isn't."

"He's a liar."

"We both know that's a lie, Julissa." I turned back to her, and met her eyes, not really giving a shit about the nasty expression she wore. "You know what, listen. I'm having a great day, and I'm not interested in letting you ruin it. As a

346

matter of fact, let me share some joy with you. Tariq hurt you. I know that. He knows that. You know that. And *everybody* that knows, wishes it hadn't happened, but it did. You're angry, which is your right. But what *isn't* right is you using your influence to try to hurt me and my daughter, who have never done anything to you.

"You want to hurt *him*? That makes sense. Key the Range Rover, put a brick through the window, I *get* it. I've *been there* – with him! But what you don't do, as a woman, is attack another one who didn't have shit to do with your pain. You wanted to affect me – that's one thing. But then you try to bring my daughter into it? Girl, I owe you an ass whooping. But here's where I'm going to spread my joy – instead of giving it to you, I'm not. But don't you *ever* mess with me or mine again."

I turned away from her for what I hoped would be the last time, and we rode the last fifteen floors in silence. I was *so* glad to see the forty-third floor I walked to the front of the elevator and waited barely an inch away for the doors to open, and then sprang off.

"Kora."

Goddamnit.

I wanted so badly to just keep walking like I hadn't heard her, but something in me made me turn around and look her way. "What?"

She swallowed hard, then ran her tongue over her lips as she stepped between the doors to keep them from closing. "I… I'm sorry. You're right. Trying to hurt you and Dawn, that wasn't okay."

347

I was stunned for a second that she'd apologized, but then I nodded. "Yeah. Okay." I started to turn around, then she spoke again, and internally, I groaned.

"It's just I was – I *am* so angry. I knew Tariq wasn't a good idea. We started as just sex, and I should have let it stay that way. I was fresh off a breakup… three years with this man, him complaining that I worked too much, that I was too independent, that I wasn't committed enough. But why should I have been, when we just were just dating, you know? I wasn't putting my all into someone who after three years, hadn't even hinted about taking the next step. And then he broke up with me. And I convinced myself that it was really just him, that he was crazy, that he would probably never marry anybody. I started seeing Tariq, and then here this motherfucker comes… engaged. Telling everybody they'd been dating for a year and half, so he'd obviously been cheating on me."

Julissa sniffled, wiping the stray tears that had started down her face as the elevator began to chime from being kept open. She stepped off.

"I don't know what got into me. *This*, this isn't… *me*. I don't *do* stuff like this," she whispered, glancing nervously around the lobby. "Tariq is an amazing man, and I guess I needed to prove that it *wasn't* me, that somebody would want to commit, but once again, somebody else gets the ring."

I let out a little breath, as my own eyes started to get a little misty. I dug in my bag for the only thing I had, a makeup wipe, and handed it to her. "Listen… don't let what that bastard ex of yours did make you crazy. There's nothing wrong with working hard, being your own woman, and needing a man for nothing except the sex, or companionship, and eventually love that he should provide, if he's expecting a commitment from you. I really, *really* get it, Julissa. I do. But me and Tariq… that was a foregone conclusion, and had nothing to do with you. When I looked you up, after he told me about you… girl, you've got it going on. Pick yourself up, dust this shit off, and trust me… the love that's supposed to be yours is going to find you. Okay?"

She met my eyes, hers filled with clear embarrassment as she nodded, and I looked away, not wanting to prolong it. I turned to head for Tariq's office, then stopped to turn around.

"My friend Nubia would tell you that you're *"too fine for this bullshit"*. You should think about it like that too."

Without waiting on a response for her, I walked off, heading to Tariq's office. After a thumbs up from the receptionist, I knocked twice and then walked in, and he smiled at me as soon as he looked up.

"So you have good news for me, right?" he asked, standing up. "You can't even keep the smile off your face right now."

I shook my head. "I sure can't. Kora Oliver *will* remain as head director at Warm Hues

Theatre, *and* my request for *Trouble Don't Last* has been approved, and will be my next show."

"That's amazing, baby!" He rounded his desk to pull me into a hug, then planted a kiss against my lips. "I see my good luck charm worked."

349

I lifted an eyebrow. "Good luck charm?"

"The ring. Remember? Make a shitty day better, or a good day great…"

"Ohh," I nodded. "Yeah. I guess so."

"So, Ms. Head Director. You have time for dinner with me tonight."

I cringed. "Uh, I don't know. I might be busy with the script, making notes, writing down poten—*mmm*." I moaned as he hand deftly made its way under my skirt, into my panties, and against my sensitive, instantly damp skin. "Okay, *okay.*"

Tariq smirked, then pressed his lips against my neck. "Is that a yes now?"

I nodded as he pushed his fingers inside me. "Mmmhmmm. Text me the details… when we finish."

-the end-

Thank you so much for taking Kora and Tariq's journey with me. If you enjoyed this book (or even if you didn't!) please consider leaving a review/rating on Amazon and/or Goodreads. Not only does it help others decide if they'd like to meet these characters, it's how I know you're out there, and I would love to know what you thought about the book!

Christina C. Jones is a modern romance novelist who has penned more than 15 books. She has earned a reputation as a storyteller who seamlessly weaves the complexities of modern life into captivating tales of black romance.

Prior to her work as a full time writer, Christina successfully ran Visual Luxe, a digital creative design studio. Coupling a burning passion to write and the drive to hone her craft, Christina made the transition to writing full-time in 2014.

With more than 17,000 books sold or borrowed, Christina has attracted a community of enthusiastic readers across the globe who continue to read and share her sweet, sexy, and sometimes scandalous stories.

Most recently, two of Christina's book series have been optioned for film and television projects and are currently in development.

Other titles by Christina Jones:

Standalone Titles:
Love and Other Things
Haunted (paranormal)
Mine Tonight (erotica) **Friends &**
Lovers:
Finding Forever
Chasing Commitment
Strictly Professional:
Strictly Professional
Unfinished Business **Serendipitous**
Love:
A Crazy Little Thing Called Love
Didn't Mean To Love You
Fall In Love Again
The Way Love Goes Love You Forever

Trouble:
The Trouble With Love
The Trouble With Us
The Right Kind Of Trouble
Trouble Don't Last (2016)